Trust in Love
by
Vashti Ann Reed

Noire Allure is an imprint of Parker Publishing LLC.

Copyright © 2008 by Vashti Ann Reed
Published by Parker Publishing LLC
12523 Limonite Avenue, Suite #440-438
Mira Loma, California 91752
www.parker-publishing.com

All rights reserved. This book is protected under the copyright laws of the United States of America. No part of this publication may be reproduced, stored in a retrieval system, or transmitted in any form or by any means—electronic, mechanical, photocopying, recording, or otherwise—without the prior written permission of the publisher.

This book is a work of fiction. Characters, names, locations, events and incidents (in either a contemporary and/or historical setting) are products of the author's imagination and are being used in an imaginative manner as a part of this work of fiction. Any resemblance to actual events, locations, settings, or persons, living or dead, is entirely coincidental.

ISBN: 978-1-60043-047-3
First Edition

Manufactured in the United States of America

Cover Design by Jaxadora Designs

Trust in Love
by
Vashti Ann Reed

Dedication and Acknowledgements

This book is dedicated to my mother and father, Lucius and Mary Boykins, and to my daughter Efia Dalili whose words of wisdom, "You're never too old to live," reminded me that a dream deferred is not necessarily a dream denied.

One

DANITA JOHNSON SAT IN the Penn-Atkinson Foundation's conference room overlooking downtown San Diego. Cullen Powers the only other finalist for a grant she was pursuing sat beside her. An African American who looked as powerful as his name implied, Cullen had a presence that exuded a keen intelligence and a gentle manner. Danita wanted to concentrate on her presentation, but she found it harder by the minute to ignore him.

She straightened in her chair and locked her gaze on the chairman across the conference table. Her life, her future everything she held dear hung in the balance. She wanted to get on with the ordeal and learn how to improve her chance to win the grant that would save her business and let her continue to employ the wonderful senior citizens she had come to think of as members of her family.

When Mr. Frederickson leaned forward, apparently charmed with Cullen Powers, Danita could barely swallow her frustration. Her attention shifted back to Cullen as he answered Mr. Frederickson's questions about the famous athletes he had helped. Under any other circumstances she could have listened to Cullen's soft clear baritone for hours, but it already seemed to have gone on for days. Enough was enough. Mr. Frederickson showed his fascination with sports in a way that made Danita feel invisible.

"You're right, Mr. Frederickson," Cullen said. "Tip Rogers did wear our knee braces most of last season."

As she watched Cullen speak, his generous mouth intrigued her in spite of herself. He had a handsome nose and an arrogantly chiseled chin. His dark brown eyes shone with intelligence and intensity. His masculinity caused her heartbeat to quicken, surprising her. She carefully shifted her gaze to Mr. Frederickson who beamed at Cullen and said to the other men at the table, "Good thing he had Cullen to help him or he might have lost the batting championship. What materials did you use in the braces?"

While Cullen answered Mr. Frederickson's questions, Danita kept an interested expression plastered on her face. Alex Frederickson, a tall red-haired man in his fifties with a military manner to match his military haircut, couldn't seem to get enough of Cullen and his company The Center for Orthotic-Prosthetic Resources, or COPR.

The chairman stroked his neatly clipped gray beard and gave Mr. Frederickson a meaningful glance. "Very interesting, Alex, but we need to get back to the agenda."

Danita sent the chairman an approving smile. If only she had to compete with someone less dynamic than Cullen Powers.

The chairman droned on. "Before I assign the advisor to these two outstanding finalists, I believe it fitting each learn something of the other's project."

Mr. Rawley the grandson of the foundation's creator turned to Danita. "Ms. Johnson, tell Mr. Powers about WAIT FOR ME."

Danita drew herself up in her seat and scooted forward, her glasses perched on her nose. "WAIT FOR ME employs seniors who house-sit for working people who can't take time from their jobs to stay home for repair persons or deliveries."

Mr. Frederickson crossed his arms and leaned on the table. "When I read your proposal, the jobs you offered appeared perfect for retired people. Where did you get the idea for your business?"

Thankful he'd given her an opportunity to expand her presentation she said, "The concept came to me three years ago when my grandmother's friends complained about the difficulty of making their Social Security checks stretch to cover those small, and not so small, emergencies that arise from time to time. Most seniors are unable to do any strenuous work, but they are responsible people who still have their pride and a strong work ethic. After brain-storming with my grandmother, we came up with the idea."

"WAIT FOR ME seems to fit the bill," Mr. Rawly said.

Danita glanced around the table, glowing confidently at the committee members. As her gaze swept past Cullen Powers a new sensation made her shiver as it zinged through her chest. She knew what caused the sensation: attraction coupled with fear.

Fear, she thought. The fear of losing the grant to this charismatic man. She might as well add her awareness of the man's sensual magnetism while she was at it.

She straightened in her chair. She knew she would lose her focus if she let her interest in Cullen sidetrack her. She turned away, opened the folder in front of her and removed her brochures. She avoided looking at Cullen while she distributed them.

She pointed to the smiling faces of an elderly African American man and a Latino on its cover. "This is Phil and Ernesto, two of my first employees. When Phil came to WAIT FOR ME, he was suffering from severe depression. He'd just had knee surgery and he was living alone. His wife had recently died and his only daughter was in Japan with her military husband. He didn't want to ask her to come home to look after him. When he got out of the convalescent center, the social worker there who had used our services told him about WAIT FOR ME.

"Since working for us he says he not only feels useful, but he has something to look forward to every day. His symptoms of depression have disappeared and he's regained his energy. The money he earns allows him to enjoy a meal out or a movie from time to time."

One of the committee members, a well-built man who appeared to be in his late thirties raised his index finger to snare Danita's attention. He had sat silently throughout the meeting. "Is your enterprise in serious financial trouble, and if so, why?"

Danita's hands moistened with nervous perspiration. "Yes, it is. A series of catastrophes hit us almost two years ago. I'm afraid if we don't get additional funding, we may have to close our doors. The loss of business could be fatal."

Mr. Rawley asked, "Care to share what the 'catastrophes' were?"

"We were previously located in a mini-mall. One of the businesses there caught fire. The firefighters inundated our unit with water, destroyed our records, ruined our computers and made it necessary for us to relocate to a more expensive site. We had fire insurance of course, but collecting it took time and we had a great many unexpected expenses. We also lost business until we could get set up again."

"Tough break," Mr. Frederickson said.

Danita didn't want to admit it, but if WAIT FOR ME closed its doors, it might never reopen. "The grant will make it possible for us to continue in business and keep our seniors employed."

The chairman made a check mark on his agenda. "Thank you for that overview. We wish you all the best." He turned to Cullen. "I'm sure Ms. Johnson would be interested in hearing about your proposal."

Cullen removed six of his company's brochures from the briefcase on the floor between his chair and Danita's. The faint woodsy scent of his after shave tantalized her. When he steadied himself on the arm of her chair her pulse speeded up and she caught her breath.

His apologetic glance as he murmured, "Sorry," disconcerted her.

Cullen distributed his literature. He pointed to pictures of braces and artificial limbs. "Many of my clients—who range from eighteen months to ninety-plus years of age—rely on Medicare and Medical to pay for their prosthetic devices."

"Lucky they have those medical plans. In my grandfather's day most people had a heck of a time getting the medical help they needed," Mr. Rawly commiserated.

"Of course the situation has improved, but because of the plans' payment structures, those clients qualify for only the least expensive braces and prosthesis which makes their rehabilitation much more difficult and time consuming."

Cullen looked each member in the eye. "This grant will supplement our neediest clients' insurance payments allowing us to fit them with more advanced designs which, though more expensive, provide the mobility they need for their self-respect and independence."

The committee members picked up their brochures and examined the photos contrasting standard models with COPR's improved ones. "I see what you mean about your designs. They are definitely more functional," Mr. Rawly assured Cullen.

Mr. Rawley's remark piqued Danita's interest in spite of herself. She examined the pictures comparing the less expensive devices with the more advanced models. She sympathized with his clients who would be denied the newer technology. She had to admit he had a good proposal.

While Cullen talked, Danita studied him, admiring the neat conservative style of his short, tightly-curled black hair and overall masculine appearance.

Her reaction to Cullen annoyed her. He stood between her and the thing she most valued: her work with her seniors. Now was no time for distracting fantasies. If he won the grant she'd lose her business. People were depending on her.

Mr. Rawley cleared his throat. "Two outstanding projects. Now you can see why you both are finalist for this year's grant."

Danita murmured her assent although she couldn't see why Cullen needed the grant as much as she did. His perfectly pressed navy blue suit looked expensive as did his gold watch. His connection to the sports world and his charisma would no doubt allow him access to all sorts of other sources of funding.

Disabled children and adults always gained the sympathy of foundations. Her grandmother used to say, "Old folks are in God's waiting room. Only their loved ones care what happens to them." Grandparents supported dreams and loved unconditionally. She for one would champion their cause with all the passion she had in her.

The chairman handed Cullen and Danita folders with pictures of young children, seniors, disabled people and teens superimposed over a map of San Diego county. The slogan, PENN-ATKINSON: A FOUNDATION FOR CHANGE stood in bold black letters above the pictures.

The chairman said, "Please turn to page two paragraph one of the enclosed agreement and read along with me."

Curious, she opened her handout, found the section and followed along while he intoned, "Grant recipients who by word or deed bring disgrace, ridicule, or censure or in any way tarnish the image of The Foundation shall forfeit the award or the undistributed balance which will in turn be given to the runner up."

For long moments he rested his gaze first on Cullen then Danita. "Any questions?" he asked. Both shook their heads.

Thank goodness she had no reason to worry. Nothing could be more wholesome than her seniors swapping stories, snacking on the treats they brought, or enthusiastically going to their assignments. "We welcome any and all scrutiny," she said.

With a benign smile the chairman said, "Good. Please sign the agreement now."

Danita and Cullen signed the papers and returned them to the chairman.

The chairman said, "Alex Frederickson will be your advisor and the link between the Foundation and the both of you. He'll visit each of your establishments, interview the employees you select, observe how you manage your business and answer your questions. Think of him as your facilitator while you pursue the grant. On his first visit he'll tour your facility and review the budget you submitted to us as part of your applications. On his follow-up visit he'll interview additional staff members."

He concluded, "If there are no questions, we'll adjourn our meeting. Thank you both for joining us today with your excellent proposals. We'll notify you of our decision by the end of June. If you have any questions feel free to contact Alex."

Danita bit back her dismay. The chairman could not be serious. Mr. Frederickson had shown his preference for Cullen's proposal throughout the entire meeting.

Alex Frederickson took out his palm pilot and turned toward Danita. "Let's see, Ms. Johnson. Today is Thursday. I'd like to meet with you at WAIT FOR ME Monday morning at nine."

Danita clenched her teeth, whipped out her organizer and checked the date in question. "Fine. We look forward to your visit." She entered his name and time and dropped her organizer back into her voluminous shoulder bag.

Mr. Frederickson shook her hand and voiced his pleasure in meeting her. His smile dismissive, he turned to Cullen. "Will Wednesday at ten work for you, Cullen?"

Danita frowned. She hadn't missed the fact that he'd addressed Cullen by his first name and had given Cullen an extra day to prepare, and had avoided a Monday morning meeting.

Mr. Rawley made his way to Danita's side and shook her hand. "No matter how this turns out, my congratulations for getting this far in the process. The publicity you receive as a finalist will help your business. Good luck."

His encouragement warmed her. "I thank you," she said, "and my seniors will thank you if I win this grant. They believe in your foundation's goals and insisted that I apply."

A headache sprang to life behind her left eye. She glanced at Cullen, silently counted to ten and ignored Cullen's too confident grin. Well, she'd show him. She'd keep trying until *she* won.

Mr. Rawly and Danita drifted over to the doorway where the other committee members surrounded Cullen. A six-footer, Cullen filled the exit and loomed over her. With a polite murmur of apology he stepped aside, and Danita eased past him.

On her way out of the door Mr. Frederickson asked Cullen technical questions about his appliances. She felt her new advisor had already forgotten she existed.

Walking toward the elevator she reached into her purse for her cell phone to call her partner. Darn. She'd left it charging on her desk. She'd have to use one of the phones in the lobby.

She thought about how Mr. Frederickson had hung onto Cullen's every word. A rush of renewed determined coursed through her. She was still in the competition, and she would find a way to win...whatever it took.

Cullen rode down in the elevator, fuming at Mr. Frederickson's insensitivity toward Danita. The committee had kept Cullen talking and now it was probably too late to intercept her and...what? He couldn't change what had happened in the conference room.

Danita's brave smile haunted Cullen. Even though he intended to go all out to win the grant, he flinched at the memory of the distrustful look she'd given him before she'd left.

When his elevator arrived at the lobby, Cullen lounged against the nearby wall and took out his cell phone to call his secretary and let her know he'd be late. He heard Danita's sexy alto voice which seemed to come at him from nowhere. At first he thought he was imagining it.

He made his call and while his secretary was finishing up another call he swore he heard Danita's voice again. Looking around the corner of the wall he spied Danita about eight feet away talking on one of the public phones, her back turned toward him. When his secretary came back on the line, he couldn't take his eyes off Danita. He finished his call, and dropped his cell phone into his pocket. He started to leave until he realized this would be his chance to talk to Danita and apologize for Frederickson's insensitive behavior.

He watched her as he leaned against the wall fascinated by her animation. Her entire body moved when she talked. An energy field sizzled around her. Her fire drew him and he couldn't look away.

Her voice hummed with vitality. "An Etna's pizza sounds great. I want Hawaiian on my half. I'll be back at the office by the time it arrives."

Danita's mellow voice melted over him like warm chocolate. The first time Cullen had heard her speak, that seductive quality coming from a woman who was barely five feet three and probably weighed little more than one hundred pounds had surprised him. He found himself straining to hear her every word. Listening to her order pizza even turned him on. He wondered what that voice would do to him if she wanted to seduce him.

She ran her fingers through her jet-black bangs. "You don't want to know. The other finalist, Cullen Powers, lives up to his name. He's a powerhouse of a speaker and his project is great, but we're still going to win."

Cullen admired her fairness and honesty, but was surprised as well. Maybe she wasn't as upset as she had appeared.

He was about to approach her when she stepped out of her high-heeled pumps, flexed her toes and rested her feet on the black and white marble tiles. Cullen felt rooted to the spot. He couldn't remember when he had seen such dainty feet and shapely calves. The thought of massaging them...*Whoa! Back up! She hasn't given me a second look, let alone an encouraging smile.*

She set her purse onto the counter and shielded it from view. "Mr. Frederickson our advisor is going to be a tough sell. He's the one we'll have to impress. Powers boosted his own project, not on its merits alone, but on a bunch of his famous athlete-patients who keep him in business."

Cullen bristled at the unfairness of the charge. He had simply answered the committee's questions. She was probably annoyed because she knew he deserved to win.

She lowered her voice. "We've got to do something...anything. Maybe we can get the committee's attention with a bungee-jumping contest for our workers." She laughed.

Cullen grinned at the picture she created, but her laugh made him realize he cared what she thought of him. He hadn't encouraged Mr. Frederickson's asinine behavior; he had no intention of using his connections with athletes as an unfair advantage.

Danita rubbed a spot over her left eye. "Think about what we can do to win. Maybe you'll have a plan by the time I get there."

As he waited until Danita completed her call, Cullen wondered if he had given her a headache. He'd offer her a cup of coffee and get her to relax a few minutes with him. He stepped up next to her and tapped her on the shoulder.

She stumbled over her shoes and looked up into his face as she clutched his arm. The touch of her slender hand sent a jolt straight to his gut. Her faint aroma that reminded him of lemon blossoms captivated him.

She jerked her hand away, placed it on the shelf of the booth and stepped into her black pumps. "You startled me."

Her smile warmed his insides. She was cute when she was flustered. From the stubborn tilt of her chin, her gray power suit and her intense expression, he knew better than to say so. "I'm sorry. May I have a word with you?"

"About what?"

"I want to apologize for our advisor's behavior. I had no idea there'd be so much interest in our local athletes. If you have a few minutes, let's grab a cup of coffee and talk."

She stared at him, disbelief reflected in her narrowed dark brown eyes. "Thanks for your concern, but I'm in a hurry."

"Surely you have a moment. Can't we be friendly rivals? We both have worthwhile projects. You can apply again next year if you lose this time."

Danita picked up her briefcase and stepped forward as if to leave. "Next year? I needed the grant last year."

What a damn shame the first woman who had attracted his attention since his wife's death would be his competitor. He wanted...needed... a few more minutes to warm himself in Danita's presence. "Does that mean we can't be friends?"

Danita leaned against the shelf and brushed her bangs out of her eyes. Her impatient gesture almost made him back off.

She squared her shoulders. "No, it means I have to get back to work, and right now you're in my way."

He retreated a step and lifted his hands in a gesture of surrender while still blocking her path. "Worried you might give up once you admit how important my project is compared to yours?"

"Not at all."

Cullen watched as she tightened her full sensuous lips. A dimple flashed in her left cheek and softened the harshness of her glare.

"Maybe we have more in common than you think. Afraid to have a cup of coffee with me in a public place?"

She looked him up and down. "I'm not afraid of anything. I can spare about fifteen minutes."

"I know you're expecting a Hawaiian pizza for lunch, so let's get going." *Before you change your mind.*

Her eyes widened. "You eavesdropped! Gentlemen don't eavesdrop!"

The censure in her voice made him smile. He wouldn't have been surprised if she shook her finger in his face. "I couldn't help overhearing when I made my call."

He looked her straight in the eye until she turned away and headed toward the coffee shop. Now if only he could figure out a way to get past her defenses. For reasons that made no sense he wanted them to become more than friendly rivals.

Cullen caught up with her and walked beside her to the coffee shop before she changed her mind.

Fifteen minutes, she says. We'll see about that.

❧

Sitting next to Danita in the Penn-Atkinson Building's coffee shop, Cullen watch her dash a tear from her eye. She shook so hard he was afraid she'd spill her coffee, and every time she said, "Third floor rear" or "Simple" she'd laugh again.

Cullen chuckled along with her. Her now-familiar lemon-blossom scent gave him a curious sense of intimacy. "Not many people your age still read Langston Hughes' *Simple* stories let alone quote lines from them. You surprise me."

He smiled, remembering with affection how when he was six years old his father had read Simple stories instead of fairy tales to him at bedtime.

"When you told me your full name is Cullen Hughes Power some of the Langston Hughes tales came back to me," she said.

"Unforgettable, aren't they? So, your dad used to read those same stories to you, too."

"When I got my first library card I checked out every Hughes book I could find." She sipped her coffee.

"Me, too. I think I learned to read in order to read them for myself anytime I wanted. How did you happen to memorize so many lines? Did you father make you learn them?"

She looked at him, surprise in her gaze. "Of course not. No one can forget a line like 'He tore those signs down then tore them up'. Hughes' choice of words was perfect."

"That line is classic Hughes, all right. I guess that's why I remembered it, too."

She grinned. "I can imagine the expression on the landlady's face when she looked for all those 'Don't Nobody' signs only to find out Simple had ripped them up and thrown them away. I hate unreasonable rules. If I'd been Simple, I'd have pulled them down, too."

"My best friend Mitch is the same way."

He rested his gaze first on Danita's tantalizing mouth then on the dimple in her cheek. Unable to resist, he enveloped her elegant hand with his. He gave it a gentle squeeze.

Cullen loosened his red-and-blue patterned tie. He knew he was being immature when he settled his arm along the back of the booth. Hoping to impress her with his masculinity, he let his suit jacket gape open so that his well-toned chest was outlined through his stark white shirt.

Danita froze.

For the first time since they had entered the coffee shop, Danita realized that indeed Cullen had distracted her from her goal. Well, she wouldn't be fooled by a handsome face a second time in her life. Been there done that.

She had been so busy taking him up on his dare that when they had started recalling their favorite authors, her enthusiasm for books and writers made her relax her guard. She knew he was watching her struggle to breathe but she didn't care. Her heart filled her throat and threatened to suffocate her. She had to get out of there.

Cullen leaned close. His leg brushed hers. "What's wrong? You don't look so well."

The moment he touched her, jolts of awareness arrowed straight to the pit of her stomach. She snatched her bag and flung its strap over her shoulder. "I have to go. I've been here over half an hour. My partner must wonder what happened to me."

When she rose to leave, he lightly clasped the strap of her shoulder bag. "May I see you again?"

Her hands shook as she pulled away. She leaned away and picked up her briefcase. She swallowed. The grant may have slipped her mind this time, but she had no intention of letting it happen again.

She slid out of the booth and nearly lost a shoe. "I don't think that's a good idea."

"I'll walk you to your car." He grabbed the check and fumbled in his wallet for a tip.

Intent on leaving, Danita never slowed. She exited the coffee shop and strode past the bank of phones and toward the heavy double doors leading to the parking lot.

Cullen reached the outside door before Danita did and opened it for her. Ramrod straight she exited nearly colliding with a middle-aged woman wearing a deep red and black African-print dress. She backed through the door and into Cullen's path. He took a quick sidestep, held out his hand and steadied the woman.

"Cullen, what in the world are you doing here?" she exclaimed.

Saved by a whirlwind, Danita thought, and hurried to her car.

Cullen's former mother-in-law stood before him, her brow furrowed. He smiled at the sight of another small bundle of energy like Danita. "Kay. What an entrance!"

He noticed the contrast between her conservatively cut steel-gray hair which flattered her sharp features and her flamboyant outfit which flowed in a swirl around her body. Outlandishly high heels and intricately-designed dangling gold earrings announced her artistic flair. Except for grayer hair and a few more lines around her big brown eyes, Kay looked the same as she had when he'd married Ayana eleven years before.

She looked back at the door as if she couldn't decide whether to come in or leave. "Cullen? Is everything all right?"

A whisper of guilty relief flashed through him that she had not run into him when he was with Danita. He wasn't sure how she'd react to seeing him with another woman on his arm, no matter how innocent the situation.

"I've thought about you a lot lately." He draped his arm across her slim shoulder.

He bent over so she could give him an exuberant hug. "What's new with you?" she asked.

He told her about his meeting concerning the grant and how well the committee had treated him.

"I hope you win. You do such wonderful work. I'm proud of you, son."

"Thanks, Kay. Haven't seen you for a couple of weeks. How's the art show coming?"

Her gaze scanned the large elegant lobby. "Fine. In fact, that's why I'm here. I'm seeing my lawyer about some last minute problems with the show."

Cullen looked down at her. That explained the troubled look in her eyes. Danita's dramatic exit had his imagination working overtime.

Kay moved around him. "We're blocking the door."

"Come on, I'll walk with you." He took her arm and steered her toward the bank of elevators. She winced.

"Did Aaron drop you off?" Cullen asked.

"No way. I don't ride with my husband if I can help it. Not only does he drive over eighty on the freeways, he's reckless. He makes me so nervous I told him I'd walk rather than get in the car with him again."

"Your little blue Bug still running?"

"Sure, and it gets me where I'm going."

"How is Aaron?"

She sighed. "He's fine. Busy with lots of new accounts."

"Give him my best. He must feel good about the way his political consulting firm has expanded."

"He does, but you know Aaron—he's never satisfied. He wants me to help him entertain. When I leave here I'm meeting him for dinner with some of his clients and their wives. He claims my impressions of them help him decide how to design his clients' campaigns."

Cullen's lips tightened at her unintended criticism. He knew Aaron blamed him for Ayana's death. If she had lived she would be entertaining for Aaron and leave Kay free to concentrate on her art.

Kay didn't sound happy about the prospect of entertaining. Between the growing demand for her work and her responsibilities as Aaron's hostess she must be overwhelmed.

When they reached the nearest elevator Cullen punched the up button. "How are the paintings coming for my open house? About ready for me to look at them?"

"Sure. Why don't you stop by my studio next Friday? You can choose the kind of frames you want."

"I take it Aaron will be out of town."

Kay's gaze wavered. "Um-hmm. We can talk without interruption, and you can concentrate on picking what you want and not worry about Aaron and his moods."

"I wish they were moods. I'd know how to handle that. The last time I saw him he acted as if he hated me. He still holds me responsible for Ayana's death, doesn't he?"

"He'll get over it. If he doesn't, and soon, he'll drown in his own bitterness."

The heavy elevator doors swished open and several people exited it. Cullen blocked the door while he kissed Kay on her cheek. When he pulled away he noticed a faint purple bruise under her collar.

Before he could comment on it, she entered the cage and said, "See you Friday. Maybe you'll tell me then who that was you found so interesting that you didn't see me coming into the building." She laughed as the door closed.

Cullen laughed, too. Damn, he'd almost forgotten how well she knew him.

He pulled Danita's brochure out of his inside coat pocket and checked the address.

What would Kay think if she knew he was on his way to confront a woman who had snared his attention?

Two

DANITA'S SECRETARY CARLOS called out a greeting as Danita hurried toward her small office.

"Hi, Carlos," she said.

He leaned his tall gangly body back in his chair. "How did the meeting go?"

"It was the pits. What a morning. I met my competitor. We sure have our work cut out for us."

He tugged at his black pony tail. "Anything I can do to help?"

"If I think of something I'll let you know. In the meantime hold my calls and take messages until Virgie and I get a chance to figure out what we have to do."

"No problem." A smile lit his handsome face.

Danita walked into her office and slid into her plush red swivel chair behind her uncluttered oak desk. Like all her other office furniture, her desk was a Salvation Army purchase. She tossed her briefcase on it, popped the locks on her case and extracted a folder labeled Penn-Atkinson even before she opened the bottom desk drawer and stashed her purse. The time had arrived for her and her partner Virginia Washington to come up with a plan to impress their advisor.

At the front desk Carlos talked on the phone. Danita stood on tiptoes and peered through the half-window behind her to look into Virgie's office. Drat. Virgie was also on the phone.

Danita dropped down onto her chair. She opened the folder and Cullen's handsome face looked up at her from his brochure. She caught her breath. Every system in her body went on alert.

Recalling her encounter with him, she realized she was upset with her behavior. While he'd been a perfect gentleman, she'd run out on him as if Tyrannosaurus Rex had poked its nose through the door and roared. In disgust at her adolescent response, she slapped the pamphlet face down on the desk.

She had to admit she had enjoyed their coffee break...until he'd stretched his arm across the back of the booth and the strain of his muscles nearly popped his shirt buttons. All at once she had vividly imagined him lying next to her.

Sheesh! He was her rival for heaven's sake. She certainly wouldn't want him to try to save WAIT FOR ME. She would do that for herself if only she had a fair shot at it. She'd started WAIT FOR ME on a shoestring three years before, and she'd fight to keep it. Would she never learn that when it came to most men, they took what they wanted no matter who got hurt?

She absolutely had to get hold of herself—stop seeing danger where none existed. But, oh, Cullen Powers *was* dangerous. Her fascination with him spelled danger with a capital D. Cullen wasn't the problem. Her attraction to him was.

The phone light went out on line two. Good. Virgie had finished her call. With the Foundation's folder, a notebook and pen in hand, Danita rapped on Virgie's door and went in without waiting for an invitation.

Virgie looked up from the note she was scribbling and, from the "you're-next" look in her eyes, Danita knew what was coming. When Virgie worked on the accounts for WAIT FOR ME, her eyes lit up behind her glasses like a detective discovering clues.

Annoyed with herself, Danita remembered she had been so busy preparing her presentation to the committee she hadn't reviewed the materials Virgie had given her on Friday.

Virgie had a new accounting program, and she had told Danita she lived for the day when she could get Danita to sit still long enough to get acquainted with it. Virgie believed if Danita had learned more about the financial end of the business, Robert the Rat couldn't have taken advantage of his position with WAIT FOR ME. Though Danita would trust Virgie with her life, she knew Virgie was right.

"I smell pizza. I'm starved," Danita said, hoping to distract Virgie. "Has it been here long?"

Virgie turned to retrieve a square Etna Pizza box from the top of a tall file cabinet and set it on her conference table. "The guy brought it a few minutes ago. You made it just in time. I could eat a tree."

Danita was glad she remembered that food always seemed to divert Virgie. Five feet ten and slim as a pencil, she appeared both fragile and competent in her black denim pants suit. Her exotically slanted eyes enhanced her caramel-colored flawless skin. She wore her naturally wavy hair, which hung midway down her back, in a neat braid secured with a crunchy.

While Danita went to get cans of soda from the mini fridge, Virgie brought out paper plates and napkins. They both selected a slice from their side of the box: Hawaiian for Danita and Pepperoni for Virgie.

Before taking a bite Virgie asked, "Now tell me, was the meeting as bad as you said? Cullen Powers sounds like something else. Did you like him or was he a jerk?"

Danita didn't have to think about her answer. "The meeting was awful, but Cullen is definitely not a jerk. He seems sensitive, smart, and funny."

"Oh-oh. If he's anything like Robert the Rat you definitely won't be standing in his line."

"It's too soon to tell what he has up his sleeve. Robert pretended he loved me as much as I thought I loved him, but all the time he was working behind my back to ruin WAIT FOR ME."

"In the end he did you a favor. What if you had married him before you found out what a sleaze ball he was?"

"Tell me about it."

"Let's get back to Cullen. How old would you say he is?" Virgie took a bite of her pizza.

"He says he's thirty three. Tall, tan and unattached."

"You left out handsome."

"He's a James Blake look alike with hair. Just right for you."

"You mean James Blake the hot stud muffin pro tennis player who was voted the sexiest man alive? Oh my gawd! Who wouldn't want him? But if you're trying to fix me up again, forget it. I don't have time for a meaningless but oh-so-satisfying relationship." Virgie's chuckle didn't hide the pain Danita knew lay behind her words.

Three months before when Virgie had received her final divorce decree Danita had convinced Virgie to become her partner and take over the accounting end of the business which had been a shambles thanks to Robert the Rat. Not only had she hoped to help Virgie deal with her feelings of regret and betrayal, but Danita needed Virgie's expertise as a CPA.

Danita toyed with the idea. If Danita could get Cullen interested in Virgie she could pierce two hearts with one arrow. She could get rid of the conflicting feelings she had for Cullen, and help Virgie get over her disastrous marriage. As soon as the idea took shape she rejected it. She'd never use Virgie that way. She'd handle Cullen herself.

Virgie tapped Danita's hand. "What happened after the meeting? Obviously you two had a chance to talk. I want all the gory details."

Danita hesitated, reluctant to tell Virgie about her precipitous exit after having coffee with Cullen. Instead she said "Virgie...we've got a big problem. If we hadn't applied for the grant ourselves, I'd say he deserves to win. Cullen has a wonderful proposal. I could see he really cares about his clients and wants to help them."

She told Virgie about Cullen's project giving only a brief sketch of the time she'd spent alone with him.

"You guys have a lot in common," Virgie commented.

Her remark reminded Danita that Cullen had said the same thing. Too bad they had to be rivals. "We do. Including our determination to get the award."

Virgie reached for her orange soda. "Where do we go from here? Any ideas on how to tip the ledger in our favor?"

Danita frowned. "I wish. A week barely gives me time to master the new accounting system you've installed, so I'll have to let you deal with Mr. Frederickson. You know how my eyes cross when it comes to reading budget printouts. I just got used to the old system. I need a crash course. Can we meet after work at your place this week until I can learn the new one?"

"Good idea. We can start tomorrow night. Pack some clothes and you can sleep over after a night of cramming."

"Thanks, I'll do that." Danita handed Virgie a sheet of paper from the Penn-Atkinson folder. "Here's the agreement they had us sign. The chairman made us read a clause about scandals in it in concert. Can you believe how controlling they think they have to be? Those guys were adamant. If we have a scandal we'll get no money. What possible scandal could we have?"

Virgie tossed her heavy black braid over her shoulder. "None I can think of." She studied the page without further comment.

While she waited impatiently for Virgie to finish reading, Danita sipped her drink. "I wish we didn't need their money. WAIT FOR ME is terrific, and our people need us. If we can make the committee take us seriously and forget Cullen's athletes, we'd have a good chance."

Virgie grabbed a pencil and a note pad. "Okay. Let's start with Mr. F's visit. Get the ladies to bring goodies."

"I like your devious mind. No one can resist Mrs. Sanders'

chocolate chip cookies."

"Right!" Virgie wrote on the pad. "Then we'll get Phil Carver and his cronies to stay all day in case Mr. F. wants to interview some of the employees."

Danita raked her fingers through her bangs. "Phil's perfect."

"Mr. F. needs to see how important it is for people like Phil to earn extra money. A month before Phil's property taxes came due he used to eat peanut butter and jelly for his three squares. The possibility of losing his house sent him into a panic. Since working here, he's stopped worrying." The prospect of Mr. Frederickson getting acquainted with her seniors revived Danita's optimism. Even he would be unable to disregard their heartbreaking stories.

"By the time he leaves he'll realize we're the only ones who can protect our people from financial hardship without stripping them of their dignity. Basically, Cullen wants to upgrade his patients' devices. They could probably do almost as well with the ones their insurances fund. With our folks it's not a matter of an upgrade. It's a matter of survival."

Virgie snapped her fingers. "I've got it! What we need is publicity. Does your brother-in-law J.V. still have a connection at the *Tribune*?"

Danita brightened. "He sure does, and from what I remember his friend owes J.V. a favor. I'll see if J.V. can convince his connection to write an article about WAIT FOR ME."

Danita jumped to her feet and went to her own office phone. She punched in her sister's number.

"Sis. I need to talk to J.V. for a few minutes."

Laureen said in her dry way, "Nice to hear your voice, Dani. I'm fine. And how are you?"

Danita chuckled. "Are you guys at home tonight? I need a big favor."

"Sure, we'll be here. What's up?"

"I need J.V. to get his friend at the Union-Tribune to do a feature about my organization. Think he can manage it?"

"I don't know. His friend is always looking for a good human interest story. Dinner will be ready at seven. Get here by six, if you can, and maybe we can convince him."

Danita hung up, grateful for a sister who was always in her corner and a brother-in-law who was always willing to help. While thinking about the best way to approach the subject with J.V., she glanced out the window.

She widened her eyes. Her heart fluttered then picked up

speed. She whispered, "Cullen Powers. What's he doing here?"

She gripped the edge of her desk. The smooth wood indented her palm. Embarrassed at the way she had left him earlier that day she realized she wasn't ready to face him again so soon. As she watched him get out of his white Buick she unlocked her desk drawer and grabbed her bag. Heels tapping a frantic rhythm on the gray vinyl imitation-marble tile, she left her office.

She dashed into Virgie's office. "I've got to run. Sorry to leave the lunch mess. I'll call you later and let you know what time I'll get back."

Virgie gave Danita a surprised look. "What rang your register?"

"J.V. can see me today. I've got to pop home and pick up some materials to show him. I also forgot my cell this morning. I need to pick it up. After that if there's an emergency, call me on my cell."

Danita clutched her keys. "If anyone except my family comes looking for me, say I left and won't be back 'til tomorrow."

Not waiting for Virgie's reply, she went to the front desk and let Carlos know she was leaving and how to contact her. Danita rushed through the lounge behind the reception area. She waved to the men and women who waited for their afternoon assignments and scooted out of the back door which banged shut behind her.

With unsteady hands she unlocked her beige Taurus, jumped inside, and fumbled getting the key into the ignition. Trembling, she drove down the alley to the nearest side street.

At the corner she slowed to glance at the parking lot in front of WAIT FOR ME and caught a glimpse of Cullen standing beside his car. She kept her face averted as she drove away. "Coward, coward, coward," she muttered. "I can't believe I'm doing this."

I've got to stop this. Intelligent thirty-one-year-old women don't run away from unwanted attractions, they deal with them. If only he hadn't snuck up on me.

Caught in the grip of her confusion she promised herself that the next time she'd show more spunk.

⁂

Laureen dropped the last piece of broccoli into the top of the steamer and replaced the lid. "Did Virgie tell you what Cullen wanted?"

Perched on the brown bar stool at the beige ceramic-tile breakfast bar in Laureen's spacious kitchen, Danita diced tomatoes. "She said he asked for me, and when she told him I was gone for the day he left."

"Doesn't sound like the Virgie I know. I'm certain she gave him the third degree when she found out who he was."

"If she did, she didn't mention it."

"If you'd stayed at the office instead of rushing away, you'd know what he wanted."

The rich aroma of baking chicken filled the kitchen, but Danita wasn't hungry. She was sorry now that she'd told Laureen as much as she had about Cullen. "You don't have to rub it in, Laureen. I admit it was stupid of me to take off, but Cullen makes me feel crowded...overwhelmed."

Laureen placed sour dough rolls in a pan. "Seems to me you do a lot of running whenever a good-looking guy comes along and shows any interest in you."

"Don't start. I need to get ready for Frederickson's visit on Monday. I simply wasn't expecting Cullen to show up. I've decided I can deal with him if I see him again. He doesn't scare me."

Laureen laughed as she pushed up the white sleeves of one of her husband's old dress shirts which she was using as an apron. Though she was five feet six, the shirt nearly reached the knees of her designer jeans. "You expect him to turn up again, then?" She grinned. "Fascinating."

"I didn't mean it that way. The committee chairman said Cullen and I'll see quite a bit of each other before they decide who wins the grant. Win or lose, I'll have to see him when I attend the banquet where they'll hand out the award."

"R-i-ight." Laureen gave Danita a Cheshire-Cat grin. "Tell me more about him. He sounds cute."

"I wouldn't call a six-foot man built like a mega athlete 'cute'."

"Well, let me decide for myself."

"He's attractive, has eyes the color of onyx, a great smile, broad shoulders and chest, and he's slim from the waist down."

"Yeah, he's cute," Laureen said. "You should give him a chance, unless you're still hung up on Robert."

"I wouldn't say 'hung up, but I did learn a lesson. Guys want all the glory when it comes to their women. They want to be the important one. When a woman has a responsible career he still expects to come first. We're the ones who are supposed to understand when they're too busy for us, but when we have commitments we can't break, they accuse us of not loving them enough, or being too ambitious.

"I'll never forget how Robert did everything to distract me including spying on me, demanding that I cancel meetings and go out with him and his friends, and generally being at his disposal whenever he decided he needed some 'loving'."

"All men aren't like that. J.V. understands when I have to work, and he's always willing to pick up the slack here at home," Laureen said, and gave Danita a hug.

Resting her head against Laureen, Danita said wistfully, "My mind tells me you're right, but when a man like Cullen gets too friendly, I get suspicious."

"If Cullen asked you for a date, would you go?"

"Certainly not."

"Why not? You say he's attractive, fun, you respect him and he's built like a brick…"

Danita sat up straight, "All right. All right. I don't need a road map to see where you're headed. I admit he has a certain appeal. I'd never get involved with a man who's after the grant I need to save my seniors their jobs. Besides, I can't imagine doing...you know...with him, and given the chemistry between us, I'm afraid that's what he'd expect."

"What you call 'you know' I call lovemaking. How did you think Adam got to be a member of this family? With the right man, the bedroom turns into a paradise where two people engage in the most earth-shattering experience known to humans. You get what I mean, don't you?"

Danita concentrated on tossing the salad. Her face warmed at the images she failed to suppress—images of her and Cullen wrapped in each other's arms.

"Don't tell me you've sworn off men for the rest of your life because of Robert."

"These days it doesn't pay to be promiscuous."

Laureen put her hand on her hip. "Who mentioned promiscuity? I'm talking love here. Are you saying no man since Robert has kissed you until you were greedy for more than kisses? Until his touches left you so hungry you had to make him part of you? And when you came together you exploded into a thousand pieces, your breath drawn from your body, and you knew you'd never breathe again and didn't care? Is that what you're telling me?"

Laureen's graphic description painted such a clear picture of Danita and Cullen locked in passionate abandon that Danita's body quickened.

"I'm telling you that I haven't met anyone in the last eighteen months who turns me on that way. To me sex means love and love means commitment, and right now I'm committed to saving WAIT FOR ME."

Laureen made a derisive sound. "You always have an excuse when a man gets too close. Better watch out, kid. Cullen sounds as if he could turn you around and upside down before you know what happened."

Danita admitted to herself that Laureen was probably right. Maybe Robert had taken more away from her than her money.

Laureen's unwavering gaze showed she meant to pursue the subject. "Unless you plan to spend the rest of your life alone, you'll have to 'you know' with somebody. What's it going to be?"

"You have it all, and I'm happy for you. Sometimes I even envy you and J.V. and Adam, but..."

"You didn't answer my question."

To get Laureen off her back Danita said, "When this competition is over, I promise to get my act together. If Cullen doesn't wring my neck when I win the grant and if he asks me, I might go out with him."

Laureen handed Danita a glass of white wine. "From what you've told me about him, he won't wait two months."

꽃

Just as Danita started toward the family room, J.V. sauntered into the kitchen. He stroked his thick but well-trimmed black mustache. A lanky six-footer who couldn't weigh much more than one hundred seventy pound, he went over to greet Laureen with a hearty kiss. She gave him a grin and a glass of white wine. "Sip this. Dinner will be ready in a few minutes."

"Smells like dinner's worth waiting for." J.V. patted Laureen's bottom as she turned away.

With a husky laugh she sashayed back to the kitchen.

Joining J.V. on the family room's comfortable but sturdy gray sofa, Danita smoothed the colorful afghan draped over its back.

J.V. turned to Danita. "Laureen didn't tell me you'd be by tonight. How's business?"

"That's one reason I'm here. I need a favor." Danita described her meeting with the foundation's committee and explained her determination to impress them."

Danita grinned. "I've always wanted a good ten-minute presentation. Maybe you could put a promotional together for us."

"Glad to do it," JV answered. "In fact, I can squeeze you in next week. Too bad I didn't think of it myself."

"Another thing. Do you still get together with your friend, the feature writer for the family section of the *Union-Tribune*?"

J.V. leaned back, a sly look on his face. "We're having dinner with her tomorrow evening."

"Do you think you can convince her to write an article about WAIT FOR ME anytime soon?"

"That sounds like two favors to me, but I'll see what I can do. It'll cost you, though."

Danita knew what was coming. J.V. lived to bargain with her. Although he always came through, he loved to tease her first.

"How about you sit with Adam next weekend? Laureen and I need a second honeymoon."

Danita suppressed a laugh. She liked his bargain and she suspected he knew it. She loved spending time with Adam.

"I can manage that only if Rena gets the article written and in the paper within two weeks."

"You haven't given me much time. Maybe if you sit with Adam for the next two week-ends I'd have more incentive."

J.V. looked doubtful, but by the hint of humor in his dark brown eyes she guessed he was giving her a hard time just for the heck of it.

Laureen called from the doorway. "Jeremiah Vernon Spencer, admit you can do the favors and quit stalling. Dinner's ready."

The kitchen phone chimed. While Laureen went to answer it, J.V. said, "Okay, you've got it. Two week-ends with Adam for a nice big spread in the UT and a DVD from my studio."

Laureen called out, "It's for you, Danita. It's Virgie."

Danita hurried to the kitchen phone. "What's up?"

Virgie sounded distressed. "I hate to spoil your evening, but Mr. F. has to change his visit to tomorrow."

"Oh, no! We'll never be ready by then!"

"Oh, yes we will. We'll show Mr. Frederickson that we can handle a little surprise visit. WAIT FOR ME is in the business of dealing with emergencies. How soon can you get back to the office?" Virgie's voice rang with confidence.

"I'm on my way. Thanks, friend." She hung up the phone.

Laureen went to Danita's side. "Let me fix you a plate to take with you."

Danita hugged her sister. "I don't know what I'd do without you."

Laureen took a large plastic dish and its cover from the cupboard and filled it with enough food for two people. "Just get back to the office and come up with a kick-butt game plan."

※

Midmorning on Friday Danita sat next to her advisor at a conference table in a corner of WAIT FOR ME's spacious lounge. Her favorite seniors, Phil Carver and two of his friends took up chairs on both sides of them. The aroma of coffee and the subdued hum of familiar voices provided a reassuring background for Danita's frayed nerves.

Phil Carver, a spry and still handsome sixty-something with a full head of salt and pepper hair, placed his empty mug on a paper napkin. "One thing your questionnaire doesn't cover, and that's love," he said in his rich Southern accent. "You hang around this place long enough and you feel lots of love. Ms. Danita spreads it around like honey on a bun. Carlos and Ms. Virgie, too."

Danita's heart filled with pride. She had tried to make WAIT FOR ME more than a place to work, and her employees appeared to recognize her efforts.

Mr. Frederickson pulled out a blank sheet of paper and laid it on top of the questionnaires. "Can you be more specific?"

John Fitzpatrick's speech still carried a touch of native Ireland. "These folks show they care what happens to us. They have people from different agencies come in here and explain new regulations and different kinds of insurances."

Danita watched Mr. Frederickson, but his expression told her nothing.

Mr. Frederickson wrote on the paper though he kept his gaze on Phil. "Ms. Johnson has speakers come here? I didn't know that."

Phil turned to his friend Ernesto Moreno. "Tell him about how they had the people from the state's senior advocacy program come in and explain long-term-care insurance to us last month."

Short, wiry and sporting a San Diego Chargers T-shirt, Ernie sat upright, with a look of self-importance. "These two ladies make sure we know what's happening, and help us do what needs to be done to make life easier for us. And if they can't, they find somebody who can."

John raised his shaggy red brows. "Danita found a good lawyer for Zenia's grandson. Everybody knows the kid's innocent. The D.A. keeps delaying the case, but now it looks like his lawyer's going to get him off."

Danita winced. She had hoped to keep that little fact from Mr.

Frederickson. He might think she helped felons.

"Yeah." Phil smiled widely. "They get us free tickets to dress rehearsals for the opera, the symphony and plays, too."

John, his hazel eyes alight, added, "They take more time with us than our own kids. That's what I call 'love' at work."

Danita smiled. One thing she had over Cullen: she didn't fix her people and send them on their way. She took responsibility for their welfare over the long haul.

With a nod of his head, Ernie indicated the twenty or so seniors in the lounge. "This is one place where we're always welcome whether we go out on jobs or just hang around. Some of us guys help out——fix little things. Beats sitting home alone, and with so many of us here, we keep Ms. Danita and Ms. Virgie safe."

Mr. Frederickson wrote furiously on the paper, and shoved it into the folder. He glanced at the clock over the door, stood and shook hands with Ernie, Phil and John. "If you'll excuse us, Ms. Johnson and I need to meet in private. Thank you again for your cooperation."

When Mrs. Sanders handed a covered plate filled with cookies and brownies to Mr. Frederickson he beamed and took it. "Thank you. They're great." He followed Danita out of the lounge and through the reception area. Apprehensive, she opened her office door and proceeded to a small conference table next to her desk. The good part's over. Here comes the hard stuff, she thought.

Danita passed a budget folder to Mr. Frederickson and opened her own copy. He went over every line and column and asked for clarification from time to time.

Mr. Frederickson made no comment, but completed his examination of her budget. He looked up from the spreadsheets, his demeanor serious. "You've done a good job with WAIT FOR ME. I'm prepared to confirm the committee's opinion that it serves a necessary and unique community service."

"Thank you," Danita said with relief.

"However," he said, "You must assure us you'll find a way to cut back on your expenses in the future. You appear to have used your assets well, but there are ways to save money if you look carefully at your budget."

"My partner and I have already started exploring ways to cut back."

"Make certain you stick to your guns." Mr. Frederickson's level look told her he meant what he said.

"Yes sir," she said in a subdued voice.

Mr. Frederickson unbuttoned his gray suit jacket. "Penn

Atkinson wants to help worthy enterprises, but only if they use fiscal discretion. Your business is thriving. You have a good concept and in general WAIT FOR ME is well run, but unless you learn to manage it more efficiently, you'll be in financial trouble again within a year."

"We're making the corrections as part of our new operating policy."

Frederickson crossed his arms. "I have a little story to tell you. Two years ago the foundation rescued a concern on the verge of going under. It, too, was an asset to the community. When we told its managers to discontinue their speculative investments with the son of one of their owners, they gave us their solemn word they would."

Nervous, Danita smoothed her navy blue suit skirt.

"After we gave them the grant they decided they were out of danger, so they returned to their old practices. They soon ran out of the grant money and the business had to declare bankruptcy. When the story hit the papers, heads rolled at the foundation because of that little fiasco." Mr. Frederickson frowned.

Danita's gaze didn't waver from his. "I assure you we don't plan to make the same mistake."

"I hope not." The smile he flashed held no warmth. "I haven't made my site visit to COPR yet, but from what I've seen here today, you're still in the running. Take my warning seriously. I won't jeopardize my job by making a recommendation likely to blow up in my face."

Danita hid her shaking hands in her lap. "We're well aware of the committee's position regarding scandal, and we intend to run this business in an even more responsible manner just as our already changed policies indicate."

Mr. Frederickson closed his folder and put it into his briefcase. "See that you do, Ms. Johnson."

The idea of Cullen's COPR winning the grant over WAIT FOR ME made Danita's stomach clench. She had to talk to Virgie and see if there was any way the business could survive without the foundation's money.

Picking up his briefcase, Mr. Frederickson stood and so did Danita. He shook her hand. "The committee will want to view the DVD your partner mentioned. The originality of WAIT FOR ME's mission impressed Mr. Rawley, our founder's grandson. Will it be ready anytime soon?"

Danita recalled the kindhearted committee member. She wished she had tried harder to impress him. "We expect to have it next week."

"Give our office a call when it's ready. I want the committee to get a feel for what I've seen."

"We appreciate the opportunity to show the program. We're proud of WAIT FOR ME and welcome the chance to share our ideas."

"I'll call you when I return from Sacramento. We'll get together one more time before next month's reception honoring past grant winners. You'll receive an invitation in the mail, but I'll give you the date now."

Mr. Frederickson took his organizer from his inside jacket pocket, and read the date to Danita. He waited until she penciled it in on her desk calendar before putting away his Palm Pilot.

Her spine stiff, Danita led the way to the exit. When the door closed behind him, she slumped against it and fanned her face with one hand.

Things could have gone worse... a lot worse. Although Mr. Frederickson had said they were still in the running she knew they couldn't rely on him to recommend WFM over COPR.

Resolute, she strode to the front desk. They needed a back-up plan to save WAIT FOR ME.

ஐ

Danita checked with Carlos their part-time secretary/part-time community college student, and learned Virgie had no one with her in her office. After a perfunctory knock she barged in, sank into an armchair next to Virgie and kicked off her shoes.

"How did the interviews with our employees go?" Virgie asked with a tired smile.

Danita gave Virgie a weary grin. "Great. We'll have to do something special to thank them for keeping us in the game."

Virgie smoothed her full beige miniskirt over her knees. "What did Mr. F. say?"

Danita gave a brief account of her meeting with Mr. Frederickson, including his thorough examination of their budget and his final warning. "The man is unyielding. There's got to be a way around the grant."

Virgie fingered her gold necklace. "Sorry, partner, but we'll go toes up in six months without the grant money."

"'Go toes up'?"

"Be out of business. Unless we can come up with ten grand in the next three months, it's good-bye WAIT FOR ME."

Danita sighed. "I've cut back every way I can. I've put all my savings back into the business. No more gourmet dinners, no more shopping at Nordstrom's. I buy my shoes at Marshall's. I even let my housekeeper go. I don't know any other way to economize."

"We'll keep it simple around here and stay out of trouble. I can't imagine what kind of scandal we could get ourselves into, but we'll watch our step."

Danita dipped her head in agreement. "One way I know of is to keep our minds on the business, get some free publicity, and keep our personal lives squeaky clean."

"You mean we can't date until this is over?" Virgie asked with an impudent smile.

"You're welcome to go out all you want, but I have no plans to date until we have the grant money in the bank," Danita vowed.

"Cullen will be disappointed at that bit of news."

Danita jerked upright remembering Laureen's comment about Virgie. "You did give him the third degree, didn't you?"

Virgie's expression was pure innocence. "Of course not. He came in, asked about you, then left."

"What did he ask?" Danita sat up in the swivel chair.

"He wanted to know if you were in. What time you'd get back. What you said about him. Did you date? Just stuff like that." Virgie waved her hand in a dismissive gesture.

Danita's cheeks warmed. "Did I date? I hope you told him my private life didn't concern him."

Virgie grinned. "Sure did, but I think he's kind of cute, He reminds me of the big brother I always wanted when I was a kid."

Danita had wondered if Cullen would make more than a big-brother impression on Virgie. "You mean you found him comfortable and easy to talk to?"

"Right. And I could tell you're his main interest."

Danita didn't like the way her pulse speeded up and her heart lurched at the thought of Cullen being interested in her. "What makes you think that?"

"The way he said your name and the dreamy look he gave your office door." Virgie paused dramatically. "He was almost fidgeting before I told him that you weren't dating anyone seriously."

"You didn't...! Why'd you tell him that? You know I can't get involved with anyone." She uncrossed her legs.

"The man looked so worried when he came in here I didn't think about it. He said you ran out of the coffee shop like Lucifer had come after you with a pitch fork, and he hoped he hadn't done anything to offend you. Did he come on to you?"

Danita's face fairly burned. "No."

"I invited him to help me finish your share of the pizza, but he said he had to get back to his office."

Danita thanked her guardian angel Cullen hadn't grilled Virgie. She wondered what Virgie wasn't telling her, but she didn't want to discuss Cullen one more second. Thinking about him confused her, and she didn't need the distraction.

She suppressed her runaway emotions without examining them. "I still want to learn the budget program you're using. I faked it today with Mr. Frederickson, but I won't get away with that forever. Can we get together in the evenings this week-end?"

"No problem. See you tonight," Virgie turned to her computer.

Danita halted at the door. "I'm out of circulation until June first. Don't get any ideas about Cullen and me. Understood?"

Virgie raised one hand as if taking a pledge. "I know how important the next two months are going to be. I wouldn't dream of playing matchmaker. I know it would be a lost cause anyway."

"And don't you forget it." Something in Virgie's guileless tone aroused Danita's suspicion. Virgie may be hiding something but Danita would find out what it was soon enough. In the meantime she had a business to run and a grant to win.

❧

Friday afternoon Danita looked around the Golden Hyacinth. "I can't believe this. It's only four o'clock, and happy hour has already moved into high gear."

"I told you this would be fun," Virgie said in a voice loud enough to be heard over the hubbub of the crowd. "We need a short break before we start on that new program of mine."

Danita shouted into Virgie's ear. "Okay, so I'm not sorry you talked me into coming, but we have to leave soon. I'm exhausted."

"Just a few more minutes. I want to finish my food." Virgie took a dainty bite of her miniature quiche.

Talking required too much effort in such a noisy environment. Danita leaned against the back of the booth and scanned the crowd. She loved to people-watch. Fifteen more minutes couldn't hurt.

Two men had been eying them since they sat down and ordered the night's special drink, but she and Virgie had ignored them. They had earned this evening's moments of relaxation, and

Danita didn't welcome any over-eager unknown males.

She squinted at the crowd, regarded the people milling about the entrance, and wondered where newcomers could possibly find seats. All at once she did a double-take.

Cullen Powers and a tall, lanky hunk came toward their booth as if they had been expected.

Quelling a giddy sense of pleasure, Danita turned an accusing glare on Virgie who enthusiastically waved the pair toward them.

Danita smiled and said between gritted teeth, "I'll get you for this, friend."

"What a surprise!" said Virgie, still waving. "I had no idea Cullen would show up here."

Danita's heart thumped in an erratic rhythm. "I'll just bet you didn't. I'm out of here!" She pushed her plate away and grabbed her purse.

Virgie put a hand on Danita's wrist. "What's the matter with you? Do you want him to think you're afraid of him?"

Danita could answer that as soon as she figured out how to breathe again. She sank against the green leatherette seat. Virgie had a point. Danita had to show Cullen he couldn't intimidate her, and then she'd leave.

"Lucky we ran into you two! All the other seats seem to be taken," Cullen said with an infectious grin which Danita tried but failed to resist.

He and his friend stood in front of their table. Cullen's gaze moved from her eyes, to her face, her breasts, and the hand gripping her bag, before it returned to her eyes. Every part of her body Cullen's gaze had touched tingled to life.

She set her bag down between her and Virgie. "Fancy meeting you here." She reached for a remoteness she didn't quite capture. Something in her coiled, waiting. She met his gaze and wished she hadn't. His eyes darkened, his pupils dilated. Quickly, she glanced away.

Virgie scooted closer to Danita to make room for Cullen's tall handsome companion. Six feet four, his curly lashes framed deep brown eyes that twinkled with mischief. His hair was closely cropped beneath a Padres cap. His chestnut-colored skin was as smooth as Cullen's. When he smiled, deep dimples winked at them. "Have a seat. There's plenty of room at our table."

Cullen bent close to Virgie and spoke into her ear loud enough for Danita to hear him. "This is Mitch Stone. He designed the myoelectric hands we make for our three to six-year-olds. We've had one hell of a week and came to do some mindless unwinding."

Cullen slid into the seat next to Danita. His face was close enough for Danita to kiss. She examined his smooth skin. A whisper of beard covered his chin.

He looked tired. She almost touched his cheek. She gave herself a mental shake. Who cares if he shaves or if he's tired?

Cullen's friend, Mitch, approached the booth and sat on the far end next to Virgie who immediately engaged him in conversation. Because of the noise, Danita didn't stand a chance of including herself in their discussion. A waiter came to take drink orders, affording her a few moments to gather her wits.

Mitch's bulk, added to Cullen's, crowded Danita in the limited space. She took a deep breath and inhaled the faint aroma of Cullen's woodsy aftershave. She clamped her knees and ankles together hoping to keep Cullen's thigh from touching hers.

Each time his leg brushed against hers she sat straighter until she was rigid. She had to relax soon or get a cramp in her thigh. *Where is that waiter?*

As if by magic, the waiter returned with their drinks. Cullen calmly raised his glass. "To a chance meeting with new friends," he said into Danita's ear. His breath fanned her skin sending a shower of sparks to the pit of her stomach.

She touched her glass to his and took a healthy swallow of raspberry iced tea. The smooth fruity drink slid down her throat but did nothing to cool her off. Cullen's body heat made her want to sink against the back of the booth and fan her face, but she restrained herself.

With inexplicable fascination she watched Cullen place his glass on the table next to hers and run a finger along the moisture that had already beaded on its side. He loosened his tie with his free hand. "I'm glad I ran into you. I'm still curious. Did I say something to annoy you the other day?"

Danita stared at her drink. "No. I simply needed to get back to the office. I had an important business appointment that evening, and I'd planned to get ready for it." Danita halted her rapid-fire speech, amazed. She never babbled. She picked up a baby-back rib and held it, not sure how she came to have it in her hand.

"Good," he said. "Glad I didn't do anything to upset you. I hoped you liked me as much as I like you."

He pointed to one of her ribs. "Do you mind?" he asked. When she shook her head, he picked up one rib and took a bite.

Gawd, the man has the nerve to look sexy even when he's eating. She watched him lick his lips. Annoyed with herself at being turned on by him, she dropped her own rib on her plate and tried to inch away, but bumped into Virgie.

Danita's voice caught in her throat. "It's not that I don't like you, but I have a lot of work to do running a business, looking out for my seniors, and working to win the grant. I don't have time for new friends right now. I'm sure you can understand."

His brown-eyed gaze snagged hers and wouldn't let go. "Not really. Let's have dinner tonight and you can explain it to me. We'll give Virgie and Mitch a chance to get acquainted."

Danita looked over at Mitch and Virgie. They had their heads together, laughing. At any other time she'd have been gratified to see Virgie shed her don't-speak-to-me attitude, but Danita didn't want to spend time with Cullen. "I'm sure if Virgie and Mitch want to see each other they can work that out for themselves. I don't think it would be wise for us to get... involved."

Cullen laughed. The rumble of his baritone vibrated through her body and set off new tremors of awareness.

"I wouldn't call dinner in a crowded restaurant 'getting involved'," he said.

Danita couldn't think of a retort. She wanted to avoid his company until she could control the way his nearness made her pulse speed up and her hands tremble.

She glanced at her watch. "Good gracious. Look at the time. Virgie, we've got to go. Now."

Mitch stood and moved aside, his black brows raised in surprise. "So soon?" he asked. Disappointment throbbed in his voice. "I just asked Virgie if you two could join us for dinner."

"Sorry she can't. We can't. Virgie and I have some serious work to do this weekend. I'm driving so she has to leave with me. Now." She cut Virgie a meaningful look. "Let's go."

She tugged Virgie to her feet and gave her a light warning pinch. Cullen eased out of the booth and stood back enough to let them pass.

He towered over Danita. She stared at the knot in his tie, refusing to tilt her head to meet his eyes.

He placed his hands on Danita's shoulders, leaned down and spoke in her ear. "I'll give you a call soon. We'll do lunch."

His touch shook her. Danita squeezed past him, pulling Virgie in her wake. "I don't think that's a good idea," she said addressing his hand on her left shoulder. "Lunch is my busiest time."

"I'll bring Chinese and watch you work your miracles." he said with an enigmatic smile. He dropped his hands and backed away.

Danita gave a noncommittal shrug, pivoted away from him and hurried as fast as the milling crowd permitted, Virgie lagging at her side. When Danita got near the exit she looked back in time to see Mitch slap Cullen's back and say something. Cullen had a determined look on his face.

She snapped her attention forward and hastened through the heavy doors. The din of the crowd faded when the doors swung closed behind her, shutting out Cullen's gaze which she had felt at her back every inch of the way to the door.

She breathed in the fresh, misty spring air with relish. She had made another successful escape, but she also knew she had not seen the last of Cullen Powers.

Three

AFTER DANITA TOOK VIRGIE home, Virgie stood by the breakfast counter in her condo waiting for coffee to brew. She threw up her hands in a gesture of surrender. "All right, already! I'm sorry if I meddled where I shouldn't have, but I did it for your own good."

Famous last words before heading down the road of good intentions on the way to perdition, Danita slid onto a stool. "You maneuvered me into going to The Golden Hyacinth to meet Cullen, didn't you?"

Virgie looked like a kid caught at the dinner table with a mouse in her pocket. "Cullen's a nice guy, and he's obviously interested in you. I felt sorry for him."

Danita narrowed her eyes. "You can't resist match-making for everyone but yourself, can you? This time you've gone too far. Aren't you worried about WAIT FOR ME? Will you feel sorry for us if we lose the grant?" She threw up her hands in exasperation. "You promised you wouldn't do this again."

Virgie gave a contrite pout. "I talked to him before you told me you wanted to avoid him. I didn't know how to get in touch with him to let him know I'd changed my mind."

Danita shook her head in disgust. "If you'd let me know what you were up to I could have told you how to get in touch with him. I want you to promise me you won't do this again."

Virgie grinned ruefully. "I promise."

As quickly as her annoyance had surfaced it melted away at the contrite look on Virgie's face.

Danita said, "Hold out your hands. I want to make sure you don't cross your fingers...and don't cross your legs or your eyes.

Don't try to get Cullen and me together ever again."

Virgie stood at attention. She lifted her hand facing forward and shoulder high with four fingers raised and her thumb crossing her palm. "I promise I'll butt out."

Danita erupted into laughter and Virgie joined her. Danita said, "You'd better. Now, how about that coffee?"

Virgie filled two cups, carried them into the living room, and they both sat on her very modern very bright blue sofa scattered with jewel-toned pillows.

"I don't get it," Virgie said picking up a bright green pillow and hugging it to her chest. "Cullen doesn't strike me as anyone who'd deliberately hurt you or anyone else. From our talk the other day and what I could see of him tonight, he seemed like a decent guy. What's got you running scared? And I don't want to hear about the grant, Robert, or how your Uncle Walker terrorized your cousins and beat up on your aunt."

Danita hated it when Virgie made her look at her real reasons for avoiding attractive men. From previous conversations along the same line, she knew she'd have to level with Virgie or spend the next hour squirming under her cross examination.

Danita took a swallow of her coffee. She still tingled every time she remembered how her pulse had speeded up when she was sitting next to him at the club. "It's a combination of all of the above, but it's more than that. Cullen...makes me nervous."

Virgie laughed. "That's a new name for it. From what I could see he turns you on. I've never seen you so rattled."

"I don't see the humor in the situation."

Virgie turned toward Danita, kicked off her shoes and tucked a foot under herself, her laughter lingering in a smile. "I do. You're always telling me to forget Ben. You say all men aren't like him, but you won't take your own advice."

"Ben never hit you."

"Maybe not, but he verbally abused and deceived me, and that's just as bad."

Danita patted Virgie's arm. "I'm sorry. I shouldn't minimize what you went through. You had a horrible time."

Pain clouded Virgie's eyes. "We're talking about you and Cullen. I could tell by the way you hustled us out of there that he got to you. You're attracted to him. Admit it."

Danita hesitated because she didn't want to answer the question. "I think I'd recognize 'attraction' when I felt it. This is different—not a comfortable feeling—more like flustered, excited, disturbed, but not attracted. I want to shake him and laugh at the same time. He confuses me."

Virgie's face lit with a knowing smile. "Maybe you should consider getting to know him better. Then you could figure out what's going on between you."

"You and I have our futures and the futures of the people who work for us at stake right now. I don't dare do anything to wreck our chance to save WAIT FOR ME. You know that even better than I."

"I know. I'm sorry I interfered, but sometimes if you don't take chances you lose them."

"If I weren't willing to take chances, WAIT FOR ME wouldn't exist, but I'm not willing to chance losing it over a man we know little about. Are you?"

Virgie squirmed. "You're right, but I liked him on sight. I'm seldom wrong about people, unless my own heart's involved."

"I agree. I depend on you to screen our people, and you have yet to be wrong about any of them." Danita took another sip of her coffee.

"There's something else I haven't told you. Before I do, I need you to swear you'll never tell another living soul."

Virgie leaned forward and frowned. "Sounds serious. You have my promise."

"It's about Kevin and my family heirlooms."

"You mean the ones from Africa that your grandmother passed on to you?"

Danita shifted uneasily. "Yes. Now be quiet and listen before I lose my courage. I needed some ready cash after Robert cleaned out our operating account. I told Kevin he could borrow the bronzes and put them on display at his gallery if he would lend me $10,000. He liked the idea, but said if I didn't repay him by the end of July, he'd consider them his."

"Tell me it's not true! You know Kevin has been after you to sell them to him for years now. Why didn't you come to me?"

"At the time you and Ben were having real problems, and from what you said, I knew you'd already maxed out all of your credit cards. Besides, I was sure we'd be in the black by now."

Virgie stood and placed her arm around Danita's shoulder. "What are we going to do?"

"We're going to go all out for that grant, and we're going to get it. Then I'm going to mend my ways. The business is too important to a whole lot of people for me to lose it now. That's another reason I don't want to get sidetracked with Cullen. He may or may not be another Robert the Rat, but right now I don't want to take that chance. Do you understand?"

Virgie looked as if Danita had delivered a body blow. She blinked back what looked like tears, reached for her coffee and drained the cup. For the first time in twenty plus years Danita realized Virgie was at a loss for words.

"It's been a long week and an even longer evening. Let's call it a night." Danita stood, hugged Virgie and headed for the door. "I'd better get home. It's too late to start on that new program now. I'm really worn out. I plan to get a good rest tonight. I'll see you around nine tomorrow morning. I don't want to show up with these bags under my eyes when J.V. and his crew show up bright and early Monday morning to make that promotional DVD for us." *And I need time to get Cullen out of my mind.*

Virgie trailed along after Danita. "Everything seems to be happening at once. First we spent hours while Rena interviewed us for the article that's coming out in Sunday's Trib. Next we have to get ready for J.V. I hope Sunday's feature turns out as well as I think it will. We need some good news. The photographer took enough pictures to fill an entire Sunday supplement," Virgie said.

Danita gave Virgie a weary smile. "I'm counting on it to make those folks at Penn-Atkinson sit up and take notice."

"I can't wait until Sunday."

Wanting to lighten the mood a bit, Danita asked, "Think you'll ever see Mitch again?"

A secretive smile lit Virgie's face as she walked Danita to the elevator. "I might."

Danita gave Virgie a thumbs-up sign. "Go, girlfriend! Just because I won't date Cullen doesn't mean you can't date Mitch. I could tell you two hit it off. Good luck. You deserve to be happy."

Danita walked to the elevator and pushed the down button. As the elevator door opened Virgie called out to her, "You do, too, Danita, and don't forget it."

Danita wondered if she did deserve it. Thanks to trusting the wrong man she'd brought her business to the brink of bankruptcy. If she hadn't needed the grant she'd never have met Cullen, and he wouldn't be making her crazy now.

She thought about him all the way home. The way he appeared out of nowhere to drive her nuts. But she had a chance to make up for misplaced trust, past decisions, and financial mistakes, and she couldn't blow it again. She needed her wits about her when she was with someone as sharp as Cullen Powers.

While she fumbled with her keys trying to open the door to her townhouse the phone rang four times. She hurried inside. The message machine kicked on before she could pick up the receiver. She almost regretted having her business calls forwarded to her home. She hoped a new client didn't need service over the week-end.

"Hi. This is Cullen. Hope you have a nice week-end. Called to say you missed a great dinner. See you soon."

Danita stared at the machine. He must have thought I'd hear his message when I got to the office first thing Monday morning. He wants to shake me up. Well, he hasn't.

The machine clicked off, but Cullen's sexy baritone lingered in her ears. She had no idea why she smiled and replayed the tape. She listened to it twice more, then poised her finger over the delete button, but didn't press it.

She could erase it later.

❧

After spending all day Saturday at Virgie's going over the new budget program, Danita had to shift gears on Monday for J.V. and his crew. They had arrived at seven in the morning, two hours before WAIT FOR ME opened.

Danita welcomed the morning's controlled chaos which gave her no chance to think about Cullen. The seniors came in at nine on the dot and added to the chaos. By noon the turmoil had her frazzled, but it looked as if J.V.'s people had finished for the day.

J.V. said, "I'll send a couple of people back here right after lunch to interview you and Virgie." He handed two sheets of paper to Danita. "Here are the questions. Be ready by one-thirty."

Danita laughed. So much for getting rid of J.V. "Will do. Thanks, Bro. I owe you more than one."

"You're right about that. I'm planning to collect." He blew on his nails and rubbed them on his imaginary lapel in a self-congratulatory gesture. "The UT article was great, thanks to me."

"Better than that. I got a call this morning from my advisor. He complimented me on the story and said Mr. Rawley was so impressed he had copies made for his files. The phones have been ringing all morning, seniors looking for jobs, and potential clients looking for help."

"We can discuss it Friday night when you pick up Adam. He's looking forward to spending the week-end with you."

After she saw J.V. and his people off, she walked toward her office, reading the questions he'd given her.

Carlos motioned her to his desk and pushed the hold button. "We've got a guy named Powers on the line who insists on speaking to you. Says he has an emergency, and wants to know if you can work him in first thing in the morning. Want to take the call?"

Danita's heart nearly leaped out of her chest, but she nodded as nonchalantly as she could while searching for her voice.

Carlos spoke into the phone. "She'll be right with you. Hold on please."

Danita hurried into her office, closed the door and sank into her swivel chair. Her pulse skittering, she wiped moist hands on the slacks of her grape-colored suit, picked up the phone and punched line two. "Cullen? What can we do for you?"

"I'm in a bind and need your help."

She swallowed and twisted the telephone cord around her forefinger. "What's the problem?"

"I had a fire at my place last night."

A wave of fear swamped her. She remembered the damage the fire had done at her old location. "Oh, my God. Were you hurt?"

Cullen's voice held a strange note. "I'm fine. The smoke made a mess of my kitchen, but no serious structural harm was done. When I walked in the door the smoke alarm was blasting in the kitchen. Luckily I was able to put the fire out myself."

Remembering the fire that had wrecked WAIT FOR ME Danita was still shaken from what could have been a serious situation. "How did it happen?"

"I did something stupid and caused the fire myself."

"What did you do?"

"When I was washing dishes, my cooking mitt fell into the sink and got wet. I stuck it in the oven to dry and forgot to turn the oven off. I had a lot on my mind, and took a walk in the park."

"You didn't."

"Told you it was something stupid. Lucky I came home when I did."

Relief flooded her. "Yes, you were."

Cullen said, "I tracked down some painters who can do the job in one day. I need someone from WAIT FOR ME to let them in and hang about until they finish. Is tomorrow too soon for you to send someone?"

"Let me check our schedule."

She put him on hold and signaled the front desk. "Carlos, how's the schedule for tomorrow?"

"Pretty tight, but we can cover an emergency if it's for one day. Only problem is, the pair we can send out has to leave promptly at five o'clock. Will that do?"

Danita said, "Get on line two. Let's see what we can arrange."

After a lengthy three-way discussion Danita agreed to send two of her house sitters to Cullen's place the next day. When Carlos rang off, Danita told Cullen, "You'll need to drop off your keys today, sign a contract and pick up your information packet."

"I'll bring sandwiches and sodas and we can do it over lunch?"

"Sorry, now's not a good time. We're taping a promotional for the business and I've got a script to go over before one-thirty. Can you drop by at five-thirty?"

Danita heard a note of disappointment in Cullen's voice when he said, "No problem."

Danita penciled him in on her schedule. "Fine. See you then." She hung up before he could say anything more.

She leaned back in her chair wishing that she didn't have to see Cullen again so soon. She knew she'd have to deal with him when he came because Carlos and Virgie would be busy logging their employees in for the day.

Under ordinary circumstances she enjoyed meeting and welcoming new clients. Often she gave them brief tours. She took them to her office and served them coffee and treats while she went over their contracts with them. They usually left with good feelings about her business and recommended it to their friends.

She had every intention of giving Cullen the red carpet treatment. That ought to help him realize what a great service WAIT FOR ME offered. As long as she had to be alone with him to fill out the necessary papers, she'd concentrate on impressing him. If she asked anyone else to do it they might get suspicious. How she hated her unwanted attraction to him. She only hoped she wouldn't have to see him again after they completed their business.

With a frown Danita rolled her chair up to her desk and picked up the papers J.V. had left with her. With dogged determination she blanked Cullen from her mind and concentrated on how to answer the questions The afternoon flew by with so much activity she was mystified as to how it was possible Cullen kept intruding into her thoughts. At four-thirty, Danita was tired but elated when J.V. and his people left. The raw tape she and Virgie had viewed looked great. They could hardly wait to see the completed program.

She went into her office to unwind. Twenty minutes later Carlos brought in the materials she'd need for her appointment with Cullen. "Can you stay for another hour?"

Danita looked up as Carlos shifted uncomfortably in front of her desk, a somber expression on his face. Danita's protective instinct surfaced. "What's the problem?"

"I got a call from my mom. My sister's baby is on the way, and there are complications. I've got to get home right away to stay with my niece."

Danita sat up straight, immediately alert. She had been so involved with her own problems she hadn't noticed anyone else's. He had been worried about his sister. She hoped the baby would be all right. "You should have told me sooner. Anything we can do?"

"Virgie said she'd drive me home if it's okay for me to leave now. It'll take too long to get there by bus. Phil told me he'd wait 'til you're ready to leave and make sure everything is locked up tight."

"Of course you may go, but is there something I can do?"

"No. Is it all right if I arrange for Mrs. Sanders to cover for me in case I can't get back here tomorrow?"

"I'll call Mrs. Sanders. You get going, and don't you dare come in tomorrow. You'll be exhausted."

Danita walked around her desk and gave Carlos a sympathetic hug and a pat on the back. "Mrs. Sanders has been dying to use her office skills. She knows the routine and will be glad to fill in for you. Take as much time as you need. Now get out of here."

Carlos bit his lower lip, his eyes suspiciously moist, his voice husky. "Thanks, Dani." He left, closing her door softly behind him.

Danita called Mrs. Sanders and told her the problem.

"I'll be delighted to cover for Carlos for as long as necessary," Mrs. Sanders said. "He's such a dear boy."

Danita remembered the reserved reception Carlos had received when he'd arrived at WAIT FOR ME, but she had been determined to introduce a younger element into the business. "I don't know what we'd do around here without him."

Mrs. Sanders voice became more businesslike. "What time do you want me there? I can come in early and stay until six."

They were winding up the details of their conversation when Cullen stuck his head in the door to her office. She searched his face. He had deep shadows under his eyes and their usual sparkle had disappeared, but she saw no sign that he had been injured in the fire. Relieved, she almost lost her train of thought. When she motioned him to come into her office, he strode to the chair in front of her desk and took a seat.

Danita needed time to pull herself together, put on her

business face. Stalling, she scribbled nonsense phrases on a blank piece of paper in front of her. "Okay, see you tomorrow morning at eight-thirty. And thanks."

Although Mrs. Sanders hung up, Danita held the phone to her ear a moment longer to give herself time to calm down. "Bye," she finally said and replaced the receiver.

She had been expecting him, so why had her heart gone out of control when he'd walked in the door? If he affected her that way every time she saw him, she was in big trouble.

❧

Cullen could tell Danita was stalling. He suppressed a smile, enjoying her obvious discomfort.

Danita's brows were creased and her full lips pressed together in a prim line. Her stare could have burned a hole in a sheet of paper on her desk as she scribbled on it with quick jerky strokes.

So. He had not imagined her loss of cool when they were thrown together at the Golden Hyacinth. He had lost his, too. He had believed no other woman existed who could bring him the rush of exhilaration he had experienced when he had first met Ayana, his wife.

From the moment he'd met Danita she had turned him on. Though he knew she wanted nothing to do with him, he blessed the fire for getting them together so soon.

If he didn't blow it, he'd show her he didn't want to upset her. He simply wanted to be near her, share her warmth, feel alive again.

While Danita talked on the phone, Cullen looked around her office. Its cheerful informality suited her. The candid pictures of her workers that adorned the walls drew his attention. He wondered if she took time to smell the one perfect pink rose which sat in a crystal vase on her desk.

At last Danita hung up and looked at him, a smile on her trembling lips. "Sorry the call took so long. We have an emergency."

He could have told her he could sit there all evening and watch her face, and listen to her sexy voice. He wanted to tell her how much he enjoyed her special fragrance; how he imagined her petite body nestled against his.

Instead he gave her what he hoped was his most guileless smile and said, "No problem. I know I caught you at a busy time. I'm grateful for your help."

He sensed a note of desperation in her voice when she said,

"Our mission is to help in emergencies."

He had a notion she might stand, click her heels together and salute. Instead she reached into her in-box and removed two folders with the distinctive WAIT FOR ME logo on their covers.

She bumped the small vase with the single rose in it. They reached out to catch it at the same time. When his hand touched hers she jerked away and toppled the vase into her lap. Water splashed on her pale pink blouse.

Fascinated, Cullen watched the liquid spread. It soon covered one perfect breast, the blouse's material clinging to a peaked nipple. A blush spread over her cheeks.

He knew he shouldn't stare at the spot where a puckered nipple poked against her blouse, but only a sudden fit of blindness could have checked his gaze. Finally looking away, he took a clean handkerchief from his pocket and extended it to her. "Sorry."

She grabbed it and dabbed at the stain. Reaching behind her, she tugged a purple jacket from the back of her chair and shrugged into it. With unsteady hands she returned his handkerchief. "No harm done. Now where were we?"

His voice husky, he said, "I believe you wanted to show me one of those folders." He pointed to the folders.

She handed him one with his name written in bold black letters on the cover, and kept an identical one before herself. "Let's get to it."

She went over its contents, explaining how WAIT FOR ME operated, and details of the work order, answering his questions as she went along.

While she filled out the forms in her matching folder, Cullen enjoyed the graceful movements of her small hands. She asked for his keys; he handed over his spares. She dropped them into a padded envelope and explained, "We'll keep your keys with specific instructions in our safe overnight. Each key has a special number assigned to it. No name. I take the addresses home with me. In case we are ever burglarized your keys are secure with us."

"Seems you've thought of everything." He grinned to himself.

She lifted her brown-eyed gaze from the folder in front of her. "Any questions?" Though on a roll and all business, her voice was slightly breathless.

He smiled. She had no idea what an enticing picture she made, sitting there in her tailored outfit which accentuated rather than diminished her femininity. He wanted to keep her talking a little longer. "A couple. Why do you send your employees out in pairs?"

"Each helps the other. While one explains the client's directions to the service person, the other takes notes and checks the appropriate boxes on their work order form. We bond and insure all the seniors, but each acts as a witness for the other in case of an accident or a dispute over any missing articles. In addition, if one of the employees gets sick, the other can call for help. The system has worked well with no incidents."

Impressed by the thoroughness of the planning needed for a simple job like sitting and watching some men paint, Cullen reassessed the woman before him. Danita might be sexy, but she was a smart cookie, and he'd better not forget it.

He rubbed his chin. "Two more questions. Who will you send to my place tomorrow morning, and what time will they arrive?"

She handed him the form she had filled out while they had talked, and pointed to two names. "John Fitzpatrick and Ernie Moreno. They'll get there at eight sharp."

"I believe I met them when I stopped by last week," He remembered them well. When he had stood at the front desk eying Danita's door, they had come over, introduced themselves and sung her praises like a pair of match-making grandparents.

Danita flashed him a look he couldn't interpret. "There's one problem. The seniors have to leave at five. You'll get home to relieve them by then, right?"

"I'll be home before five, barring emergencies." A shuffling and the slight motion of her body told him she was searching for a shoe under her chair. He smiled, remembering her dainty little feet.

"Let's pray your day remains crisis free," she said. "When the residents arrive home late, either Virgie or I have to cover for them. This is a busy time for us, and we'd appreciate it if you get home on time." She stopped shifting in her chair.

The primness of her remark tickled him all the way to his toes. This seductive package of raw energy turned him on, and he had a hell of a time sticking to business. If he got home late he wondered if she'd turn up at his... He squashed the idea before it developed. "Tuesdays are light at COPR. I plan to knock off early."

She shoved the contract in front of him, laid a red, white and blue pen with the WAIT FOR ME logo beside it, and indicated the signature line. "Please sign here. The folder's yours to keep." She focused on the contract as if it would disappear should she look at him instead.

After he scrawled his name, she kept the pink duplicate, placed his copy in an attractive folder, and handed it to him, still focusing anywhere but at him directly. Though he knew the meeting had come to an end he took his time putting it into his briefcase.

He refused to budge. She had to get up and walk around the desk to shake his hand. He waited.

As if she had read his mind, she stood up behind her desk. He scooted back his chair and came to his feet, but made no move toward her or the exit. She skirted her desk and headed for the door. He reached it the moment she opened it and held out his hand. "It's nice doing business with you. Thanks again."

When she shook his hand her pulse leaped at her throat. Its rapid flutter intrigued him, and he held her hand longer than he intended. She jerked her fingers from his grasp and turned away. Marching toward the door at a no-nonsense pace, she opened it for him.

"Good night," she said, her gaze somewhere between his chin and his tie.

"Good night," he answered. His husky farewell echoed her murmured one.

His heart pounded all the way from her door to his Buick. He searched his back pocket for his keys, then realized he had them in his hand. His hand was so moist with sweat he almost laughed aloud. He was a wreck just from being around Danita for a short while. He wondered how he would feel if they shared a whole evening together.

From the time he'd spent with Danita, he knew that until she won the grant she would avoid him like a kitten avoided water. And if she lost, he might never see her again.

He couldn't let that happen. He wanted to stake a claim in her heart before any decision was made about the grant. But how could he get her alone long enough to show her that she had nothing to fear? When would he have the chance to show her that after the competition ended, they had a chance to build something good between them? He had to find a way to make her acknowledge the surge of attraction between them and follow it where it led. At the thought a kernel of an idea formed.

He'd make sure he got her over to his condo the very next day and feed her a meal she would never forget. He knew it was a long shot, but he had all the next day to set up his plan.

He loved a challenge, but he had never dealt with a tougher one in his life.

In his office at COPR the next afternoon, Cullen said, "I'll be by to pick up the food in fifteen minutes. Will that give you enough time? ... Great. See you," and hung up the phone. He rubbed his hands together like an old time villain in a silent movie and chuckled aloud at his own craftiness. John and Ernie the house sitters from WAIT FOR ME had fallen in with his plan easier than he had hoped, and the painters had unknowingly cooperated, too. Danita would be at his place when he got home.

Cullen checked his watch: four thirty. If he hurried, he could pick up the carry out food he had ordered and get home in less than an hour. He hoped Danita would forgive him for being late.

He jogged to his car, keys in hand. In less than ten minutes he pulled into a curbside parking space a few feet from Jingo's Jamaican Restaurant. Sitting on a large corner lot, it sported spotless picture windows and a colorful neon sign proclaiming that Jingo's had the best Jamaican food in the west.

When he arrived at his door laden with packages, he had to push the bell with his elbow. He heard the click of heels and imagined an eye scrutinizing him through the peep hole.

Danita flung open the door. She wore a pink pants suit and a frown. Shoulder-length hair spiraled around her face. Soft wisps kissed her brow. "You said you'd be home early," she declared without preamble.

She looked soft and inviting rather than austere. He had the urge to give her a welcoming hug but the bags of food he carried made that impossible.

"I'm only a half hour late," he said. "I called your office and explained. I'm sorry. I had a last minute emergency. A business woman like you ought to understand."

Eying him with suspicion, she opened her mouth to speak when three men in paint-spattered coveralls trouped toward the door and stopped in the entryway. One of them looked at the bags. "Smells great," the painter said as he passed Danita and stepped into the hallway. He turned to Cullen. "Been to Jingo's I see. Too bad we can't stay. I could eat his food every night."

Cullen grinned. "I know what you mean. I've been smelling this all the way home. I can't wait to dig in." After he thanked the painters they left.

Cullen walked past Danita and into his condo. He hoped the aroma of Jingo's food would tempt her to stay, but her bland expression gave no clue to her thoughts. She closed the door behind them. Spicy smells filled the entryway. She licked her lips. His midsection tightened at the sight of her pointed little tongue moistening her full lips. He smiled. *I think she's hooked.*

He led the way to the dining area. "I knew the kitchen would be too full of fumes for me to cook," he said and nodded toward the bags he set on the table. "How does the kitchen look?"

Her face held the expression of a woman who had discovered a rare jewel. "Come see. It's terrific. The painters cleaned up after themselves, too. I have their card. I'd recommend them to my clients any day."

"They know their business, all right." He followed her to the kitchen. Dishes, covered with sheets and towels sat on counters. Shiny white cupboard doors stood open. He groaned at the thought of replacing dishes, pots and pans when the shelves dried.

He placed his packages on the counter near the kitchen door. Together they inspected the still-wet coat of yellow paint glistening on the walls. Someone had opened the windows, but the strong smell of paint lingered.

"All right," he said. "You can't tell I had a fire in here."

When she asked him how he had located the painters, he told her one was the father of one of his former patients. "Adibu can use all the work he can get. He's still paying huge medical bills. It's a shame how hard it is for self-employed people to get affordable health insurance these days."

"True," she said. "Well, I'll be on my way. Glad you got home when you did. I was beginning to worry about you."

Cullen raised his brows in surprise at her expression of concern for him. "You intend to leave now and make me eat all this food by myself?"

"Oh, I can't stay."

"Got a hot date for dinner?"

"No, but..."

He didn't wait for her to continue, but gathered silverware and heavy-duty white paper plates, took them to the dining room and deposited them on the oval mahogany table. "Come, join me. You have to eat, and it's the least I can do after I held you up here."

He dropped his suit jacket on the back of a dining room chair and directed the same innocent look at her he used to give his mother when he wanted to con her. It worked every time, and from the appreciative glance Danita gave his bags of food, it seemed to be working again.

"Okay," she said with a lilting laugh, "Who am I kidding? I'd love to stay. I haven't had Jamaican food since my cousin and I went to Montego Bay three years ago. The smells alone bring back memories of the good time we had."

Cullen turned his back to hide a triumphant smile. Retracing his steps to the kitchen he started a pot of coffee. He grabbed some napkins, serving spoons, cups, and saucers, poured glasses of water and loaded them on a tray.

When he carried the tray to the dinning room, she had already placed the containers of food on hot-plate pads and set the dishes on Kente-style patterned place mats. "Mmm, this smells wonderful," she said.

They filled their plates with a pork loin, cod fish cakes, and baked green papaya halves.

She used her fork to pick up a small cube of papaya. "Everything looks wonderful. This is almost too pretty to eat."

Cullen tried to swallow the lump in his throat as he followed the fruit's path to her mouth. He added a spoonful of mixed greens, nearly spilling them. "The Stamp and Go is my favorite," he rasped.

With each mouthful of food, she appeared to relax more and more. Halfway through the meal he wondered if inviting her to dinner had been such a good idea. He knew that echoes of her warm laughter, her soft alto, and the quick smiles that aroused and frustrated him would haunt his lonely home and leave him wishing she would stay for more than a quick meal.

To break the ice, he told her about his parents who lived nearby and were on a teaching sabbatical at the University of Ghana in Legon.

"My mom and dad both teach at San Diego State. My dad's in the English department and my mom's teaching courses in ethnic studies."

Talking about his parents didn't work. He found himself even more focused on her than what he was saying. When she examined a bite of roast pork loin her smiled broadened. She closed her eyes and slid the delicacy between her lips. She chewed; an ecstatic look appeared on her face.

Sensual hunger washed over him. His body tensed. He shifted uncomfortably. He watched this diminutive woman with the healthy appetite and hungered for her, wanting to keep her with him all night and explore all of her other appetites.

While she described her large family who sounded lively and supportive of her efforts with WAIT FOR ME, he fantasized. He imagined her in his bed lying against his pillows, her eyes filled with desire. He saw them walking for miles on a deserted beach. He fancied coming home to a house filled with laughter and promises of passion to come.

When she sat back with a sated look on her face and glanced at her watch, he jumped to his feet. "You can't leave without a slice of Jingo's Planter's Cake. It has mocha butter-cream icing. People have been known to kill for one small crumb."

"You don't have to convince me. I saw it when I unpacked this banquet," she said with a wicked grin.

"I'll get more coffee if you'll cut the cake." Hurrying to the kitchen, desire pounded through him. He lingered there, willing his taut body to calm. When he thought he could keep his hands to himself, he returned to the dining room with their coffee.

ಌ

Too content to eat and run, Danita settled into a comfortable position in the fan-back dining room chair. Strains of John Legend singing newfound love seemed to intensify the sensual tension growing between them.

She searched his face. His cheerful mood had vanished. She wondered what had caused it. Seeking to erase it, she encouraged him to talk about growing up in San Diego.

She learned he had lived ten miles north of where she had been reared. Their high schools had been sports rivals. They knew some of the same people. She was surprised she had never met him.

"When I went to work for COPR, I rented a house near my parents. After my partner Mitch and I bought out COPR, Ayana and I moved to this neighborhood. We both enjoyed standing on our balcony and gazing over at Balboa Park. I also have a shorter drive to work. It's peaceful around here," he said.

A stillness came over his face for the first time that evening. He sat quietly as if a million miles away. She sensed his loneliness and guessed he was thinking of his wife. She longed to comfort him, but didn't know how.

Danita placed her hand on his arm and waited, unwilling to break into his quiet contemplation. Her own fears seemed less serious in light of his loss.

Cullen appeared to emerge from his musings. "Have you heard of Kay Burdell?"

"The artist! Who hasn't? My sister and I worked in her husband's campaign when he ran for councilman in our district. He did a great job on the council. I don't hear about him anymore.

What happened to him?"

"Still in town, but instead of running for office he has a political consulting firm. He does quite well." he said. She heard a note of reservation in his words.

Danita said, "I went to one of Kay's shows at the Educational Cultural Complex last summer. Her work is stunning."

He covered her hand on his arm with his. "Would you like to go to her show next week in Balboa Park? She's my former mother-in-law. Come with me and I'll introduce you to her."

Sounds too much like a date, she thought. She eased her hand from beneath his, stood and busied herself carrying the dirty paper plates to the kitchen. Cullen followed with containers of left-over food which he stowed in his all-but-empty refrigerator.

She turned and almost spilled the remains of her unfinished coffee on his white shirt. Putting the plates in the trash she struggled to hold on to her caution. "I've promised myself I won't do anything for fun until I win the grant."

With that, she hastened back to the table and picked up more dishes; sorry she had mentioned the grant.

"Whoa," he said. "You're the guest, remember."

"You don't want me to help clean up?" She asked while she inched away from him.

"No, I'm a big boy. I think I can handle it."

"Fine, then I'll be on my way." She gave him an impish grin and, returning to the living room, gathered her purse and jacket from the black leather sofa. She sauntered to the front door unwilling to let him see her wariness.

Cullen followed. "You're one skittish lady." He cupped her shoulders, and with a light touch caressed them with his fingers. He towered over her, a hint of defeat in his eyes.

"Thanks for dinner. I especially loved the dessert," she said.

"I know why you're in such a hurry to leave. I feel the same way," he said. In spite of his matter-of-fact tone, he wore a roguish grin.

Puzzled, Danita asked, "What way?"

"Great food, terrible dinner partner."

"You're calling me a terrible dinner partner?" She sputtered.

"You made me sit through dinner and watch your sweet little mouth nibble on cod fish cakes, sample roast pork, savor papayas and sip coffee without an invitation to do this," he said. He leaned down and touched his lips to hers.

Taken by surprise, she didn't know whether to laugh or slug him.

"I controlled myself quite well," he continued, "until you made those noises."

An uncertain laugh spilled from her. "Noises?"

"Mmm-mm, aaah, oooh, yeees" he mimicked in a falsetto. "You made those noises every time you took a bite of the cake—and made faces."

Danita's cheeks flamed. "Oh, I hope I don't make faces when I eat."

"Yes, you do. You scrunched your brow...", he said touching his lips to her forehead, "closed your eyes...", he said kissing her temple until she shut her eyes, and pursed your lips until I almost choked on my food," he whispered against her parted lips.

Danita chuckled helplessly. "Get out of here!"

"I don't see what's funny," he said in a bantering tone. "You'd better leave right now or I'll have to...'

She tilted her head back and gazed into brown eyes filled with laughter. "You'll have to what?" She asked.

Without haste he lowered his head towards her. His teasing had allayed her fears, and she made no move to retreat.

"You're a nut." She pursed her lips.

Four

CULLEN INTENDED TO TEASE Danita with a memorable but lighthearted kiss, one that would weaken her defenses. He wanted to keep her like this...trusting, relaxed, and carefree.

Her black leather shoulder bag dropped to the floor. Her jacket slithered down his leg and settled at his feet. He ignored them both.

Still holding her gently, he eased her closer. His fingers skimmed her shoulders and his lips touched hers. She caressed him with her soft whimpers and the fragrance of lemon blossoms.

He stroked her lips with his. The rose-petal softness of her mouth drew him back again and again. He played upon it—patient, sure, focused.

Certain her sweetness came from the mocha-flavored dessert clinging to her lips, he lingered longer than he had intended. When she did not pull away he drew her closer. He wanted to restrain himself, but when her small firm breasts nestled against his chest and her arms stole around his waist, he knew he had lost the battle. He concentrated on her lips, and with a groan sought the nectar he knew was hiding inside her mouth.

He tempted her with soft nips and tender nibbles until her lips parted. Her response invited him to explore.

She intoxicated him. One kiss led to another, then another, each more intimate than the last. Drugged by the taste of her and aroused by the way she strained against him; he braced his legs apart and cradled her between his thighs.

His body grew even tighter, burgeoning against her. She stiffened, moaned and pulled away, but he held on, needing to absorb the essence of her spirit. He tried to ease the intensity of his arousal by pressing his body closer to hers but it only increased.

"Stop." She sighed into his mouth and parted her lips farther. He pursued the opportunity she offered, attempting to bind her to him with his kisses.

Her hands clung to his white shirt even as she pushed at his chest. He loosened his embrace while he returned for one last sample.

She stepped back. "Enough. Please. I'm not ready for this."

He caressed her spine to calm her while he gazed at her half-closed eyes and moist lips now devoid of lipstick. "I know," he said. Nevertheless he found himself still holding her. When she stumbled away from him, he steadied her with his hands, cupping her elbows.

"I didn't mean to... I'm sorry if you think... I've got to go. She leaned over, snatched up her bag, and grabbed her jacket. Without a backward glance, she left.

Speechless, his body still hard with desire, Cullen hurried to the window and watched her stride to her car, fumble in her purse for her keys, insert one and jerk the door open. She threw her jacket and purse onto the back seat, eased herself inside, and shut the door behind her.

She slumped over the wheel for a moment before she straightened, started the engine, and drove away.

Long after her car drove out of sight he stood looking at the deserted street. Street lamps cast pale orange circles of light here and there on the sidewalks. A dog barked. All else was silent, as if she had never been there.

He wondered if he should go after her to make sure she got home all right. *Damn, I blew it. She got away from me again. Better give her time to simmer down.*

He could still taste her, smell her, feel her in his empty arms, and he wanted to finish what they'd started. He knew he had to handle their relationship just right, or he'd never get a foothold in her heart or her life during the time it would take the committee to decide which one of them would win the grant. He also knew he'd have a snowball's chance at the equator if he won the grant before he won her heart. He'd see her again and soon or die trying.

He returned to the dining room table and began removing the remnants of their meal. He needed a plan, and kissing her until they were both senseless hadn't worked.

Then an idea took shape in his mind. He was certain Danita thrived on challenge. Why else would she start a business like

WAIT FOR ME and put everything she had into it? He already knew she couldn't resist a dare, either. He'd phone her in the morning and lay a proposition on her she couldn't turn down and still keep her self-image alive.

❧

The next morning he drove to WAIT FOR ME determined to make his plan work. He stopped at a flower shop and bought a pot of miniature roses.

When he'd called her that morning to let her know he wanted five minutes of her time, she'd balked but had finally agreed. He hoped five minutes would give him enough time to convince her to see him again.

He spotted Carlos when he entered the building. On the wall above Carlos' desk a banner declared "SAY UNCLE". Carlos looked up, a smile of recognition on his face.

For a second Cullen wondered if the message was aimed at him. He said, "May I take it congratulations are in order, Uncle Carlos?"

Beaming, Carlos walked up to the counter. "Got it in one. My sister had a boy, nine and a half pounds. She's fine, though she gave us quite a scare."

"Glad to hear she's all right. Are you a first-time uncle?"

Carlos poked out his chest. "I have a six-year-old niece, but this is my first nephew."

"Congratulations." Cullen shifted the pot of roses to his free hand and gave Carlos a high five. "Any chance Danita's ready to see me now?"

"Let me get her on the line." Carlos went back to his desk. After a brief pause he announced Cullen's presence. He hung up the phone and said, "Go on in."

With feigned confidence in his steps Cullen strode toward her office. Before he could knock, she opened the door and ushered him inside, leaving it open behind him. He inhaled her now-familiar fragrance as he followed her into her office. She took a seat behind her desk as far away from him as possible.

Though she hid her expressive eyes behind her glasses, she looked delicious and approachable. Her coral-colored pants suit brought to mind a tasty sherbet, cool but sweet to the taste.

Danita's formal smile was as plastic as a picnic spoon. She seemed determined to act as if nothing had happened between them. "Have a seat. Would you like some coffee?" She busily poured a cup and offered it to him.

The nutty aroma of the coffee reminded him he'd skipped breakfast. When she offered a plate of chocolate chip cookies he took one and laid it on the napkin she had given him.

He noticed she had not asked him what he took in his coffee. Good sign. She remembered he liked it black. He handed her the small pot of bright red roses.

"How lovely. Thank you." Though she seemed taken aback she could not hide her pleasure. She gave the fragile blooms a tender touch and bent to inhale their nonexistent fragrance. She set them down on the conference table next to her desk.

The prim look on her face told him she had no intention of repeating the fiasco of knocking over the flowers. Her rigid posture warned him she had erected a wall of reserve between them. He would let her get away with it...for now.

"Thought I owed these to you after knocking over that beautiful rose the other day. I hope it survived."

"It was fine. I revived it with a little water. What was so important you couldn't tell me over the phone?" She settled herself behind her desk and got right to the point.

An undercurrent of noise in the office outside her door forced Cullen to pull his chair closer to her desk and lean forward. "I came to pay my bill and apologize for my behavior last night. I suspected if I called, you might hang up on me."

"There was no need to come in to pay. We send out our bills." She leaned back a bit in her chair. "As far as an apology goes, forget it. It was no big deal."

It was for me, he thought. "Glad to hear it. I'd like to get to know you better. I wouldn't want any misunderstanding to ruin our new friendship." He unbuttoned the jacket of his light gray suit and settled back in his chair.

"What friendship? We can't be friends, at least not until this competition has ended. I can't allow anything or anyone to divert me from going all out for the grant. My staff and I need time to prepare properly for our meetings with our advisor. I'm the only one some of the people who work here can depend on. Too many people have either let them down or ignored them. I can't fail my seniors. Surely you understand."

"I understand, but I don't see how our friendship can interfere with what you have to do." He took a bite of his cookie and caught the crumbs in his napkin.

"You don't want to understand. You're trying to shake me up, make me forget what's important."

"You are one suspicious lady. Why would I do something so

underhanded?"

She pushed her glasses up on her nose and smoothed her bangs. "You tell me. After seeing your home I gather you're not hurting for money. I'm surprised you even applied for the grant."

Though he knew she was fighting her attraction to him, her accusations still stung. No way would he believe she could respond to his kisses the way she had and not feel something for him. "I need the grant, but you're so blinded by your prejudices you won't believe it. I can prove my need, but I doubt you'd be fair enough to find out for yourself or admit it when you do."

Danita leaned forward and folded her arms on her desk. "And how do you expect to prove you need the *Gotcha*! Come to my open house this Friday. Meet my staff and some of my patients. Find out about our special Africa project. Take the tour, then tell me I don't need the grant—unless you're afraid you might like what you see."

He didn't dare breathe. Maybe she wouldn't fall for his ploy.

She peered at him over her glasses. "Are you serious? You want me to come to COPR?"

"Exactly. Anytime Friday evening between four and eight. If you come, you'll even meet Kay Burdell." He threw the last bit in to sweeten the pot, and extended his business card.

"Kay Burdell? Really?" When she took his card, her hand touched his. She jerked away and busied herself reading it. He felt as if he had won a small victory when she didn't hand it back.

She hesitated, studying her desk calendar. "All right, but I have an engagement that evening. Mind if I bring him along?"

Cullen's satisfaction went up in smoke. *Him? What him? Virgie gave me the impression Danita's not seeing anyone.* He shrugged to show her an indifference he didn't feel. "Sure, bring him along."

Danita wrote on her desk calendar and paper-clipped his card to the sheet. She turned a saccharine smile his way. "Thanks for the invitation. See you Friday.

"Great. As long as I'm here, I'll stop by the desk and settle my account with Carlos. Bring your appetite with you. There'll be plenty to eat and drink."

"We will."

Cullen scowled. He didn't like her smug smile one bit. *She's trying to distance herself from me, but it won't work. Once I meet the competition I'll figure out how to get rid of him.*

❧

That evening Cullen carried the last of Kay's paintings into his office. His mind continued to dwell on Danita. He recalled the way she had returned his kisses, and he still burned. Her obvious desire to keep him at arm's length challenged rather than discouraged him.

He needed a woman's point of view, and since his parents had extended their stay in Africa, he would ask Kay for advice. He hoped she would accept his interest in a new relationship.

He stalled while he tried to figure out how to broach the subject. "I can't wait to see how the framing turned out."

"I special-ordered them."

"When my guests get a look at these you'll probably get several orders to do more."

"That, my son, would be really, really nice."

They cut twine, unwrapped the paintings and lined them against his office walls. Cullen stood back to admire the sensitivity apparent in the way Kay had captured the strength of her subjects and the bright colors she had used.

He moved from one painting to another. "These are terrific. I like the subtle way you incorporated physically challenged people. The stark mahogany frames make the eye go straight to each painting"

"Glad you like them, but you needn't feel you have to buy them. They were such a hit at my art show. I could have sold them on the spot."

"Oh, I want them all right." Cullen took a deep breath. "Kay, I need your advice. You're a woman."

"Nice of you to notice," she grinned. "Tell me about her."

He chuckled surprised at how transparent he was. "Maybe you can give me some ideas on how to pursue a friendship with a woman I admire and respect very much."

Kay moved to a couch in the waiting area and took a seat. Cullen sat next to her. "Go on," she said.

"Her name is Danita Johnson, and the two of us are locked in a battle for the Penn-Atkinson grant."

He told of his frustration and confusion over his attraction for Danita, and how she rejected every one of his overtures. He didn't tell her how she turned him on, set his body on fire, and stole his breath every time he looked at her. And he didn't mention luring her to his condo and plying her with food...and kisses.

As he talked he searched Kay's face for disapproval or annoyance, uncertain how much of the depth of his feelings he had revealed. Instead he saw compassion, humor, and interest.

"I do believe you've finally met someone you like and could

get serious about. I want to meet this lady," she said.

"She's coming to our open house Friday. She's one of your fans. I'm afraid I used you as bait to get her here."

Kay's rich chuckle chased away the last of his reticence. "Fascinating. Danita has good taste. I hope we get a chance to talk. What does she look like?"

"Petite, a little over five feet tall. She has a sophisticated air about her. She wears her shoulder-length hair in springy spiraling curls that frame her face. She's constantly brushing her bangs back from her forehead." He shifted in his seat remembering how he'd brushed a kiss on that forehead.

"And..."

Cullen hesitated and wondered what else Kay wanted to hear. "Her bangs accentuate her eyes. When she's not hiding behind those glasses of hers she has the most expressive eyes I've ever seen."

"Sounds cute."

"She is, but I don't think she'd like to hear you say that. She has one dimple that flashes in her left cheek when she laughs. I'm usually pretty serious, but I find myself making her laugh in order to catch a glimpse of her dimple."

"I'll have my work cut out for me looking for a small woman with one dimple," she said with a grin which he couldn't help return.

"*The Union-Tribune* ran an article on her in the Sunday supplement. I have a copy here somewhere." He went to his desk and, without searching, pulled the paper from one of the piles there.

He looked at the paper before he handed it to Kay. Danita's warmth reached out to him from the color photo layout. Her expression in the picture contrasted sharply with her heavy-eyed languor before she had pushed him away and marched out of his condo. His body tightened at the memory.

Kay studied the pictures and perused the article. "From what it says here, she must be a bundle of energy."

"She's that all right, and since the feature ran, she's busier than ever."

Kay placed the paper on the table and covered Cullen's hand with hers. "Honey, I hope you aren't uncomfortable sharing your new friend with me. You deserve happiness. You've earned it. I don't expect you to spend the rest of your life alone, contrary to what Aaron thinks."

"I hope you mean that because I think Danita may well become an important person in my life."

"Don't chicken out. You made a wonderful husband for Ayana, but she's gone." Kay's expression saddened, her voice barely a whisper. "Life goes on. You need a family of your own...children, a home, someone to pass the business to, and you don't need to apologize for wanting to get on with the business of living."

At her words of caring and support, a lump clogged Cullen's throat. His eyes prickled. He cleared his throat. "I may not get very far with Danita. She's bringing some dude to the open house with her. I think she's trying to tell me something."

"Jumping to conclusions only exercises your imagination. Better wait 'til you meet him. Meanwhile, I think you should relax, be yourself, and let her see she can trust you before you try to establish a deeper relationship with her. Give her a chance to know you. Try to see her as often as you can without pressuring her. From what you've said she sounds like a smart lady. If she's right for you I'm sure she'll recognize what a gem of a man you are."

"I'll try it your way. Thanks a lot." *Now, if only I can resist the urge to touch her, hold her, kiss her.*

"Anytime. I can't wait to see how things progress. I wish you all the best."

"Thanks, I need all the encouragement I can get."

"You certainly have mine." Kay pointed to the pictures. "Now, let's decide where to hang these."

They roamed around his office, discussed where each painting should be hung, placed each against the wall, and marked the chosen spot with colored tape. "Will Aaron bring you to the open house?" Cullen asked. "It's past time we buried the hatchet."

Kay tugged at the long sleeves on her blouse. "Before we start hammering why don't you give him a call and invite him yourself."

She picked up the phone on the table and dialed. When she got Aaron on the line she handed the phone to Cullen.

"Hi, Pops. Thought I'd give you a call and find out if you can make it to the open house at COPR Friday evening between four and eight."

There was a long pause before Aaron answered, "Cullen?"

"Yep."

"Can't. I have a heavy schedule trying to get ready for the special election in June. Can't get away right now." His voice sounded cool as he bit out the words.

"Sorry you can't make it, sir. Maybe we can get together some other time."

"Yeah. Some other time." Unfriendly harshness colored Aaron's tone. "Let me speak to Kay."

Kay spoke in monosyllables. "Yes...I know, but...I just thought... I can't. I promised to be here, and I'd hoped you might like to join me." She listened a while longer and with a heavy sigh she said, "All right, Aaron. I get the message."

She hung up, her brow knitted in obvious frustration. "That man. He's been through a lot, but haven't we all? He had the nerve to ask me to skip your open house to attend another function."

Cullen studied Kay, sorry now he'd mentioned Aaron. "I hope I haven't caused you any problems."

"None whatsoever." She drew herself up. "Aaron knows I've been planning on Friday for a long time. He's being stubborn. I'm kind of glad he won't be here with his attitude. I'm afraid I'd let it rub off on me and spoil my evening. Anyway I'll feel safer coming alone. I don't like it when he drives. Besides, if I come by myself, I can spend more time with Danita and her date."

She gave him a smile that didn't persuade Cullen all was well, but he let it go for the moment. If Aaron blamed him for Kay's decision it might give Aaron another reason for resenting Cullen. Cullen would hate it if Kay had to end their relationship. He valued her friendship and looked forward to the rare occasions they had a chance to spend time together.

She stood. "Let's start with the reception area."

After hanging two paintings there, they continued around his office working in genial silence.

When her sleeves slipped to her elbows Cullen saw a bruise. He grasped her right arm and examined the purple discoloration circling her wrist.

"I caught my bracelet on a hook the other day when I moved a picture," she said.

"It looks pretty bad. Have you seen a doctor?"

"It's nothing, but I'll be more careful in the future," she said and kept her gaze on the job at hand.

After she left he wondered again at Aaron's unreasonable anger and what consequences Kay might face because of her determination to meet Danita. Aaron and Kay had been married over thirty years. They understood each other.

Maybe his imagination was working overtime again.

After the week's hectic activities, Danita wanted to take a long soak in her tub and relax. Friday evenings were made for running errands, straightening up her apartment, unwinding, and watching a good DVD. Instead she dashed home, took a quick shower and jumped into an outfit she thought would do for the open house.

She refused to think about the better part of the two hours she had spent the night before going over her wardrobe, trying on various clothes, and experimenting with jewelry and scarves for just the right effect.

She would not admit to the feelings she had every time she looked at Cullen's roses. She had nurtured the blooms until Virgie began to ask about them with a suspicious grin. From then on she made it her business not to look at them when Virgie was around.

For a man of his height and apparent strength Cullen amazed her with the gentleness of his kisses. He nearly made her forget the grant, her determination to avoid entanglements and her worry over WAIT FOR ME.

Cullen was driving her crazy. The last time she'd seen him at her office, she'd actually tingled in all the places he had touched. It was becoming a struggle to keep her mind on the business at hand.

Carlos and Virgie were no help, either. They sang his praises and watched her closely to see how she reacted to their teasing over the roses. It was all too obvious Carlos had told Virgie that Cullen had brought the flowers.

Laureen's words about the joys of lovemaking kept coming back to her. Laureen provoked her thoughts, and Cullen's kisses ignited her feeling. The man sure could kiss, no doubt about it.

Disgusted with herself for letting Cullen maneuver her into seeing him again, she examined her reflection in the mirror. She wore her favorite dark-blue silk suit with a full ankle-length skirt. She teamed it with her long dangling silver earrings and lucky silver bracelet. She would need all the luck she could get.

Quickly she fluffed her hair into its neat no-fuss style and applied her make-up before she rushed out of the door. *Slow down. You act as if you're in a hurry to see Cullen.*

She sauntered to her car and took her time driving to pick up Adam and J.V. who had agreed to go with her to the open house. Though the community around COPR was safe, she had convinced J.V. she needed a man to escort her.

She congratulated herself on her plan. Cullen would think she was in a serious relationship and back off. Any foundation committee members in attendance would never suspect Cullen had any interest in her.

Surprised when Laureen opened the door, Danita exclaimed, "When did you get back from San Francisco?"

"About three hours ago. I've had my hands full trying to talk J.V. into going with you tonight. He..."

J.V. called from somewhere inside the house, "If that's Dani, tell her to get in here."

Apprehensive, Danita hurried into the living room. J.V. had on a suit and tie. "Good, you're ready."

"Sorry, kid, but since Laureen's home I'll have to beg off. Take Adam. I plan to start our anniversary celebration early."

"But you can't. I need you."

J.V. had the look of a man who couldn't wait to be alone with his wife.

Laureen came to her rescue. She slipped her arm around his waist and looked up at him with a slow sexy smile. "Come on, J.V.. You promised. Besides I'd like to meet Kay Burdell. We can pop in, stay an hour and leave. Danita's doing us a favor keeping Adam for the week-end."

He scowled down at her, but his expression held a look of surrender. "I can't believe you'd rather spend time with Kay Burdell than me."

"Only this evening," she said and winked at him.

Adam catapulted into the room, backpack in one hand and a case of computer games in the other. "Hi, Aunt Dani. I'm ready to go."

J.V. grinned at his son, then turned to Danita. "One hour, then we're out of there."

"Thanks, pal. I owe you another one."

J.V.'s grumbled reply followed Danita as she hustled Adam out of the door and into her car before J.V. could change his mind. Plan A just went out of the window. Cullen would never believe she and J.V. were a pair with Laureen there. She would simply have to come up with another idea to keep her distance from Cullen.

So far the lucky bracelet isn't working. What else will go wrong before this evening ends?

Adam chattered all the way to COPR. By the time she drove into COPR's parking lot which surrounded the sprawling one-story brick building, he was throwing questions at her faster than she could field them.

"You'll have to wait until you get inside. I'm sure there will be plenty of people to answer your questions," she said.

"I remember passing this place a hundred times, but I didn't know what Orthotics/Prosthetics meant." Adam stumbled over the pronunciation of the technical term. "Sure are a bunch of cars here."

Danita parked just as J.V. pulled up next to her. She surveyed the lot and thanked the fates the place would be full of people. She waited while J.V. and Laureen joined her and Adam. With any luck they could tour the place, grab a few appetizers and be out of there before Cullen noticed them.

J.V. aimed a lascivious grin a Laureen, "Let's get this show on the road. Adam needs his sleep, and I need, period." Laureen poked him in his side with her elbow and gave a sassy laugh.

Danita chuckled at their antics. She wondered if the man she ultimately married would look at her that way after twelve years of marriage.

A tall young woman with a short sculpted Afro met them at the door. Her COPR name tag identified her as a marketing coordinator. She invited them to join her group which was about to take a tour of the facilities.

Glad to delay seeing Cullen, Danita jumped at the chance. Surrounded by seven other people, she knew it was impossible for anyone to see her.

They moved at a leisurely pace toward the attractively decorated reception area in which a table of treats stood against a wall. The group paused long enough to get snacks and drinks. Danita spotted Cullen standing across the room beside a diminutive middle-aged woman dressed in a beige and black African-print caftan. Danita immediately recognized her as Kay Burdell. He seemed absorbed in what she was saying. She gestured toward a series of pictures above a long oak table and talked to a group of onlookers who hung onto her every word.

At the sight of Cullen, Danita's heart thudded against her ribs. She stepped in front of J.V., and, foregoing refreshments, followed the coordinator down a short hallway and through a variety of rooms.

The woman led them into a room whose walls were covered with mirrors. She said, "This is the walking room. The bars steady the clients and the mirrors help them monitor their own movements."

Danita had never thought about what Cullen's patients must have to go through to be fitted with his devices. She imagined that a lot of hard work must take place in that room.

While Adam asked questions, Danita almost forgot to worry about the possibility of Cullen's joining them. After they passed through the Cast Room and the Pediatric Room without any sign of Cullen, Danita began to relax her guard.

They entered the Lamination Room where containers of enamel of various skin colors hung from the ceiling and dripped into small vats of melted plastic. "For those who want lifelike prostheses we can make artificial limbs which match their skin color. Before a limb, or prosthesis, is completed we can even insert actual hair to match that of the amputee's," the marketing coordinator said with obvious pride. "No longer do people have to wear limbs of those non-human colors of twenty years ago."

The tour leader went on to explain the increasing need for braces and artificial limbs. "As you may know, there are less than a thousand orthotists/prothetists in the entire United States. San Diego is a military town. It has a growing population of injured military returnees. Then there's the large number of senior citizens, the increase of automobile and other accidents, as well as children with congenital or acquired physical handicaps which keeps COPR busy and on the cutting edge of new technology."

She talked about the Penn-Atkinson Grant and how COPR intended to use the money to help their disadvantaged clients.

When she explained how COPR used a large share of its profits to participate in the Medics for Africa Project, Danita's ears perked up. "There are many small towns and villages in West Africa where the use of braces and artificial limbs is nonexistent. Even before Cullen Powers and his partners bought out COPR they participated in the project. They hope it won't be necessary for them to discontinue their affiliation with the group for lack of funds."

"Why would they have to drop out of the project?" One of the people in the group asked.

"All of the Americans bear their own expenses to and from West Africa, and donate their expertise. In our case we make, fit and donate limbs and braces as well. The expense is considerable. We may soon have to choose between helping our African friends or helping our disadvantaged clients get the types of limbs and braces they need," she answered.

Danita thought about the information the tour leader had given. She had to admit Cullen's project deserved support. From what she could determine, he was indeed committed to sharing both his expertise and his money to help others. She wished she could find something to convince herself that he didn't deserve the grant, but to be fair, he did deserve it as much as she did.

When the thirty-minute tour ended, the group moved toward the reception area and disbanded. Adam held a sample of carbon fiber in his hand. The fiber, used in prostheses and said to be stronger than bulletproof vests, fascinated him. While he continued to ask the woman questions, Danita, deep in thought, gazed over his head at the paintings lining the walls of the hallway.

A blond youngster with a decided limp came up to Adam. Around Adam's age, he had joined the group near the end of the tour. He said he could answer Adam's questions if the woman wanted to take another group on tour. "Come on, Adam. I'll show you something you've never seen before...real twenty-first century bionics." He led Adam back to the Pediatric Room, leaving Danita alone to think about Cullen, COPR and the important work he was trying to continue in Africa.

She didn't realize she was standing alone in full view of the other guests until Cullen came up beside her. She looked around for J.V. and her sister, and spotted them talking to Kay Burdell.

"I've been looking for you," he said. "Glad you made it. Come with me. I have someone I know you'd like to meet."

Danita's throat tightened so much she could only nod. She walked beside him in silence.

"Enjoying the open house?" he asked.

"Very much?"

"Where's your date?"

"In the pediatrics room with one of your patients."

"Ah, yes," Cullen flashed a knowing smile and led her to Kay's side.

After he made the introductions, Danita said to Kay, "I love those paintings lining the hallway? They're yours, right?"

"Yes, and thank you. I did them some time ago. My style's changed since then. I'm surprised you recognized them. Cullen's one of my best customers. He flatters me into thinking he can't live without a Burdell hanging about. He even covers the wall at his place with them."

"I know. I envied him the ones I saw."

Kay raised an eyebrow. "Really. I had no idea..."

Danita sputtered. "It's not what you think. Cullen had some smoke damage from a fire in his kitchen, and he hired my company to sit with the painters until he got off work. He was so late getting home I ended up having to stand in for my employees who couldn't stay until he came home."

"Your employees? Tell me about your company," Kay asked.

While Danita and Kay talked, two men ambled over to Cullen and drew him aside. When she glanced their way she recognized Mr. Frederickson and Mr. Rawley, the grandson of The Foundation's founder. She stiffened, hoping they had not heard her say she had visited Cullen's condo.

The three men joined Danita and Kay. Mr. Frederickson said, "Great open house, don't you think, Ms. Johnson?"

"Great," Danita said.

"I had no idea the technology that went into making these appliances was so complicated," Mr. Rawley said with awe in his voice.

"We've only scratched the surface. A company in Pennsylvania has developed a below-elbow myoelectric arm so sensitive its wearer can detect weight, heat and cold. The first time one of their clients wore it and touched his wife, he said he had the same sensation he had before he'd lost his limb," Cullen said.

"Right after the grant is awarded, Cullen plans to leave to study with that company," Kay said.

"I'd like to offer the device to some of the kids we work with," Cullen said.

Danita didn't want to admire his dedication, but she could feel pride for him swell within her. She knew she couldn't keep her polite smile in place much longer. She edged away from the group. No one appeared to notice her leaving. She scanned the area for somewhere to go for a few minutes of privacy and spotted a door with an employee lounge sign on it.

She slipped inside and left the door ajar in case anyone would notice she had closed it and suspect someone had entered uninvited. The lights from the parking lot bathed the room in a golden glow.

Deep in thought she walked over to the window. Cullen was not the opportunist she had originally suspected. From the praise he had received and the comments she had heard, he wanted to serve his clients as much as she wanted to help her seniors.

When she had agreed to come to the open house, she had hoped to prove to herself that Cullen wanted the grant for the prestige connected to it and to promote his company. Clearly he needed it for unselfish reasons.

What a predicament. If she got the grant his clients would suffer. If he got the grant, hers would. She didn't want to worry about his clients. She had no choice but to win. She could only hope he wouldn't hate her when she did.

Shivering from the chill in the air conditioned room, she hugged herself. She swallowed a lump in her throat and blinked back a hot stinging pressure behind her eyelids.

She still had hope. She needed a few minutes to pull herself together. When she showed J.V.'s tape to the committee on Monday, maybe she could make up the ground she had lost at the open house.

Someone tapped her shoulder. She spun around and came face to face with Cullen.

Deep concern etched his features. "I looked everywhere for you. I wanted to ask you something." He peered at her in the semidarkness. "Are you all right?"

"Just fine. Never better."

"You don't look fine. Anything I can do?"

"You don't need to worry about me. I'm a little tired. I've had a long week."

When he draped an arm around her shoulder, she unconsciously moved closer to his warmth, soothed by his loose embrace and the now-familiar woodsy aroma of his aftershave.

Her voice sounded wistful when she said, "You really do have a wonderful business. Your family must be proud of what you do."

"Thank you. From what I saw, WAIT FOR ME fills an important need, too. We're quite a pair. We both want to help people. Too bad we have this crazy competition to endure."

His deep baritone reverberated through her, both calming and arousing her. His warm breath ruffled her bangs. Drawing her against him, he ran a comforting hand up and down her back. With his thumb he lifted her chin. Unbalanced and torn between the pleasure of his touch and her desire to let him know she cared what happened to his projects but had no intention of giving up on her pursuit of the grant, she leaned against him to steady herself. His gentle caress lulled her senses and the next thing she knew her eyes drifted closed.

At first he simply placed his lips against hers. When she slid her arms under his jacket and wound them around his waist for support, he groaned and intensified his kiss. Before she could stop herself, she offered her mouth to him.

Weakness swamped her. She leaned into the slow drugging kiss. It went on and on until she broke away gasping for breath, but before long she sought his mouth for more.

Through a fog of desire she heard voices and footsteps pass by the door. She took a quick step away from Cullen who opened his arms and released her but kept his hands on her shoulders.

"We can't do this. What if Rawley or Frederickson walked in on us?" she whispered.

"I need to talk to you alone."

"This is not the time or the place. I need a few moments to think and catch my breath. In fact, I don't think we should be anywhere near each other until this grant thing is over," she said as she headed for the door.

Though he did not pursue her, his husky voice followed her out of the door. "But we will, and sooner than you think."

୬ଈ

Danita could not stall in the powder room one more minute though her cheeks still burned, and she was still rattled by her response to Cullen...and still aroused. She couldn't deny her attraction to him any longer. She had lost herself in his kisses and wanted them to continue.

She wondered how she found the strength to pull away from him. She had left Cullen in order to give her heart time to stop pounding and her hands time to stop shaking. It seemed to take forever to freshen her make-up.

She had to do something to keep herself from falling deeper under his spell. *I'll stay way, way, way away from him. I won't let him touch me again. No more kisses. No more giving in to his challenges. No more nothin' until this grant business is over.*

Two women came into the powder room. They seemed impatient to take her place at the mirror. While they waited they talked about how COPR had helped their children.

"Isn't Mr. Powers wonderful?" a harried-looking young woman said to her companion. "When he was working with Jon, he was so sweet and patient. Without his encouragement Jon would have given up long ago."

"How's Jon adjusting at school? Do the kids still tease him about his braces?" her friend asked.

"Jon took Mr. Power's advice and showed them off to his classmates. Now the kids think his braces are 'cool'."

Danita couldn't help admiring the way Cullen had handled the situation. *Sounds like something Cullen would suggest. He must have good instincts when it comes to children.*

She turned from the mirror and looked at her watch. She had stayed at COPR almost an hour.

Ready or not, it's time to get back to Adam before J.V. comes storming in here looking for me. It's a good thing I can leave now before something else happens between Cullen and me. I've got to come up with a strategy to get that grant and a way to stay away from Cullen in the meantime. If I let him into my heart, I know I'll sabotage my own project without meaning to. I can't afford to care for Cullen. My own employees need WAIT FOR ME.

Danita hurried back to the reception area. The crowd had doubled. Kids and adults stood in groups waiting for tours. One little girl clutched two cookies, one in each hand. The noise level, no longer a polite undertone, swirled around Danita.

Intent on getting her family out and away, she nearly collided with a teen-aged boy in a wheel chair. Slowing her pace and watching for roadblocks, she joined her family.

His back to Danita, Cullen stood on one side of Kay while J.V. and Laureen stood on the other. Cullen's hand curved over Kay's shoulder as he said to her, "Too bad you have to leave so early. I thought you'd stay a little longer."

Kay's uneasy expression passed so quickly, Danita thought she must have imagined it. With a lighthearted chuckle, Kay said, "Sorry, the master calls. That was Aaron on my cell phone. He has an emergency and needs me at home."

Laureen said, "I'm glad I got a chance to meet you. I hope we see you again soon."

"I do, too. You have a lovely family," Kay said with a grin. "Since Cullen's met Danita he's a changed man, and all for the better. He's not as somber, and that old devilish gleam has returned to his eye."

"Must be the anticipation of battle. He's definitely out to get that grant, and I'm the only one standing in his way," Danita said.

From the way Cullen started and turned toward Danita, she knew her presence had surprise him. Danita smiled. For once she had caught *him* off balance.

"Must be it," Kay replied. "It's going to be a tough call. I wouldn't want to have to cast the deciding vote." She looked uncomfortable, and Danita was sorry she'd mentioned the grant.

Kay said her good-byes and made her exit, her red African-print caftan floating around her. What had Cullen told Kay? She seemed to think there was something going on between Cullen and her, in spite of Danita's not-so-subtle denial.

J.V. shook Cullen's hand. "Time to get on our way, man."

Adam almost jumped out of his black and purple Nikes. "But you didn't ask Aunt Dani about Sunday."

Danita turned to J.V.. "What about Sunday?"

"Cullen invited Adam to a picnic for his young clients. When I told Cullen you would be sitting with Adam this week-end, he asked if you could bring Adam. I told him I didn't think you had anything else planned, and you've always wanted to visit Verdant Valley Ranch. It's up to you guys. I'm out of here," J.V. said, and without another word, hastened a mildly protesting Laureen out of the door.

Danita stood there, her mouth open, unable to believe J.V. and Cullen had outmaneuvered her. Before she could round on Cullen, the youngster who had taken Adam into the Pediatric Room, squeezed through the crowd and joined them. "What did your aunt say?" he asked Adam.

Adam answered in a loud whisper, "Nothing, yet, Jon, but I think it'll be okay."

The youngster who was about Adam's age turned big blue eyes on Danita, "Can Adam come to our picnic?"

She looked into Adam's excited face. He fairly danced with anticipation. She had never been able to disappoint him, and she couldn't do it now. "Sure, why not? You need the fresh air. It'll get you away from my computer. You can get acquainted with your new video games another day."

While the two boys exchanged high fives, Cullen leaned over and whispered in her ear. "Thanks. That's why I came looking for you. To tell you about the picnic and ask you to bring Adam. It's important to have as many able-bodied kids at the picnic as we can, and we always need additional adults to help with games and wait on the kids."

Danita shivered when Cullen's breath fluttered along her cheek. Her stomach muscles quivered in reaction to the butterflies swarming there. She was glad she had slipped her hands in her pockets so he wouldn't see them shaking.

She turned away to hide her agitation, smiled at Jon and tugged Adam's hand. "Then we'll see you at the picnic. Right now I need to get Adam home. It's been a long day."

"I'll pick you two up Sunday at ten o'clock," Cullen called after her.

She looked back at Cullen, surprised at his unexpected ploy. "That's not necessary. I'm sure I can find the place."

"I insist. Since, as you say, you've had a hard week, you don't need that long drive. I'll be by at ten."

Unwilling to create a scene, Danita agreed. While the two boys discussed computer games, Danita gave Cullen her address. He took his time writing it down, as if to allow the boys a few more minutes together...or as if he hated to see her leave.

No matter what his motives, she held onto her calm facade, refusing to reveal the turmoil he created inside her while she waited. Finally, he walked beside her to the door and bid her and Adam good night. She resisted the temptation to look back as she marched toward the parking lot.

As she followed Adam who did an exuberant dance all the way to her car, she wondered if she could...or even wanted to...avoid being alone with Cullen at the picnic.

Five

ADAM READ ALOUD A rustic-looking sign, one of many announcements he had continually made from the back seat. "Verdant Valley Ranch, one mile ahead." Danita had thought he would jump out of his skin with excitement when he'd spotted the first yellow and black triangular sign with a silhouette of a horseback rider.

He practically shook the car as he bounced in his seat, straining against his seat belt. His nonstop observations and opinions and Cullen's humorous comments kept Danita chuckling.

She welcomed the distraction. Sitting next to Cullen for so long left her restless and tingling with awareness. The aroma of his aftershave made her want to inch closer to him. The vibrations of his voice quickened the rhythm of the blood flowing through her veins.

She scooted as close to the passenger door as possible and concentrated on the view from the window. She had spent too much of this trip watching his hands move effortlessly while he drove. They seemed to caress the wheel. The fact that she could go weak merely watching a man drive made her question her sanity.

She wrenched her gaze toward the rolling foot hills and the masses of tall yellow mustard plants growing along the roadside. As they passed several ranches surrounded by rail fences, Adam's excited questions escalated.

"Can anybody come to Verdant Valley Ranch today?" Adam asked.

"Nope," Cullen said. "Our local prosthetist association gets this place to ourselves once every year this time in May."

"Cool. When will we get to ride the horses?"

"Last year the kids rode about an hour after lunch. While you wait until your food settles, you can take a look at the animals in the barn," Cullen said.

"Man, it's a good thing we're almost there. I can't wait much longer."

"Save some of that energy for the games," Cullen said.

"What games?"

"There'll be wheelchair baseball and basketball, horse shoes and over the line."

"Do I get to play, too, or do I need to help the other kids?"

"Both. You'll help the kids on your team who need it, but you'll have to play, too."

"I've got a great idea. My school's having a career day. Can you come talk to the kids about what you do?"

Danita gritted her teeth. It was too much to hope Cullen would be busy and unable to accept.

"Sure, Adam. Give me a call Monday after you talk to your principal. I'd like to come. We need good people in our field. We're always happy to talk to young people who might be interested in our profession."

"The tour leader told us there weren't many people who do what you do."

"No, son, it's nowhere near as many as are needed."

Cullen glanced in the rearview mirror, his strong white teeth flashing when he smiled at Adam. Her heart gave a little lurch.

Adam and Cullen continued to chat while Cullen drove through the gates of Verdant Valley Ranch. Danita tried to figure out how and when she would get Adam alone and make it clear she did not want him involving her with Cullen in their activities. Knowing Adam's enthusiasm and friendliness, it might already be too late.

While Cullen pulled into the parking area, Adam's attention was riveted on a dozen or more picnic tables in a large grassy rise near the ranch house. Children of all ages sat talking and laughing. Adults hurried between the tables setting plates of food in front of the young people.

"Looks like we got here just in time. I'm glad we didn't eat a big breakfast, Aunt Dani. I'm starved," Adam said plunking on the cowboy hat Cullen had brought for him.

Danita got out of the car, reached into the back seat and grabbed her backpack. "You're always starved, and you did have a big breakfast."

"Well, yeah, but that was hours ago."

She laughed and slung her backpack over her shoulder. As they made their way to the picnic table, Adam spotted Jon the youngster he had met at the open house. He called out to him and took off at a run, leaving Cullen and Danita to themselves.

When Danita stepped carefully over the uneven ground, Cullen took her hand. At his touch a warm sensation swept over her. Her face warmed and her fingers tingled.

She was so engrossed in the sensations washing over her that when Mitchell Stone the good-looking hunk Danita had met at the Golden Hyacinth, came to a stop in front of them she looked up in surprise.

He said hi to Dani then turned to Cullen, "The Association decided to have a short lunchtime meeting. We need you in the ranch house. Can you get away for a while?"

Cullen dropped Danita's hand. His voice barely hid his annoyance. "We just got here. Can't it wait?"

Before Cullen could answer, Danita said, "You go ahead. I think the servers can use some help with this brood. See you later."

Without a glance in Cullen's direction, she slipped on her small brown back pack. Pretending a nonchalance she did not come close to feeling, she strolled over to the chuck wagon area and offered her services. Saved by a meeting, she thought. If her luck held, she would keep herself so busy Cullen wouldn't see her again until the end of the day.

Every five minutes when thoughts of Cullen crept into her mind, she pushed them aside and concentrated on serving the children assigned to her. When she finished her task she grabbed a plate filled with a burger, slaw and baked beans for herself.

The sun shining through a bank of low-hanging clouds warmed her though a cool breeze drifted by from time to time. Danita used her napkin to swipe at the moisture beading her forehead. Feeding so many children had kept her hopping for over an hour, and she gladly sank onto the only vacant space on a bench at a picnic table.

She scanned the other tables for Adam, but he and his new friend had disappeared. She sat there enjoying her food and the repartee between the kids at her table. It was nearly time to go to the barn and keep an eye on the children as they visited the animals.

A shadow fell over her shoulder. She looked up into Cullen's smiling eyes.

"Having fun?" he asked.

"This place is terrific!"

The young boy next to her jumped up with his empty plate and offered his seat to Cullen. Cullen thanked the child and squeezed himself into the small space. At his nearness Danita caught herself before a sigh escape her.

She waited in silence, dreading his next words. She expected him to make some overture. Instead, turning slightly away from her, he exchanged small talk with the children at the table.

Only when the children finished their meals and drifted away leaving Cullen and Danita alone at the table did Cullen break the silence. "I tried to convince Kay to join us today, but she couldn't get away."

"She's a neat lady—not at all conceited about being a popular local artist."

"I wish her husband and I got along better. I've tried everything I can think of to make peace with him, but Aaron wants nothing to do with me."

Danita puzzled over that bit of news. "Why?"

"He never wanted his only child to marry me. He wanted her to marry someone already financially established who could give her all the things she was used to. Ayana and I went ahead anyway. Only after we were married and he realized we were happy and getting along fine without his help, did he appear to forgive me for taking his 'baby' away from him."

"Where did you meet her?"

"I met her when I attended San Diego State."

"Were the two of you in the same field?"

"No. I majored in health sciences and business administration, and she in political science and sociology. She had planned to help her father with his political career."

"Did she?"

"She never got the chance. We married right after I got my bachelor's degree when she was a junior. She dropped out of school and we moved to Los Angeles where she went to work while I took my training in Prosthetics and Orthotics at UCLA."

"I thought you came back here to practice. Why couldn't she help her father then?" Danita asked.

"I wanted to take some graduate courses in Orthotics at New York University, and she encouraged me to do it. We spent a year in New York. Those first five years of our marriage were the happiest of my life, though at the time we had to struggle. I worked part-time because I didn't like the idea of Ayana supporting me. Though she had a way of helping without making me feel guilty for not bringing home the bacon, I still had my pride."

"She sounds like she was a wonderful woman."

"She was. We had it all planned. As soon as I finished my courses, she would go back to college and complete her degree. I looked forward to helping her. She was a natural student, and I admired her abilities and wanted her to do what would make her happy."

Danita watched Cullen as his gaze seemed to settle on a distant cluster of eucalyptus while he talked about the wife he had lost. The trees drooped and swayed like weeping willows in the soft breeze. They echoed the sadness lurking in the depths of his brown eyes.

As if he had forgotten Danita was there, he continued speaking of Ayana. "She helped me study for my exams and saw to it I didn't have to sweat the small stuff. When I finished my training I went to work for COPR, and she went back to school and finished her degree. I was one proud husband when she marched up on that platform and received her diploma."

"Her father must have been happy to see her return to school. Why didn't she help him after she finished her degree?"

"Two months after she graduated she died in a freeway accident. She was pregnant at the time. I felt I'd died with them. We'd been married eight years. That was three years ago. Aaron... still blames me for her death."

Danita remained silent for a long moment, wondering how to phrase her next question without bringing Cullen more pain. Her voice softened.

"Were you driving?"

"No. Ayana insisted I fulfill my commitment and go to Africa. I was there at the time, but Aaron believes that if I'd been here Ayana wouldn't have been driving alone."

Relief and indignation flooded Danita. Relief that he hadn't been driving, and indignation at the unfairness of Aaron's attitude. "That doesn't make any sense. Highway accidents happen all the time. I hope you don't blame yourself," she said.

"At first I did, but we had both agreed that I go with the project. I wanted to take her with me, but since I'd be gone only six weeks, and since she wasn't expecting our child for four months, she insisted it would be safe for her to stay in San Diego.

"After their deaths I sank into such a deep depression I ached all the time. I didn't want to eat, and had trouble sleeping. My work kept me sane during the day, and the support of my parents, friends, and especially Kay, kept me going when I wondered if I had any reason to."

Danita's heart ached for all Cullen had endured. Not only had he sustained a tragic loss, but he probably took some of the blame for not being there for Ayana when she was driving. She could understand why he dedicated himself to his career. Sadness for him clogged her throat.

She covered his hand with hers. "I'm so sorry. I'm sure you must have suffered, must still suffer."

"I think it would be easier if Aaron and I could mend the rift between us. It's so senseless. He must know I loved Ayana and wanted our child. I still miss her and grieve for our child. I wish she could have been here when Mitch and I took over COPR. She would have been so proud."

"For the last three years I found it a struggle to get on with my life, but since I met you it's as if I've awoken from a bad dream. You made me realize how much I've missed having a woman my age as a friend."

"I'm grateful to have had my profession and my work with the Africa project. They've filled a big hole in my life, but I'd like more. I'd like your friendship. Can we be friends? I'll try not to push you for more...until or if we're both ready."

He turned his hand over and entwined his fingers with hers. The strong current of understanding and compassion that had flowed through her, shifted; her heartbeat sped up to triple time.

The smell of new grass and horses carried on the soft breeze. Children's voices and their laughter drifted over Danita. Insects darted past. She sat without moving or speaking, aware of life pulsing around them—trying to decide just the right thing to say.

Though she had denied it, she had realized he was special from the moment she'd met him, but she'd had no idea he'd been carrying around such pain. She would give him her friendship, not out of pity, but because he was a good man and she wanted his friendship—but only his friendship—as well.

"Yes," she said, "I think we can manage a friendship, but we need some rules."

"Rules? What kind of rules?"

"No more of those hot kisses. No more sneaky hugs. No more conspiring with my family to get me alone."

Cullen ran his hand over his face as if a heavy load had been lifted from his shoulders. Then he gave her a smile so sweet and guileless all of her doubts about his motives crumbled. She wanted to believe his interest in her wasn't about the grant, but about his reawakening to life. She hoped she was right. If he was trying to distract her in order to win the grant she would never be able to trust another man again.

Besides, he might change his mind if she won. He might even hate her. The thought saddened her. So she'd keep things simple for the time being. Friendship would work as long as she didn't allow her heart to get involved.

She must have let her dejection show because he said, "If that's what you want. I didn't tell you my story to ruin your day or make you uncomfortable. I'm fine, now. I hope you don't decide I need mothering, because I don't. Just a friend." He leaned forward to peer into her eyes.

Still lost in the emotions of the moment, Danita could not quell her desire to soothe his heartache. When he put his free hand behind her neck and caressed its nape, she leaned into his touch. His breath fanned her lips, his distinctive male aroma drifted around her.

He leaned closer, his lips nearly touching hers, then abruptly moved away as if he didn't want to spoil their truce. "Danita, I don't want your sympathy. I want..."

"Aunt Dani." Adam dashed up the grassy slope to the table. "I was looking for you and Mr. Powers. You want to watch me ride?"

She pushed aside her momentary surprise at Adam's interruption. She wished Cullen had had the chance to tell her what he wanted. "Can't. I promised to help some of the parents with the little kids. We're going to take them to the barnyard to see the animals."

"No problem," Cullen said to Danita. "You go ahead. Adam's my guest. I'll watch him."

The rest of the day flew by. Though Danita didn't see much of Cullen, the memory of his voice, his touch, the sadness in his smile intruded upon every minute they were apart. That evening as they neared Danita's apartment, Adam gave a big yawn and said, "That was the best picnic I ever went to."

"Glad you enjoyed yourself," Cullen said.

"My mom says when someone invites you to something special you have to reciprocake."

"Reciprocate?" Cullen corrected with a grin.

"Yeah, so I'm inviting you to my birthday party next Saturday."

Oh, no! If Cullen meets the rest of the family, I'll be in for the biggest match-making campaign in the history of the Johnson-Spencer clan. Maybe Cullen will refuse to come. After all, he told me he planned to spend Saturday with Kay.*

"You want an old man like me at your party?" Cullen asked.

"Sure. Besides us kids, there'll be lots of old people there. Aunt Dani, all of my uncles, and my grandparents."

Cullen glanced at Danita and chuckled. "I don't think I can make it, Adam. I promised to take Kay to a poetry reading in Hillcrest."

"B-o-r-i-n-g. Bring her to the party. She'll have more fun than at any old poetry reading."

Danita rushed in to head off Adam. "Don't pester Cullen. He has other plans, and I'm sure it's too late to change them. Perhaps you can plan something with him another time." *When I won't have to be there; when I've had a chance to talk to you about me and Cullen not being close friends.*

Cullen pulled his car next to the curb in front of Danita's apartment building, turned off the ignition and swiveled in his seat to face Adam. "Thanks, Pal. I'll check with Kay, and if she's agreeable, we'll be there. What time?"

Adam bounced in the seat, his cowboy hat almost hitting the ceiling of the car. "From two until the grown-ups decide to go home. Come on in. I'll give you my address and phone number."

Adam bounded out of the car and slammed the door. Cullen and Danita followed. Adam called over his shoulder, "Man will my mom be surprised when Kay Burdell shows up at my party."

Danita's shook her head. She had lost control of the situation. How would she explain Cullen to her family? She had enough trouble fighting her attraction to him.

Knowing how her family embraced her friends and made them a part of the clan, she wondered if she could stop them before they got started.

She inserted her key in her door and looked up at Cullen. He had a grin on his face worthy of Tom the cat of "Tom and Jerry" cartoon fame.

જીત

Danita disappeared upstairs with Adam. Cullen prowled her living room, proud of himself for the way he'd followed Kay's advice. It seemed to be working. He had every intention of getting Danita to trust him and get to know him before he made his move. And he intended to make his move, but only when the time was right.

Now if I can keep my promise of no more kisses.

He smiled at the memory of her attempt to get rid of him before he could take a seat. Instead, at Adam's insistence, he ended up ensconced in her living room with Adam's address in his pocket, a cup of coffee in his hand and Beyonce for company.

She had chosen accessories and paintings which reflected her African heritage. A foot tall bronze statue of a warrior stood alone on one shelf in a lighted wall-cabinet between an almond beige sofa and a matching easy chair. A dozen other smaller intricately crafted brass figures sat on two narrow shelves below it. The large statue dominated the display and appeared quite old. It reminded him of those he had seen when he visited a museum in Ghana.

He walked closer and examined the statue's strong male features and the details of its intricately arranged braided hair. If this statue were authentic, it must be worth a great deal.

He sank onto the comfortable beige sofa. His heart thudded as he imagined her stretched out beside him on the couch, watching her favorite DVD. He would hold her in his arms, feed her popcorn and listen to her sigh through the sentimental parts as he licked the salt from her fingers.

Danita took a seat on the ottoman at his feet. "Sorry that took so long, but Adam was so excited we had to call his parents and tell them all about the picnic and about your coming to his party."

His body hardened at her nearness. Her familiar scent had tantalized him all day. At first her fragrance had seemed at odds with her casual figure-hugging jeans and short denim jacket. Yet the combination of lemon blossoms and denim reflected both her femininity and her vivacity.

Cullen resisted the temptation to lean toward her and plant a kiss on the dimple in her left cheek. "That's all right. I was enjoying the quiet. Tell me about the statue and the figurines." He pointed to the lighted cabinet.

"When my Grandfather Thomas attended Fisk University in the fifties, he sang in their choir. They traveled to the Gold Coast, now called Ghana, and gave a series of concerts. One of the families he stayed with there gave him the statue and those two brass figures which were used to weigh gold. Before he died he passed them on to me."

"They're beautiful. Did he give you the other things you've collected?"

"Actually I bought everything else you see here at a local discount import store or The Wild Animal Park." Danita laughed, and the sound skittered through his chest, making it hard for him to breathe.

Determined to discover the real reason Danita persisted in holding him at arms' length, Cullen searched doggedly for the right words to breach her resistance. Before he could stop himself he blurted, "Tell me why you're so desperate to get the grant that you're afraid to be friends with me?"

"I said we could be friends, but I guess I do appear desperate and cautious."

"Can't you tell me why? Maybe if I understood, I could help."

"There's nothing to tell. Like every business we've had some unexpected reversals. We need a hefty dose of cash to keep our doors open until we start making a profit again."

Cullen shifted the decorative pillow behind him and patted the cushion next to him, but Danita remained on the chair. The way she averted her gaze and twisted her fingers in her lap made him realize there was more at stake than a business failure. Either her ego was at the heart of the problem or she really was distressed about what would happen to her employees if WAIT FOR ME closed its doors for good.

Cullen strained to hold back his impatience. He wondered if he was the only one affected by the kisses they had exchanged. "Then why do you seem uncomfortable with our friendship?"

"You're here, aren't you? I'd say we aren't exactly enemies." She gave a careless shrug.

"You've avoided me all day, and you would have liked nothing better than to have me drop you off at the door. If it hadn't been for Adam, I'd be in my cold, lonely condo all by myself."

"Sure, and my name is Gilda Gullible. You can't expect me to believe you'd spend the evening alone unless you chose to do so."

"Why do you say that?"

"You must know you're a good-looking guy. You've got class, style and a way of paying attention to a woman that would make her think she's the only one in the universe."

"You think my interest in you is all an act?" he asked, stung by her implied accusation.

"I didn't say that."

Cullen tamped down the irritation rising in his voice. "You didn't have to, and you're wrong. I may be many things, but I'm not a phony. Why do you keep pushing me away?"

"I'm not. Until this grant thing is settled, I can't afford any diversions, no matter how tempting."

"Does that mean you find me tempting?" he asked with a grin.

An answering smile tugged at her lips. "It might."

Hoping she would admit to the attraction growing between them, he asked, "Then if this grant didn't stand between us, would you give me a chance to get to know you better?"

Danita looked down at her hands, her lips pressed together as if choosing her words with care. "Maybe, but it does."

"I think WAIT FOR ME is an excuse, though I grant it's a good one. I don't know why I feel that way, but I do. Am I wrong?"

"How can you say that? I've been honest with you."

"Then let me help. Let me visit WAIT FOR ME. With my background in business, I'm sure I can come up with some way you can save WAIT FOR ME in case you don't get the grant."

Danita looked up at him. Her gaze searched his. "Why do you want to help me?"

He ticked off his reasons on his fingers. "Because the sooner we get this thing out of the way, the sooner we can both get on with our lives. Because you need to know you have nothing to fear from me. Because maybe it's time you stopped running. Because maybe I can help. Take your pick."

"Do you really think you could...?"

"Invite me and we'll see."

"I have an important meeting Monday morning, but if you're free Tuesday afternoon, you can visit as long as you want. If you see what we do you'll understand better why WAIT FOR ME is so important to us all, and why we need to keep it open."

Cullen had no intention of giving her a chance to change her mind. He stood, reached for her hand, and pulled her to her feet. "I'll be there around one."

He walked with her to the front door and paused. "I'll say goodnight now."

The soft but wary look in her eyes was too much for him. He hauled her into his arms and did what he had wanted to do all day, and in the process, took advantage of her surprise-opened mouth to taste the honey inside.

When she stiffened he gentled his hold on her. His tongue swept across hers, teasing for a response. His teeth nibbled her lips. He opened his mouth and covered hers in a caress he hoped would put out the fire that seared him all the way to his soul. Her soft body melted against his. Her breasts nestled against him. He could barely keep himself from cupping them and running his thumbs over her nipples until they rose to his touch.

When he realized she probably felt how his body was reacting to her he moved away, afraid he would frighten her with the strength of his need. He raised his head and looked at her. Her lips glistened from his kisses. Eyelids lowered, head tilted back, she looked as if she were waiting for more. With a groan he touched her lips with his before he eased out of the door, then turned for one last look.

"See you Tuesday." He took in her trembling hands and swollen mouth. She had the look of unsatisfied hunger that reflected his own. She nodded but didn't say a word.

He turned and walked away with a jaunty spring in his step. The door closed softly behind him. In spite of a misty rain, he whistled all the way to his car.

Maybe, finally, she would stop running.

Six

DANITA DROPPED ADAM off at school and still arrived at the Penn-Atkinson offices a half hour early for her appointment. She had J.V.'s promotional DVD and its back-up copy in her briefcase. The secretary led her to a conference room. He stayed with her until he loaded her disk into the player and checked to make sure it worked.

"This should do it," he said.

Nervously she smoothed her bangs. "Has it ever broken down during a presentation? Mr. Frederickson said I didn't need to bring my own."

"We use it all the time. Never had a problem. Relax. You shouldn't either, but if you do, call me on extension fourteen and I'll come in and help you out," he said gesturing toward a phone on a small table at the back of the room.

After he left, Danita still had a few minutes before the committee arrived. She wandered to the window and gazed out. The gray skies reflected in the bay made a dreary backdrop to downtown San Diego and turned the sweeping curve of the Coronado bridge a dull blue. She hoped the weather didn't forecast the outcome of her meeting. No amount of sympathy or encouragement from Cullen would save her if she blew this presentation.

Cullen. She had spent the entire night dreaming about him. She had awakened, tingling from the steamy lovemaking she had welcomed while she slept. She could not believe how eager she had been for his kisses, and more, even if she had been dreaming. She squeezed her eyes shut in an effort to make the lingering vision of their entwined bodies disappear.

In the shower, she had scrubbed extra hard, hoping to rid her body of the sensations still coursing through her. Instead, the more she had scrubbed, the more aroused she became.

She was sorry she had agreed to let him tour WAIT FOR ME. When he visited he would find out all of her weaknesses. He must already know she had no defense against his kisses. He would soon learn how vulnerable she was when it came to her business.

She wondered if he would use the information against her. Probably not, but she shouldn't have taken the chance. She checked her watch. She would call him and cancel before the committee arrived.

She took out her cell phone, but at the sound of the door opening she dropped it into her purse. The secretary walked in and set up for coffee. Before Danita could decide what to do about Cullen, the chairman arrived. Enough stewing about Cullen. She'd better keep her mind on the presentation.

The next hour flew by. The committee members' questions and comments told her better than words of praise that the program had served its purpose. She'd have to do something special to thank J.V.

With a kind smile, Mr. Rawley the founder's grandson said, "Young lady, WAIT FOR ME is obviously a godsend to the people who work for you. Your company offers a valuable service to working people and gives your seniors jobs they can take pride in doing. The cross-generational focus of your business adds another positive dimension. People are living longer and want to feel needed and appreciated no matter what their ages. They've worked all their lives and enjoy being productive."

When her advisor Mr. Frederickson added his praise, Danita felt the lump of uncertainty in her stomach dissolve. He beamed at her as if it had been his idea for her to show her disc.

"Thank you for inviting me here," she said. "WAIT FOR ME is the kind of place you have to visit to understand. The disk doesn't tell the whole story, but it does give an overview of what we do." One by one she looked each committee member in the eye. "Feel free to drop by anytime you're in the neighborhood, and I'll arrange for one of our workers to show you around."

"Thank you. We'll put your brochure on the bulletin board in our employees' lounge," another of the committee members said. "Hope you're up to an increase in business."

"With pleasure." She could not suppress a grin. She exhaled a heartfelt sigh of relief. *I have a chance. Thank God I have a chance to get the grant.*

❧

Danita sailed through the entrance of WAIT FOR ME and went straight into Virgie's office. Virgie greeted her eagerly.

"How did it go?"

Danita gave a celebratory whoop. "Great. They ate it up. You should have seen them. I thought Rawley would break into tears when Phil said we saved him from a cat-food diet. I could have kissed Rawley. As chairman of the board, he has the most influence with the committee. With him on our side we're bound to win."

"Way to go! You'll have to call J.V. and tell him what happened."

Danita laughed and grimaced at the same time. "I'll bet he'll ask for ten more favors when I do."

"Whatever he wants, it'll be worth it."

"What did Cullen say when you told him about your presentation?"

A strange sensation crept into Danita's heart—almost like regret. Cullen had offered to help her find a way to streamline their practices. She hadn't told him she was going to show the committee J.V.'s DVD. She hadn't even told him she had one. She felt unaccountable guilt, as if she had done something underhanded at his expense.

The last time they had been together she'd had trouble remembering her own name. All she'd thought about was how to control her attraction to him. She didn't want to think about the grant—or anything else that could drive a wedge between them.

Instead she'd found herself enjoying his smiles, his quirky humor, and his gentle manner. Okay, and his kisses.

If Frederickson mentioned it to Cullen—and she knew he would—Cullen would think she'd deliberately tried to trick him. She would tell him the first chance she got.

"I forgot to tell him, but I will the next chance I get. Speaking of Cullen," she said to Virgie, "he's coming over tomorrow to give me some tips on the business end of this place in case I don't get the grant," Danita said.

"You're kidding. I hope you don't plan to show him our books. Anyway, I thought you weren't going to have anything to do with him. What's going on here?"

Danita shifted in her seat. She looked at her hands, at the ceiling, out of the window. She settled her gaze on the top button of Virgie's green blouse. "I told you Adam and I were going to a picnic with Cullen on Saturday. While we were there I found out Cullen has a business degree. After the picnic Cullen and I ended up talking about how we could make our money go further. He pointed out that if we didn't get the grant we would still need a way to save WAIT FOR ME. I couldn't turn him down without appearing ungrateful."

Virgie raised her brows, her mouth dropped open then rounded into an "O". "Do you think it's wise to let him in on our problems?"

"I've asked myself the same question a hundred times since I agreed to meet with him, but he knows we need the money. Why else would we have applied for the grant?"

"Good point. Want me to sit in with you?"

Danita had thought of that, but she had agreed to see him, and she didn't want him to think she was afraid to meet with him on her own. "If I need you, I'll call you. I'm sure I can get rid of him without giving away too many of our secrets. Just don't leave while he's here, all right?"

"Don't worry. I wouldn't miss this for anything. I have a feeling you'll yell 'Virgie' before he's here ten minutes," Danita had begun to wonder the same thing. Why fight it? The man stayed on her mind all the time. She heard his name and her heart did flip flops. Maybe a big dose of him would turn her off. *Yeah, right.*

೭ఽ

The next afternoon Cullen relaxed in a comfortable chair at the conference table in Danita's office. "I'm impressed. You've made WAIT FOR ME a great workplace for your seniors."

"Now you see why I can't turn these people away. They'd have no place else to go," she said.

Cullen had spent over an hour touring her facility, talking to the workers and listening to Danita describe her business. He would have preferred spending the time taking up where he had left off Sunday night.

At first it was an effort to keep his mind on what she told him. The way she bent over to speak to her seniors showed how much she loved and respected them. When she spoke, her sultry alto seemed to embrace them...and him.

With an effort he turned his attention to the job he had set for himself: helping her save her business without the grant.

He arrived, convinced he needed the money more than she

did. Though he had seen nothing to change his mind, he would hate to see WAIT FOR ME shut its doors.

"Would it be so bad if you returned to your profession? Couldn't you help some of these same people through other community agencies?" He watched her closely while he waited for her reply.

She met his gaze, her expression intent. "It wouldn't be the same. They want to earn their way, not live on handouts and deal with a bunch of bureaucrats."

"You've got a point. Many of my clients complain all the time about the red tape they have to go through just to get the benefits they're entitled to."

Danita leaned forward. "I told you my grandmother gave me the idea for WAIT FOR ME. She took care of me when I was in school and my parents worked. She was always there when I needed her. She died the same year I opened it. In my heart I've dedicated it to her."

"I understand now why you're so determined to save it."

"There's more. I didn't tell you my entire family invested in us. I've paid some of their money back, but my savings are gone and the business is barely showing a profit."

"I see. They must have a lot of faith in your ability."

"They do, and they believe in the concept. Some of these seniors are their friends and neighbors who have lived in the community for years. If WAIT FOR ME goes under I'll let down my family and my employees, and I'll be ruined financially. It'll take me a long time to recover.

"From what I'll be able to salvage I'll have only enough left to repay my small business loan or repay my family. They would insist the loan come first. It would take me years to earn enough money as a geriatric social worker to reimburse them. Some of them may not be around by then."

Cullen felt a stab of unease. If it weren't for him she would receive the grant. If he won, he would be responsible for her family's financial losses, but he couldn't drop out of the competition. He needed the grant to help his clients, too. No wonder Danita held him at arm's length. What a mess.

He wanted her and the grant and intended to get both. "Life is full of challenges. We'll find a way to keep you going in case you don't get it."

In a light tone he could tell was forced, she asked, "Any suggestions, Mr. MBA?"

"Bachelor of Business Administration. I don't have an MBA,

but I do have a few suggestions. First, begin to think like a business woman rather than a social worker. Instead of sending your employees in pairs, get a business-plan account with your cell phone company and assign one of your workers to take calls from those on assignments in half-hour intervals to let you know they're all right and when they're ready to leave. You'll save almost half the cost of your operation."

Danita sat forward in her seat. "Great idea. And when the repair persons show up, our people won't have to call in. The repairmen would call 9ll in the event of an emergency. With the money we'll save, we can use the same number of workers but take on more assignments. Anything else?"

"Withdraw your ads from the two 'throw away' publications, but leave ads in local business publications. From what you say, your clients are pretty affluent. You need to aim for people who can afford your services."

"If I do, I can increase the size of my ads in *The San Diego Business Review* and *Working Women*."

At her radiant smile, pride rippled through him. She looked at him as if he were an efficiency guru and she had learned the secrets of financial life.

"You and Virgie should make yourselves available for presentations at business and professional group meetings. Get on The Speakers Bureau's list. Your business will definitely pick up in short order."

"I have a DVD that J.V. made for me. I could use it at those meetings," she said.

"Great. You're getting the idea."

From her sigh he could almost feel relief surged through her. "Anything else?"

"Two other things," he said. "First, as your fancy pens and folders run out, don't order any more. Keep it simple. Give out business cards instead. Your clients will pass them on, and you'll save money. Keep your brochures, but get rid of everything else."

"I love your suggestions so far. What was your other idea?"

"This one you may not like."

"Try me. You've already helped me save a bundle."

Cullen hated to mention the next money-saving advice because it would cut into his opportunity to see her. "You're open only five days a week, but many business people who work six and even seven days need your services. Whether you stay open or not, you're still paying rent on this place, right? When you're closed, you're losing money."

Danita's brow furrowed. "I hadn't thought of that."

Cullen walked to the window overlooking her outer office and turned back to face her. "Find seniors willing to work weekends. You and your partner take turns covering phones here. Your facility won't sit empty and you can charge more for weekends."

She joined him and gave him a bear hug. "You're a genius. I can't thank you enough."

He wrapped his arms around her. If she wanted to kiss him he would make it easy for her. He leaned down. The phone rang.

Still smiling, she went to answer it. She listened for a moment, the smile replaced by a tight frown. "Put him on."

Cullen watched her, still caught up in the feel of her body. She seemed to have forgotten he was still in the room. Tension radiated from her.

Danita bit her lip. "Hi, Kevin...I guess I *had* forgotten... So soon...I know I promised... Can you give me a few more weeks?"

Her grip on the phone became so tense her knuckles stood out in ridges. Then she relaxed her hold and straightened her spine as if she had decided that no matter the emergency she'd meet it full on. "Fine. I'll expect you tonight at seven."

When she hung up, she stared at the phone as if unable to tear her gaze from it. Finally she looked at Cullen, defiance evident in her pursed lips and clenched jaw.

"What's wrong?" Cullen demanded. If someone else was hassling his woman he'd take care of it. He had made points with her and he didn't intend to lose the ground he had gained to some faceless person on the phone.

My woman. Sure. Danita made it clear she was her own woman and I'd better not forget it. Yet in his heart he knew she would be his one day.

She gave him a determined smile. "Everything's fine. A little problem I thought I had more time to deal with. I can handle it, but I've got some business to take care of first. I hate to sound impolite, but I have to leave now."

Cold fingers closed around his throat. Something serious had happened and she wouldn't let him help. "You're sure there's nothing I can do?"

Her shrug told him she would not discuss this new turn of events. "No, but thanks for the offer. Truly, I can handle it. I wish I could thank you properly for your advice. You may have even solved this little problem."

He went to her, pulled her to her feet and gathered her into his arms. "I hope so. For how you can thank me, your appreciation is thanks enough. I'll go now, but I'll see you at Adam's birthday party."

He expected her to pull away, to make some excuse for him not to go to the party. When she did neither, he knew she had a big problem. He missed her fighting spirit even when she directed it at him.

He would find out what had sent her into a spin. When he did, he would help her in spite of herself.

🙵

"Kevin, you're early," Danita said ushering him into her townhouse apartment. Having recently celebrated his sixtieth birthday, his thick hair and mustache were barely gray and meticulously groomed. Of average height, his slim build, penchant for expensive casual-looking clothes, and mild manner belied his razor-sharp intellect and acquisitive nature.

She had been nervous about his visit ever since his untimely call. She had hoped he had forgotten their

Kevin kissed her on the cheek and walked into the living room. "How's everybody?"

Danita led him to the sofa. "Fine. Mom and Dad are enjoying their retirement, but I think he'd prefer his job to the 'honey-do' jobs Mom finds around the house for him."

Kevin sat on the middle cushion. "Poor guy. Doesn't pay to have any free time on your hands. My brother's wife comes up with a hundred little chores for him whenever he has two minutes to rub together. How're J.V. and his family? And Lu?"

Danita wished Kevin would get on with it, but she knew from long experience he had his idea of protocol and he would stick to it. After they discussed both their families, she offered him coffee and he admired several of her pieces.

He strolled over to the lighted wall cabinet. "I still find it hard to believe your grandfather's African friends gave him such priceless objects."

"In the 1950s few people appreciated West African arts and crafts." She took a seat on the couch and gestured for Kevin to join her. She searched for a way to convince him to give her more time to honor her promise. She knew pleading with him would be useless. She hoped her family never learned she had "pawned" her inheritance to finance the last few months of WAIT FOR ME.

When Kevin sat next to her, she took a steadying breath and said, "I wonder if I could ask a favor before we complete our business."

Kevin narrowed his eyes. "Your family and mine have been friends for years. I'll do what I can, as long as it doesn't interfere with business."

"I'll explain to my parents that you have them on exhibit, but since I plan to redeem them in a few weeks, I hope you will keep the rest of our agreement between us."

He gave her a look of pained tolerance. "Of course, but when the time is up and you haven't repaid my loan, the artifacts are mine."

In her rush to reassure him her words tumbled over each other. "Of course. The money you gave me to exhibit them saved my life. If I can't repay it, I'll keep my word, but I'd like to explain our arrangement to my family if I have to."

Kevin settled back on the sofa. His wary expression relaxed. "No problem. Now tell me, how's business? I saw your article in the *Union Tribune*. Things getting better?"

If I get the grant. If Cullen's suggestions start to pay off right away. If nothing else goes wrong. If Mrs. Phillips repays her loan. She swallowed her doubts and looked him straight in the eye. "Definitely. The way WAIT FOR ME is going, I expect to repay you by the end of June."

"For your sake, I hope so, but should you have to part with them, they couldn't have a better home."

"I know that, Kevin, and I appreciate your help."

Kevin stood and jingled some keys in his pockets as if to let her know he was ready to leave.

"Let me get a box for these," she said, moving toward her office off the living room.

Please, please. Let me find a way out of this. Don't let Mom and Dad find out what a fool I've been.

By the time she got the box and returned to Kevin, her hands had stopped shaking. An eerie calm settled over her. She watched him pack the weights and the statue without flinching. She wondered if the cold, numbing sensation wrapping itself around her soul came from confidence or hysteria.

She had to concentrate hard to keep her balance as she walked him to the door, said good-bye, locked up and returned to the kitchen to put the empty cups into the dishwasher.

She returned to the living room and looked around, frantic to find some item to fill the empty cabinet. She snapped off its glowing light. The shadow left in its place filled her heart with emptiness.

The door bell rang. *Darn, Kevin must have remembered one more detail to brighten my day.*

Though her shoulders ached, she pulled them straight, marched to the door, and flung it open. "Cullen. What are you doing here?"

"Would you believe I came here to ask what to get Adam for his birthday?"

She moved to block the doorway. Not up to any more emotional upheaval, she didn't invite him in. "You could have called me."

"Would you have answered the phone?"

Cullen's gaze swept over her face. He pressed his lips together in a tight smile. His brows lowered, he stood, feet apart, unmoving.

"Could this wait until another time? I've had a lousy evening. I want to get some sleep," she said. The jut of his chin told her he had no intention of leaving.

"If you'll let me in I'll tell you the other reason I came."

She stepped aside giving him plenty of room to enter without brushing against her, and closed the door behind him.

She wanted to throw herself into his arms and rest against his chest for a little while. Instead she moved to the other side of the room. Conflicting feelings swept through her. Her heart fluttered at the sight of him while alarm bells rang at the realization she was alone with the one person who could get her to confide her deepest fears.

She knew he wouldn't understand how she could do what she had, but she believed he wouldn't condemn her either. His acts of friendship made her want to trust him.

"Don't do it," a little voice within her said. "This is your problem to solve."

Cullen's presence crowded the room. Memories of his kisses and caresses, both awake and in her dreams, caused her to reach out and brace her hand against the back of the love seat to keep herself upright *Will he always have this effect on me*? She walked over to the easy chair which was as far away from him as she could get and sank into it.

He seated himself on the sofa and turned his concerned gaze upon her.

"What's so important you couldn't have called?" she asked.

He draped his arm across the back of the sofa. "Your reaction to the phone call today worried me. I thought you might need me to beat up somebody." He gave her a teasing smile.

His voice belied his relaxed posture and the affable expression on his face. She had to get him out of there without succumbing to an overwhelming need to go to him, lean her head on his shoulder and pour out all her worries.

She sat as upright as she could, fighting the lingering curl of fear that she might lose her most cherished possessions. "As you can see, I'm fine, safe and unharmed. Believe it or not I can take care of myself."

"Who was the man I saw leaving here?"

"You mean, Kevin? He's a family friend. We had some business to transact."

"Why here and not your office?"

"I decide where I do business."

"You're right. I overreacted. The guy who walked out of your door didn't look as if he'd threaten a flea."

Danita tensed while she watched him look around the room, his gaze swept past the now darkened display case and settled on a pair of mahogany fertility gods sitting on her book case.

She couldn't have replied if she had wanted to because her throat clenched in apprehension. Maybe he wouldn't notice the empty shelves. She was glad now she'd turned the light off in the cabinet.

"Since I can see for myself you're all right, I'll go home. Before I do, give me some clue what to get Adam? From what he says he has every gadget a kid his age could want."

The muscles in her neck were drawn so tight they ached. She dropped her head forward to ease the tension then raised it and rolled her shoulders forward. "He does, but he could always use a few more baseball cards. Even if you come up with some he already has, he could trade them for some he doesn't."

Cullen rose and walked toward her. "Great idea. I have a client who stocks them in his sports memorabilia shop."

He seemed ready to leave. Danita breathed a sigh of relief. Instead he circled around behind her and laid his hands on her shoulders.

"Relax," he said. "In my business I can recognize tension a mile away. Let me massage those tight little devils so you can unwind and get a good night's sleep."

How could she relax when his touch created more tumult than all the havoc of the day? He started with a light squeezing of the area where her neck and shoulder joined, then ran his fingers up and down in a firm movement which eased the knotted muscles.

While he murmured soft words, his breath tickled her ear.

"Trapezius. Deltoid. Sternocleidomastoid." Nothing sexy about those terms, but they tickled her senses anyway.

He ran his hands across her shoulders and back to her neck gently pushing her forward to gain better access. Pleasure skittered through her, heating her body. When her muscles eased she marveled at how his touch could be both firm and gentle.

"So soft," he said in an undertone. "You fit into my hands...perfectly."

Her breathing deepened. The tension of the day lifted. She slumped forward in total relaxation. When Cullen placed one hand on her forehead and the other at the back of her neck, she surrendered to his touch.

The dim lights in the room and the quiet hum of night comforted her. The muscles in her neck loosened and allowed him to ease her head onto the back of the chair.

He placed his thumbs on her temples and circled the muscles on her forehead. She closed her eyes, sighing deeply.

Moments later his kneading stopped. She felt him lift her feet one at a time. He rotated them before he placed them in his lap, rubbing each in turn. He must have taken a seat on the ottoman, but she was too relaxed to open her eyes and see for herself.

His touch stirred a flood of needy sensations and soothed her as well. Strange how he could lull and excite her at the same time. His quiet words held a question mark, and it took great effort for Danita to focus on them.

"What did you say?" She murmured.

"What happened to the statues and the weights?"

It took a moment for his question to penetrate. When it did, she jerked her feet from his lap, stood and walked over to the cabinet, the effects of his massage evaporated like fairy dust. She needed time to think, to determine whether to tell him the truth, or to conceal her unwise decision and salvage what respect he might have for her.

The sound of his footsteps neared. He stood behind her, his hands curved over her shoulders.

Danita wanted to move away from him, but she yearned for his touch. His heat radiated around her, drawing her closer.

"The statue and the weights? I loaned them to Kevin for a special exhibit he's giving at his gallery."

He turned her to him and held her with his gaze, his brows drawn together in a frown. "Glad to hear they're on loan. I thought for a minute you had sold them."

"What made you think I'd do something that...that..."

His grip on her shoulders tightened. "Irresponsible? Crazy? Desperate? Maybe it had something to do with the way you responded to the phone call this morning. Or it could be the way you tightened up on me when I mentioned them?"

"I 'tightened up' because I wondered why you insist on making my business your business."

She shrugged, but he didn't loosen his grip. He seemed to measure the truth of her words with his hands.

"I think you know why. I think you know I care about you and don't like to see you upset."

Danita stilled. The strength of his concern, tangible enough to touch, enfolded her. She searched his face for some sign he believed her story. His fierce frown disappeared. A gentle smile tugged at his lips.

He pulled her against him and stroked her back. "Never mind for now. We'll work this out some other time when you're not so tired."

Convinced he had bought her explanation, she allowed him to lead her to the couch. He sat beside her, pressed her cheek against his shoulder, and gathered her hand into his. "Loosen up," he said rubbing his free hand up and down her arm.

Currents of pleasure flowed from his caressing fingertips. When she spoke, she noticed her voice sounded softer than usual. "Cullen, I realize you meant well coming here, but I can take care of myself. I have a big family. If I were in danger, I could call on any one of them."

"I want to help you. That's what friendship is all about. If there's anything I can do, you only have to ask."

He kissed her ear and drew her closer. Her momentary need for comfort made her settle against him. She would stay in his arms a little longer before she asked him to leave. She wanted time to renew her strength and get on with saving her business and her inheritance.

He held her face and tilted her chin. She closed her eyes against the hunger she saw reflected in his eyes. When he kissed her, her desire spiraled. She parted her lips to say something, anything to stop the feelings swamping her. Instead she opened to his kiss, seeking relief from the cold fingers of panic which had chilled her heart the moment Kevin had walked out of the house.

He eased her against the arm of the sofa. The swish of silk stroking smooth upholstery sent a delicious shiver up her spine. She flexed her fingers, then caressed the smooth hair at his nape. When he delved deeper, she moaned into his mouth. She was drowning in the feel and taste of him.

He opened the top button of her red blouse. As she offered her mouth to his kisses, she arched against him, unable to stop herself from giving him her wordless permission to explore her body.

She sighed when he peeled aside her blouse and cupped first one breast then the other. She yielded to his touch. While she returned his kisses, he unsnapped the front fastening of her bra. She clung to him, her mouth fused to his.

He shifted his mouth to the pulse at the base of her neck. A low moan escaped her. "So beautiful. So soft. So perfect. Open to me, Danita. Let me take away the sadness. Let me make you smile again. Let me love you."

His words caressed her. "Yes, oh yes," she whimpered.

He kissed first one pouting nipple, then the other. "You taste like honey," he murmured against her breast. His voice vibrated through her.

Lost in a sea of sensations, she sought to capture them with her hands and body. Straining against him, she clutched his shoulders. His powerful muscles flexed under her fingers.

She moved restlessly beneath him, seeking relief. She arched her pelvis and the burgeoning strength of his arousal set her on fire. She melted against his hardened length throbbing with life between her thighs.

Harsh whimpers burst from her throat at the intensity of his need. Memories of her dream-night in his arms merged with the reality of his lovemaking until he moved against her. She froze.

This was no dream. They must be insane. Her heart pounded against her ribs so hard she was sure he could feel it. She struggled to catch her breath and clenched her teeth to keep back a cry of protest.

How could she stop him now without looking like a tease? But this wasn't right. They'd agreed to be friends and she'd come on to him...gave him all kinds of signals that this was what she needed. She pushed against his chest, struggling now to put some distance between them. He did not move right away. She whispered, "Cullen, please, let me go."

As if stung, he jerked away. He looked at her, the passion in his eyes mingled with such regret she almost reached out to comfort him. She stood and turned her back. With trembling fingers she rearranged her clothes and rebuttoned her blouse

"I'm sorry if I let that get out of hand," she said.

"I'm the one who should apologize. I came here as a friend to protect you and got carried away."

Cullen's muffled reply held such remorse, she went to his side and sat next to him. He leaned forward and rubbed his hand across his face.

She touched his shoulder and he flinched. Guilt overcame her. "I lost my head, too," she said. "I felt down, and you comforted me. I'm sorry. I didn't intend to lead you on. It's been a long day. Let's forget it."

He looked at her. Frustration rang in his voice. "Be honest, Danita. It was more than that and you know it. This attraction between us has grown from the moment you sat next to me at Penn-Atkinson. You're fighting it, and I don't believe it has anything to do with the grant."

The grant. The words chased away her last remnants of desire. She had been stupid to let him into her life. She had to get him out of it...now. Danita surged to her feet. "How can you say that? My so-called 'resistance' has everything to do with the grant."

"Why? Don't you think the committee realizes we're human beings? Besides, how in blazes would they ever find out we're interested in each other? No, there's something else going on here, and I'm damn sure going to find out what."

Her secret clogged her throat. She swallowed against it, refusing to display one thread of indecision.

She said, "The only thing going on here is that I need the grant to keep me in business. Ever since we met you've tried to distract me from my goal. I'm not beautiful or irresistible. I'm a working woman trying to help a group of older citizens."

"I hope you realize I've tried to help you."

"I do, and I appreciate it, but now I want you to stay away from me. I don't have time for emotional detours."

"I'm not sure I can back off, and I don't believe you want me to."

His smile sent Danita's temper into orbit. It appeared knowing and self-satisfied. She walked stiffly to the door and watched him while he gathered his jacket before he joined her. She angled her chin and looked him straight in the eye. "You men are all alike. If you can't get what you want, you get angry, or tell us our 'no' means 'yes'."

He stood stock still and raked her from head to bare toes with his gaze. His expression held a question. "What is it you think I want, Danita?"

She hugged herself, suddenly chilled. "What every man wants."

He moved past her and opened the door. "No. I want what

every honorable man wants, and I'm willing to wait for you until you admit you feel the same."

He walked out into the night, closing the door behind him with a decisive click.

Danita leaned against the door a long moment before she locked it. His presence still surrounded her. She would have to see him one more time when he showed up at Adam's party. She would show him she wanted to keep their relationship platonic. If only she could think of a way to discourage her family from their interfering matchmaking. If only she could keep her traitorous body and emotions under control.

Seven

"I CAN'T BELIEVE WE'RE doing it again," said Danita.

Laureen pushed one of her errant braids behind her ear. "Doing what?"

"All the women congregating in the kitchen while the men play cards in the dining room. It's so 1970s."

Aunt Lu hiked herself onto a stool at the kitchen counter, her back to Laureen's family room. Barely sixty and with a still-youthful figure, she wore a stylish black and white pants suit. "What do you know about the 1970s?"

"What you told me, *Aunt Lucille*." Danita laughed at her memory of the good-old-days tales Aunt Lu had spun when she'd stayed with Danita's family between jobs.

"Well, keep it to yourself, girl. No sense making the rest of these women jealous."

All ten of the women sitting at ease at the table and at the breakfast bar laughed.

Laureen asked, "Is it true, Aunt Lu? When you toured with that band in France, did Sachmo really include your name in a verse of 'When the Saints Go Marchin' In'?"

"More than once, but that story's older than dirt. No one's interested in those ancient tales any more. I'm sure Mrs. Burdell wants to hear about something more uplifting."

Seated next to Danita, Kay grinned. "Call me Kay, and I remember the seventies with nostalgia. We knew how to have fun in those days, didn't we?"

Kay launched into a tale about a civil rights demonstration and the party afterward. Glad Adam had invited Kay, Danita listened, fascinated. Kay fit in perfectly with the family.

Above the chatter of the women, the music and laughter of the children on the patio carried through the kitchen window. Hearty sounds of male voices drifted from the dining room. Danita loved family parties, and from the look on Adam's face this party was a big success.

Danita caught a glimpse of Cullen entering the kitchen for a beer. On his way back to the men, he stopped and whispered in her ear, "Thanks for inviting us. Great party."

His warm breath fanning her cheek flustered her. She wanted to remind him that Adam had done the inviting, but ducked her head and smiled instead.

Torn between avoiding Cullen and keeping her ear tuned to his remarks, Danita had experienced a frustrating evening. She feared that any minute he might mention the missing heirlooms and her financial problems at WAIT FOR ME.

Cullen appeared unaware of her wariness. All afternoon he had patted her shoulder or whispered in her ear every chance he got. She wondered how to convince him she wanted him out of her life.

She might try scowling instead of blushing when he spoke to her. Maybe she could make a general announcement: *"Not in the market for a man in my life."* She grinned, imagining the kidding and smart remarks that declaration would trigger.

His whispers had flustered her so much she'd missed part of Kay's story. Kay said, "The year they moved to New York, Cullen made up his mind to give my daughter a special Christmas present. A week after they got there he began selling his blood to a research lab to supplement his earnings. He told me later that he went every eight weeks.

"I'll never forget how excited Ayana sounded when she called to tell me he had given her the gold heart and matching earrings she'd wanted. When one of his friends told her where he got the money, she couldn't decide whether to laugh or cry. She said she took turns doing both for a week. She had them on when she died."

Danita blinked back tears. He must have loved Ayana a great deal. She almost envied her such devotion.

"Hope Cullen doesn't plan to spend the rest of his life alone," Aunt Lu said. "That boy sounds like he was a good husband." Reminds me of my fourth and last husband.

Kay gave a fervent nod. "I pray he doesn't. He's been so lonely the last few years I've feared for him. Thanks to Adam and

Danita, he seems to have developed a renewed interest in life."

Danita decided it was time to change the subject. "Last husband, Aunt Lu? Does that mean Kevin's stopped proposing? I'll have to talk to him."

Aunt Lu sighed dramatically. "That man has trouble figuring out what 'no' means. Maybe you can explain it to him."

Danita patted her aunt's hand. "Poor baby. He's just looking for a good woman who'll teach him how to live it up a little."

Aunt Lu flicked her hair behind her ear. Her lips curved upward in a mischievous grin. "Looks like Cullen's looking for the same thing."

Danita's composure nearly slipped at Aunt Lu's forthrightness. She detected the gleam of the matchmaker in her aunt's eyes.

Great. Now the family will be all over me like needles on a cactus.

Fortunately one of her cousins piped up with a story of her best friend's marriage gone sour. The women swapped stories of both good and bad husbands until Laureen announced, "Time to open the presents and cut the cake. Danita, go break up the card game while I round up the kids."

Danita approached the two tables of men playing spades. "Last hand. Time to cut cake and open presents."

J.V. looked up and grinned. "Your fella plays a bad game. He's joining our weekly card group."

Danita dropped her jaw. It was bad enough J.V. referred to Cullen as her "fella"...worse that the guys had invited him to join their informal card club.

Before she could protest, Adam and his best friend Lemar raced up to Cullen. "I forgot to thank you for the tickets," Adam said. "Lemar and I think soccer is way cool, and neither one of us has ever seen the pros. Thanks, Mr. Powers."

Cullen stood up and walked to Danita's side. "No big deal. It would be a shame to waste them, and when I heard you talking about soccer I remembered I had the tickets in my wallet." After Cullen and Lemar exchanged the handshake, the boys loped away to join their friends.

Danita felt like beaning Cullen. As she had anticipated, he had won over her family.

On impulse she tugged Cullen's arm until he leaned down so she could speak into his ear. "Please don't mention the problems at WAIT FOR ME or Kevin and the bronzes. I'll explain later."

An impish expression lit Cullen's eyes. He put his mouth close to her ear to overcome the background noise in the room. "When?"

At his nearness and his warm breath in her ear her heart did a little dance. "Later."

"Over drinks?"

Danita glared at him. She really *should* have beaned him. "That's blackmail."

Cullen winked, folded his cards and dropped them on the table.

"Okay, but I'll have to give you a call to let you know when I'm free," she said in a near whisper.

"I'll call you Monday," he said. The men stopped playing and turned toward Danita and Cullen.

She took in the men's rapt gazes and wanted to beam herself up to The Enterprise. Cool but relentless, they would not rest until they discovered Cullen's intentions toward her.

Danita clenched her teeth and retreated to the kitchen. She found no fault with Cullen's kindness to the kids. She didn't even begrudge him the fun he had with the guys. He worked hard, and she had seen the pain in his eyes the night she had eaten dinner at his place when he'd talked about Ayana. She *did* mind his intrusion into her only sanctuary—her family.

Everyone gathered in the family room. Adam opened his presents and exclaimed over each of them. Cullen gave Adam a gift certificate to his friend's shop Kollectors' Korner. Danita gave Adam two passes to a local movie theater. While Adam unwrapped his gifts, he yelled thanks over the cheerful noise of the crowd.

The rest of the day Danita stuck to Kay's side like icing on a cake—except for the times her family conspired to get her and Cullen alone with each other.

They didn't even try to be subtle. Aunt Lu sent Danita in search of an ice cream scoop.

The next thing Danita knew Cullen stood at her elbow. "Laureen told me to tell you to look in the toss-in box of utensils."

He opened the pantry door and scanned the shelves. She joined him and found herself with barely enough room to turn. "I don't see the box."

He reached around her, pressing himself against her back. His warmth enveloped her. Her pulse skittered.

"I've got it." He chuckled and removed a box from a shelf. His breath ruffled her bangs.

No fair. At his height he could probably see everything on the top shelf.

While he removed the scoop and stashed the box back on its

shelf, she turned and glanced at his chest which his designer polo shirt outlined in mouth watering detail.

She sighed under her breath. Her family knew just how to get to her. Well she wouldn't give them the satisfaction. She grinned at him and, with a thank-you, returned to the kitchen with the ice cream scoop.

Legs crossed, Adam sat on the floor among a pile of gift wrap and ribbon and opened the last of his gifts. Laureen asked Danita, "Would you mind getting a plastic garbage bag for the wrappings and ribbons?" She nodded and went to the garage. Danita dragged a short step ladder over and positioned it under a shelf. Cullen, in a laugh-laced baritone with a bad Spanish accent asked, "May I be of service, Senorita?"

Not surprised he had followed her, she rolled her eyes toward the ceiling. "By all means."

He reached to remove a bag from its box. Danita said, "I really don't think it takes two people to carry one lightweight plastic bag, do you?"

He laughed. "Maybe it doesn't," he dropped a light kiss on her lips, "...but it's sure fun watching your family think up ways to throw us together. Are they always this single minded?"

Danita's face burned. "Maybe we can outwit them. Next time they send me off, I'll wait in the kitchen. When you come in, I'll go back to the party."

"What? And spoil their fun? Sorry, Dani, we don't want to deprive them of the best entertainment they've had since Laureen met J.V.. Seems your cousins asked him to convince Laureen to jump off the high dive at pool, and when she jumped she landed on his head nearly drowning them both."

She let out a spurt of laughter at the memory. "You know about that?"

"J.V. told me the story while we played cards. I think he wanted me to know in case I had any objections to becoming a matchmakee."

Danita grinned in spite of her embarrassment. "You've been warned. We'd better get back to the party."

"I'm in no hurry." He moved closer to her.

"I am." Unsuccessfully suppressing a chuckle, she marched back into the family room with Cullen's laughter ringing in her ears.

The evening flew by with the women using one ploy after another to get Danita and Cullen alone. She treated their efforts with the faked nonchalance they deserved until they gave up.

Kay and Cullen left, along with the last of the guests. Danita heaved a sigh of relief mixed with unaccountable regret. Strange that with Cullen at the party, the world had seemed alive and exciting, but the moment he walked out of the door a letdown feeling assailed her.

She wandered around with a huge trash bag, dumping napkins, paper cups and plates into it. She carried the bag through the kitchen past her mother and Laureen and out the back door to the bin.

Laureen and her mother had their heads together, whispering. The moment she reentered the room they stopped. *Darn—here they go.*

She shut the door. "Okay. Let's get it over with. What did you say about me?"

Laureen said, "We were discussing Kay Burdell."

"What about Kay?" Danita asked, unconvinced.

Danita's mother, svelte and regal like Laureen, took a seat at the breakfast bar. "We couldn't figure out why she had on an outfit with a high neckline and long sleeves. It's unusually warm today, and with all those people at the party she must have burned up in that thing."

Cullen had absorbed her attention so much she had given no thought to Kay's attire. "Mom, you know how artists dress. They don't think about style or weather. They put on what the creative spirit of the day moves them to wear."

"But did you notice the look in her eyes?" Her mother's face reflected her concern. "The last time I saw that look, Uncle Walker's wife wore it before she took the kids and left him for good when they had their troubles."

Danita leaned forward. "Their 'troubles' Mom? Uncle Walker beat up Aunt Joan. I hardly think we can put Aaron Burdell in the same class with Uncle Walker. As for the look in Kay's eyes...she *did* lose her only child. Mom, you're tired. I think I should rescue Dad from Adam so you can go home and get some rest."

Juanita Johnson put her arm around Danita's shoulder. "Leave them alone a little longer. Grandpa gets a kick out of the child. I can't wait for you to start a family."

At the mention of family and children, Danita nearly pulled away from her mother, but resisted, unwilling to hurt her feelings. She remained in her embrace, waiting for the inevitable.

Juanita gave Danita's shoulder a squeeze. "You could do worse then Cullen Powers. Any woman in her right mind would go after him, not avoid him. Does the man have a problem we should know about? Is he gay?"

"I knew it, Mom! I knew you were going to put in a plug for Cullen. And, no, he's not gay."

Laureen said, "I know what's wrong with Cullen. He's not short, skinny and weak. You know the kind of guys Danita dates. Like that puny little Abner guy you dated once. So quiet he blended into the wallpaper. Besides, who would name his son Abner, for Pete's sake?"

"Abner's dad is a minister. He named his son after a brave Biblical warrior."

Laureen chucked. "Didn't do any good, did it?"

Laureen and her mother rocked with laughter until the tears rolled.

"M-o-m, Laureen. You guys quit it," Danita wailed in frustrated good humor, barely keeping herself from joining in their laughter. "Besides, I'm not looking for romance at the moment. Right now I'm trying to win a grant from the Penn-Atkinson Foundation. If I win it, the prestige would help the business, and I can repay the family the rest of the money I borrowed."

Danita's father, a tall robust man in his sixties, walked into the kitchen. With obvious pride, Dan Johnson wore the plaid sport shirt Danita had given him for his birthday. When he looked at his wife his face lit with a smile. He gave her a big smooch on the cheek. "Time for us old folks to go home, Nita."

Danita's mom stood. She leaned forward and said close to Danita's ear, "Ready or not, sometimes romance comes looking for you, and when it does, there's no place to hide."

૨ૐ

Bright and early Monday morning Danita sat at her desk, her pen poised over her note pad. Her mind drifted to her mother's parting words. She wondered what it would be like to give in to Cullen's obvious pursuit. Would a hot and heavy affair get him out of her system, or would she become caught up in a web of passion?

Was he really as attracted to her as she was to him? *Okay, I admit it. I guess I am a little bit in love with him. Who wouldn't be? He's sweet and funny and gentle. He cares about people, not just for what they can do for him, but because he has a kind heart. But I don't have to do anything about it.*

Was he only after the grant or was he getting serious about her? Did she dare trust him knowing how humiliating and painful it had been when she and Robert had broken up and she had to admit to herself and her family that he had used her?

She couldn't seem to get enough of Cullen's kisses and his touch. *Stop this right now.* Too many people depended on her. She couldn't, wouldn't take the chance. *After this is over and if he's still interested?*

Her mind made up she turned her attention to her notes when the phone rang.

"Hi, Danita, this is Cullen. Recovered from Adam's bash?" he asked.

At the sound of his voice she clutched the receiver. Since she had promised to contact him first, he had caught her off guard...again. "Almost. And you?"

"I enjoyed the party. I love your family. Kay had a great time, too. Knowing her, I bet she'll send you one of her creative thank-yous. I asked her to include me in her note."

Danita struggled to keep her cool in spite of her quickened pulse. "I'm sure Adam will appreciate it. Glad you could come to the party. What can I do for you?"

"You can tell me when we go for that drink you promised to have with me."

"You still want to go?"

"Looking forward to it. I have a problem to run by you. It has to do with Kay."

"What's up?"

"Can't go into it right now, but I'm worried about her. When are you free?"

"Can you make it at seven?" The question in her voice reflected her hope he would have to say no.

"Perfect. I'll pick you up at your place."

"Fine." She gently replaced the received in its cradle, unsure if she was disappointed or eager to see him again so soon.

Cullen sounded worried. A prickle of unease crawled up Danita's spine. *What problem can Kay have? She has everything-- renown as an artist, a prominent husband, and Cullen who worships her. Could Laureen and Mom be right? Could Aaron Burdell...*

She shrugged off her speculations. Cullen probably mentioned Kay's "problem" to arouse her concern and make sure she kept their date. Her curiosity would get her into trouble one day. She wondered if that day had arrived.

Seven o'clock came too soon. She had stewed all day, worrying about what to wear on their non-date, how she would keep the evening on a platonic level and what Cullen had to ask her. Her mother's words about Kay echoed in her mind. Though she believed Kay could not be a battered woman, something did seem to bother her. Danita hoped whatever it was, it turned out to be minor.

At three minutes after seven her door bell rang. On unsteady legs she walked to the door and peered out of the peep hole. At the sight of Cullen she opened the door and held onto the knob to keep from melting at his feet. He wore a dark gray suit. His woodsy aftershave drifted around her like a gentle caress. He smiled.

His gaze traveled over her basic black dress and stopped at her heart-shaped necklace that matched her dangling earrings.

"You look nice. I mean you always look nice, but I think this is the first time I've seen you in a dress."

She nearly chuckled because he seemed so unsure of himself. Feeling more at ease because of his *unease* she grabbed her purse and bolero jacket from the hall table, and stepped past him into the hallway, locking the door behind them. With his hand on her back, he guided her to his car.

"Let's try a new place in Hazard Center. My partner says they serve great drinks, and crowds haven't discovered it yet."

When they entered the dimly lit club, a well endowed blonde hostess wearing a skimpy body-hugging black dress led them to one of several empty booths. Expecting him to check out the woman, Danita glanced at Cullen who met her gaze with a placid smile. She looked away, irked he had apparently read her mind.

After a waiter took their orders, Danita and Cullen spoke in unison.

"How's Adam?" he asked.

"How's Kay?"

"I can tell our evening promises scintillating intimate conversation." Cullen laughed. "Relax. I brought you here to get to know you better...and ask for advice."

Danita wanted to relax, but her mother's words about romance still bothered her. The candlelit tables and piped-in sexy wail of Kenny G's saxophone didn't help. Cullen's nearness unnerved and...excited her. She would have to stay on guard.

All day she had consciously tried to push his image from her mind, and when his name sneaked to the surface she quickly banished it. She dealt even more decisively with memories of his touches and kisses. She might as well admit it. He'd gotten past her defenses, and there seemed nothing she could do about it.

"Why are you worried about Kay?"

Cullen moved his glass in tiny circles on the table. "Kay and I have a special relationship. She's like a second mother to me. I can tell when she's upset."

Danita wondered if his relationship with his mother was a good one. Her expression must have betrayed her thoughts because Cullen hastened to add, "My own mother's great. She's beautiful, talented and she's crazy about me. Both of my parents are only children, and none of my grandparents are living. That probably explains why I'm close to Mom and Dad."

As if searching for the right words, Cullen paused. "After Ayana died, Kay went out of her way to help me through my loss even though I knew she grieved, too. She understood my confusion and remorse. Although she knows I'll always remember Ayana, she bugs me about getting on with my life. For the last three years my work has kept me sane during the day, and Kay's acceptance has kept me going when I wondered if I had any reason to go on."

Danita could hear his melancholy. She wanted to reach out and take his hand. "Kay's a special woman."

"You're right. After Adam's party Kay grew increasingly nervous the closer we came to her house. When I took her elbow to help her from my car, she winced. I asked if I'd hurt her, and she said she'd bruised her elbow hanging some canvasses."

Danita frowned. "Sounds as if you don't believe her."

"The last few times I've seen her she's admitted to one accident or another."

Warning bells went off, but Danita wanted to use caution before she jumped to the wrong conclusion. "Some people are accident prone."

"I've never known Kay to have this many mishaps in a row. Two weeks ago she said she cut her arm when she snagged her bracelet. She was hanging a painting at the time. Last week she collided with a packing crate and bruised her shoulder. Now she's hurt her elbow."

Cullen's narrative triggered memories of Danita's Aunt Joan who had been abused. "What do *you* think happened?" she asked.

He gripped his glass. "I think Aaron's lost it and is taking his frustrations out on Kay. Ever since I've known them, Aaron and Kay have had a rather odd relationship. When they're around his cronies Kay lets him monopolize the limelight. She has a good mind, yet he treats her as if she hasn't a brain in her head."

"When he ran for council he advocated women's rights."

"You saw his public face. You should see him in private. When he's had a few drinks, the way he puts Kay down sets my teeth on edge. Sure he's subtle about it, but I don't like it. I wonder why she stands for such treatment."

Cullen's description of Aaron's behavior caused a knot in Danita's stomach. "When you and Ayana were married, did you notice any evidence of his abusing Kay?"

"No, but he's a changed man since then. When Aaron knows Kay and I are together, he finds some excuse to call her and tell her to come home early. She does what he asks, but lately, she gives me the impression she's fed up with his bullying. If she leaves him, I'd say it's about time.

"I get the feeling Aaron's become physical. I hope I'm mistaken, but if I'm right I'll make sure he never does it again."

From Cullen's angry scowl, Danita knew he meant every word. "If your hunch is correct, what'll you do about it?" she asked.

Cullen leaned his elbow on the table. "My first impulse is to confront Aaron, but our relationship is already bad. If I'm wrong, I could make matters worse."

"But you can't ignore what you've seen."

"I don't intend to, but I can't ask her about it now. She's leaving for D.C. tomorrow night for an artists' conference, and I don't want to upset her. I'll follow up on my suspicions when she comes back next week. Right now I'm trying to decide the best way to do that."

Danita found it hard to square her image of Aaron with Cullen's, but memories of Aunt Joan's husband convinced her they should come up with a plan to help Kay if Cullen was right, and pronto. She dug in her purse and extracted a card case. She flipped through it until she found a card for a battered women's shelter in Oceanside. "We can start with this."

Cullen examined the card and put it into his wallet. "Can you help me think of a way to broach the subject with Kay?"

Several alternatives occurred to Danita, reporting Aaron one of them. "You'll have to open the subject if Kay doesn't. Why don't you point out to her that she seems awfully accident prone lately and it worries you?"

Danita shifted in her seat. "Since you and Kay have a special relationship, let her know you sense trouble between her and Aaron. She may not admit it right away. Tell her you've noticed the bruises and her growing fear of her husband."

"What if she denies it or clams up on me?"

"Tell her when she's ready to talk about it you'll be there for her."

"Kay values her privacy. She'll tell me to mind my own business."

"Let her know you care and she's welcome to stay with you should an emergency arise. Assure her you're not prying or acting out of dislike for Aaron. Make her understand you have an obligation as a 'son' and a moral obligation as a man to protect her. Then give her this card."

"What if Aaron does something to her before she makes up her mind?"

"Let's hope he doesn't. If you push too hard too fast, you could put her on a stubborn path of denial that could endanger her more. Watch her and wait. She'll admit it soon enough, and when she does we'll find a safe place for her."

"Any ideas what she needs to do to get ready to leave? She may have to get out of there before Aaron finds out her intentions."

"I have a brochure that sets out exactly what she needs. I'll find it and you can give it to her.. Just make sure you're right about Aaron."

"Don't worry, I intend to, but how did you know what to do?"

Caught off guard, she stammered, "It's a long story."

Cullen's searching gaze made her uncomfortable. Muscles twitched in his strong jaws as if he were biting back more questions. "I'll call you as soon as I know something definite. In the meantime I guess I'd better get you back to your place."

They drove to her apartment in silence. Danita mulled over their conversation. Kay had always been one of her idols...a liberated woman and a local legend as an artist. If Kay ever admitted Aaron had indeed manhandled her, Danita intended to help her every step of the way.

When they pulled up in front of her apartment, Cullen said, "I'll see you to your door."

"No need. It's only a short walk, and it's just nine o'clock."

Stubborn resolve edged his voice. "I'll see you in."

Danita raised one shoulder in resignation and let him help her out of the Buick.

He followed her to her apartment door and waited while she let herself in.

She had decided to keep him outside, but the determined look in his eyes said he needed to be sure she was safe. "Come in while I dig up the brochure I have on domestic violence. It lists the important papers and records people need if they plan to leave an abusive situation. Would you like a cup of coffee...or something?"

"I'd like 'or something', but this might not be the right time. I'll take water."

Unsure whether he meant her or an alcoholic drink, she went into the kitchen and poured him a large glass of ice water. Leaving him in the kitchen she went to her office and returned with a copy of a domestic violence information guide.

He put it into his inside jacket pocket. "Thanks. I'll give this to Kay when she's ready for it."

He surprised her when he drank his water and rose to leave. She followed him to the door. He looked so bereft that when he gathered her into his arms and held her closely, she didn't back away. His tender embrace seemed to seek comfort even as it comforted her. She longed to lay her head on Cullen's broad chest but feared she'd give him the wrong idea.

She saw the bitterness in his eyes. "Why must people hurt each other?"

"Some people, Danita, not all people. Men who love their women cherish them, protect them, and would die for them. Think of your father and the other men I met at Adam's party. They enjoy their women, faults and all. You can hear it in their voices, see it in their glances and their touches."

Danita smiled through her sadness and snuggled against him.

He loosened his embrace. "Most men are unfulfilled without the love of their women and the children they create together. I know that, but a rogue husband like Aaron has forgotten...if he ever knew. I'd never abuse a woman even if I didn't love her, but if I loved her she could depend on me to honor her as long as I lived."

He lifted her chin and gave her a kiss so tender and sweet it made her heart weep. Too soon he stepped back, and with a final kiss on her forehead, he went out of the door.

The moment the door closed behind him, Danita wandered to her bedroom clicking off lights along the way. She could no longer deny she trusted Cullen. She only hoped he would justify her faith in him.

She took a shower and put on her night clothes, exhausted from the events of the evening. The moment she climbed into bed, the phone rang.

"Hope I didn't wake you."

"Cullen? Has something happened to Kay?"

Eight

"AS FAR AS I KNOW KAY'S fine," Cullen said "I'm calling about something else. Did you read your mail?"

Relieved, Danita sank against her pillows. "Not yet, why?"

"I have my invitation for the Penn-Atkinson reception."

"I've been expecting mine. It's next Thursday, right?"

"What time should I pick you up?"

Danita hesitated. She had planned to go alone. If she went with Cullen, he might get in her way when she began circulating. She intended to do a lot of networking, maybe even have time to get to know the committee members better. She believed she could improve her chances for the grant if she could find out what previous recipients had done to win.

"Danita, that wasn't a trick question. What time?"

"I'd better go by myself. I don't want to hold you up. I'll probably get there a little late."

"How late?"

"I don't know."

"Afraid they'll think we're a couple?"

"They could come to that conclusion." She hated her defensiveness, but it was too late to call back her words.

"Unless you cling to my arm and give me adoring glances, I don't think so."

A sigh escaped. "Why do you keep insisting I go with you?"

Cullen cleared his throat. His voice sounded weary and a little embarrassed. "Frederickson, our esteemed advisor, enclosed a note in my invitation. He practically commanded me to bring you. He says he doesn't want you downtown alone after dark."

Frederickson's sudden protectiveness made her smile. She searched for an excuse but failed to find one.

Cullen asked, "Now can you tell me what time to come by? Cocktails start at six."

"Around five-thirty."

"I'd bring a corsage, but I know what you'd do with it." With a chuckle he hung up.

She replaced the receiver. Cullen's sexy baritone voice rattled her. When she was near him, she found it more and more tempting to succumb to the attraction simmering between them.

If only he weren't gentle, loving and good looking. If only he weren't persistent. If only her family didn't adore him. If only there was no need for the grant.

"So much for avoiding Cullen," she muttered and snuggled into her bed prepared to try to keep him out of her dreams.

❧

Danita put the finishing touches on her hair. Except for her dress she was ready.

She had spent every possible minute collecting the final bits of information the committee had asked for, and implementing the changes Cullen had suggested at WAIT FOR ME. Now it was a matter of toughing out the foundation's decision and making sure she didn't blow her chances to make a good impression.

She finished her make-up and nodded in satisfaction. "That'll do as long as I don't rub my eyes," she murmured to herself. As she reached for her pick to give her hair one final fluff, the doorbell rang. On the way to answer it she shrugged into her kimono and tied its sash.

Padding to the door on bare feet she yanked it open and met the laughing-eyed gaze of her sexy tormentor. "Is it five-thirty already?"

He leaned over and planted a kiss on her lips, effectively halting her protestations. "Am I early?"

Heart racing, she didn't reply, but stepped aside and let him enter. He wore a light beige shirt, a midnight blue suit and a blue and beige tie with a subtle geometric design. In spite of her annoyance she had to admit he made a handsome escort.

She led him into the living room. "Please have a seat. I'll be ready in a minute."

Just as she turned to leave she halted blinking her eyes rapidly and rubbing one of them gingerly.

"What's wrong?" Cullen asked. He placed a hand on her

shoulder, stopping her retreat.

"I think I have a lash in my eye."

"Hold on. Sit on the bar stool, and I'll get it for you."

She sat keeping one eye closed. He stood at her knees and leaned over her, his breath warm on her brow. With a feather-light touch he held her right eye open. A tear trickled down her cheek and washed the lash from her eye. He took out his handkerchief and wiped the tear away.

"There, that did it." He held out the handkerchief and showed her the offending lash. Their gazes locked. The need to touch him drew her hand to his chest. She moistened her lips. "Cullen—"

"Danita—" He traced the line of her jaw with a knuckle.

Without haste he tangled his fingers in her hair, placed his lips against hers and teased her lips with his until she opened to him. His sweet taste sent her seeking more. Endless kisses aroused a warm pleasure within her that fast became a fire of need. She moved into the kiss, savoring his muffled moan.

She widened the space between her knees, and he wedged himself between them. When he pulled her to him, her kimono seemed to melt away. Her naked shoulder burned at his touch. His fingers traced her neck and back and ignited a trail of sensations so intense she whimpered.

He cupped her breast through her bra and she sighed into his mouth. She twisted into his touch and offered herself to his caresses.

He lifted her. She kept her eyes closed, the sway of his body telling her he was carrying her.

When he came to a stop, she slid down his body and tottered on bare feet. She opened her eyes and found herself staring at their reflection in her dresser mirror. Locked in his embrace, her hair mussed, her parted robe exposing the curve of her breast above her bra, she felt as thoroughly aroused as he looked.

She eased away from him, wrapped her robe tightly about her and tied its sash with a double knot. "I'd...better finish dressing or we'll...be late."

He took a deep breath. "Are you all right?"

Unable to meet his gaze, her heart pounded so hard she was sure her neighbors could hear it. "I'm f-fine," she whispered. "Fix yourself a drink. I'll h-hurry."

When he reached the bedroom door he turned and gave her a long, hungry appraising look. "Take your time. I can wait."

The heat in his eyes and the decisive click of the door closing behind him made her shiver.

She put on a bright red dress with a modest camisole top and flirty skirt that swirled around her knees. It was too late to change into something else that was not so...so *red*. With unsteady fingers she tidied her hair all the while muttering to herself about letting Laureen choose the dress for her.

She slipped on her strappy high-heeled red sandals, shrugged into her lacy multicolored jacket, and grabbed her purse and her keys. She opened the bedroom door and headed for the living room feeling like an animal trainer about to walk into a lion's cage.

She'd have to play it by ear. Cullen would show his true colors soon enough. They all did.

❧

When Cullen and Danita arrived at the Westgate Hotel's stunning ballroom, the fundraiser was well under way. They picked up their name tags at a table near the door, and proceeded to find their assigned table.

Once seated, Cullen asked, "What can I get you to drink—punch or something stronger?"

Danita would have preferred a cocktail to soothe her jitters, but she needed to stay alert. "Punch sounds fine, but not if it's red. This place is packed, and I'd hate to spill it on anyone."

Left alone, Danita scanned the milling crowd. At least two hundred elegantly dressed people filled the room, with another fifty or more on the patio. A huge display at one end of the room seemed dwarfed by the spacious room. People in earnest conversation were already seated at most of the forty-odd tables, but her table was empty.

When Cullen returned with their drinks she pointed to a display. "What's that all about over there?"

"Looks like publicity for our illustrious benefactors. Want to take a look?"

She left her drink on the table and accompanied Cullen to the extensive exhibit area. The history of Penn-Atkinson's philanthropic activities dating from 1950 to the present fascinated Danita. When she came to pictures of the grant recipients for the last four years, she committed their faces to memory along with highlights of their biographies and the type of grants they had received.

She was so engrossed that Cullen's deep voice startled her. "I see a friend of mine. Would you like to meet him?"

"No thanks," Danita replied. "Go ahead. I'll join you later."

Cullen strode away without a backward glance. Danita guessed their arrested lovemaking earlier in the evening had embarrassed him, too. Though her face burned with the memory, she quelled the sensation and searched the crowd for the four people she hoped could help her.

Over the next hour she found three of the four winners and quizzed each of them. She noted Cullen stayed one step behind her when it came to finding grant winners.

The last recipient she managed to corner, was an earnest but friendly thirty-something blonde who ran an after-school program for homeless children in a downtown shelter mere blocks from the site of the reception. She said to Danita, "Your project is terrific. I'll bet you sold Mr. Rawley on it right away."

The woman's statement puzzled Danita. "Mr. Rawley? I suppose so, yes. Why?"

"I found out, much to my amazement, that Mr. Rawley has the most influence over the committee's decision."

Taken aback, Danita said, "Mr. Rawley? That nice old man? I knew he was the founder's grandson, but I had no idea..."

The blonde grinned. "He seems like a kindly old pet, but he's the one with the power. Don't underestimate him."

"Now you've made me nervous."

"I suppose you've treated him like a friend. Good. He thrives on people thinking he's a figurehead. After I won the award last year, he told me he hated it when people shined up to him. He said anyone who uses a fake front turns him off. Be yourself. He'll think more of you."

They discussed the woman's students and the difficulty she had finding volunteers willing to enter the neighborhood where she held her classes. Her enthusiasm and dedication inspired Danita.

When three men in business suits joined them and asked the woman how they could help her with her program, Danita thanked her for her advice and excused herself. From the grateful look the blonde gave her, Danita knew that she wanted to concentrate all of her attention on the men. Danita chuckled. Since the two of them were assigned at the same table, Danita would ask more about her classes later.

Danita found herself looking for Cullen. She spotted him with Mr. Rawley. Cullen was no doubt making points for himself and Danita could not blame him. One of the women standing in a group right behind Cullen and Mr. Rawley beckoned her to join them.

When she did, Mr. Rawley's voice reached her first. "Over here, Alex."

She heard footsteps approaching, but dared not turn around in case they might think she was eavesdropping.

Mr. Rawley said, "Cullen was telling me some very interesting things about his competitor."

Danita's ears perked up. Of all the nerve. She could understand Cullen making a pitch for his project, but not at her expense. No doubt he had given Mr. Rawley an earful about how he had to rescue poor little Danita—had to clue her in on even the most basic business practices. Heat burned her cheeks at the thought of them laughing at her ineptitude.

Mr. Rawley's jovial voice boomed. "Tell Alex what you told me."

Danita was about to step around the tall man who hid her from Cullen's view, but stopped herself for fear she might cause a scene. Embarrassment colored Cullen's voice. "I merely mentioned having used the services of WAIT FOR ME. The professionalism of the seniors was impressive."

"I'm not surprised. I visited the place not long ago. The seniors were full of life and proud of their jobs." Mr. Frederickson chuckled. "The employee lounge reminded me of a hangout for adolescent old-timers. Must do those people good to have a place where they're not only welcome but safe."

Danita's heart swelled with gratitude...and love. Cullen had deliberately risked his advantage to put in a good word for WAIT FOR ME. His gesture overwhelmed her. The walls of mistrust she had built over the past two years crumbled.

Mr. Rawley's voice held a note of regret. "Too bad the rules for the grant won't allow us to select more than one winner. One of these days we'll have to look at our criteria. With two projects like this year's, we'll have a damn hard time choosing."

Just when she made up her mind to reveal her presence, someone tapped a microphone. A man's voice announced, "Ladies and gentlemen, please take your seats at your assigned tables."

The crowd dispersed and the chattering subsided.

When all the tables filled, the voice continued, "My name is Joe Rawley. Welcome to our annual preselection reception for the Penn-Atkinson Foundation. In a few days we'll know the name of the winner of this year's grant which will be delivered to him or her at the end of this month."

Danita's mouth went dry. Four more weeks and it would all be over. Thirty days until she would keep or lose WAIT FOR ME. Cullen had done what he could to keep her in the running. Win or lose she would always be grateful to him for his generous spirit.

❧

On the way home from the reception Danita castigated herself. *How could I have been so blind, so prejudiced, so frightened all this time? I let Robert win. I let him destroy my ability to trust my instincts. I let him rob me of my life as surely as he robbed me of my money and nearly ruined WAIT FOR ME.*

Danita decided then and there to make amends for all the mean-spirited thoughts she had harbored against Cullen since she'd met him.

Looking back over their short acquaintance, she realized he had offered her only kindness and consideration. He had gone out of his way to help her, even though he knew his assistance increased her chance to win the grant.

"You're awfully quiet, Danita. I hope you're not brooding about my...loss of control earlier this evening."

In spite of the seat belt constraining her, she shifted in her seat and faced him. She gave him a big smile. "Not at all. Besides, it takes two to lose control in a situation like that. Forget it. I have."

"You have?" Disappointment colored his voice, then his tone brightened. "You're not mad at me?"

"Not at all."

"Prove it. Go out with me Saturday night. Chris Rock's in town. I can get us good seats for his show."

Danita hesitated. She needed time to examine her newfound feelings before she spent an entire evening alone with him.

Cullen's voice cut into her thoughts. "I promise it's only a date. I'll keep my hands to myself...if you will."

The disarming smile he gave her melted the last of her uncertainty. "All right. Sounds like fun."

"Dinner first?" He eased the car to the curb in front of her apartment.

"Sounds fine."

Cullen threw back his head and laughed, a deep rumble which echoed with undisguised elation. "Danita, Danita. As soon as I get set for another of your fast balls, you pitch me a curve ball high and inside."

Danita chuckled. "Want me to stall? I can do that."

"No, no. Don't change your mind. We have a lot to talk about."

"Such as?"

"My visit to Adam's school. My first card party with those bandits you call relatives." He ran his finger down her cheek. "Your whole life before I met you."

At his touch her throat closed. She tried to speak, but found she could barely breathe a whispered, "Oh."

Cullen went around to the passenger door and helped her out of his car. He led her to her front door, waited while she unlocked it, and went inside with her.

"I'll pick you up Saturday at five." He stood in the doorway as if expecting her to argue with him.

"Perfect." She'd be ready by four. No sense tempting fate—or Cullen. A mischievous imp inside her made her grin. She would take the day off and have a complete beauty treatment. Then she'd "let" Laureen talk her into choosing a dress from her boutique: something sexy enough to knock Cullen's socks off.

Cullen leaned over and kissed her nose. "You're not going to back out on me?"

"Trying to renege on a date made in heaven?"

"Not a chance, my sweet Dani. Not a chance."

❧

With an impatient tap of his foot, Cullen stood at Danita's door and jabbed her bell. *The woman's driving me crazy. First she's cool then she's hot? She keeps me at arm's length, and then comes on to me. I'll turn into a raving testosterone driven fool before she's through with me.*

Danita opened the door and greeted him with a smile so warm it melted his insides.

"Come on in while I get my purse and jacket. Would you like a drink before we leave?" she asked as if this were their tenth date instead of their first.

"No, thanks. We'll get something after the show."

When she said, "I'd like that," he searched her face. *Did she realize she had agreed to drinks after the show?*

Cullen stared at her retreating figure. When she hurried into her living room the hem of her sassy bright pink dress flounced around her knees. The faint scent of lemon blossoms surrounded him. She dazzled him. The sparkle in her eyes intrigued him. She looked as if she felt as excited about the prospect of spending their evening together as he did. When she had opened the door to him with a welcoming smile, he had thought he must be dreaming.

Danita returned with her purse and jacket. He would have hauled her into his arms and kissed the reason for her warm welcome out of her, but he had learned the hard way to keep his kisses to himself.

She seemed to have stopped running. A million questions reeled through his mind. If he could figure out what he had done right, he would do it again...and again...and again.

He led her to his car. She made a comment about how clean it looked and how she needed to take time out to get hers washed. She seemed *too* relaxed.

What was she up to? Had her family changed her mind about him? Did his buddy Adam put in a good word for him? Maybe Virgie or Carlos had talked to her—or Phil. Whoever or whatever had influenced her, he was determined not to blow it.

"I hope you like Ethiopian food," he said. "Though it might take a while to get served, it's well worth the wait."

Her face lit up with anticipation. "I've never had any, but it sounds...different."

She swung her legs into the car and smoothed her wide skirt over her knees. He suppressed a groan of disappointment when the skirt hid her enticing legs. "I promise it's better than 'different'."

He closed her door, rounded the back of the Buick and slid into his seat. Remembering how she had enjoyed the Jamaican meal, he couldn't wait to see her at The Queen of Sheba where they served their meals without utensils.

When they reached the restaurant, Cullen introduced Danita to the owner who greeted Cullen by name and ushered them to a low table flanked by cushions. Thick curtains with Northeast African designs formed islands of privacy in the small restaurant.

Danita scanned her surroundings with widened eyes. African pop music played softly in the background. The aroma of herbs and spices hung in the air. "I love it. Except for the music, this place makes me think of the Arabian Nights."

Cullen grinned. She looked like a kid on her first trip to Disneyland. He hoped her delight would last throughout the rest of the evening.

A waitress in a royal blue caftan brought them a steaming pot of tea and two glass cups. She poured the fragrant brew and explained the menu.

"Do you have any preferences?" Cullen asked Danita.

She spread her hands in a gesture of perplexity. "To tell the truth, I'm overwhelmed. I trust you. Please choose for me."

Cullen laughed and ordered his favorite dishes. After the waitress left he said, "Relax, Danita. It'll take awhile for the kitchen to prepare our meal. Let's enjoy our tea while we wait."

Danita settled against the large overstuffed pillows. She sipped the hot sweet beverage and gave an appreciative "Mmm-mm".

She directed a flirtatious look at him over the rim of her cup. "If you spent the evening with J.V. and the gang you know plenty about me, I'm sure. Tell me about yourself. What got you interested in prostheses and braces?"

Cullen did a double take. Danita? Flirting? No way. He searched her face. All he saw was interest and expectation. He must have imagined that look. "It's a long story. Sure you want to hear it?"

She leaned toward him. "Unless you don't want to tell me."

"Remember, you asked. In elementary school my best friend and neighbor was Kandoo Singleton.

"Kandoo was born with one healthy leg and one leg which extended from his hip to a few inches below his knee. Until he started school, Kandoo's mother was so protective of him she never let him play outdoors, and never left him alone. She hovered over him as if she thought he would splinter."

"He's an only child and I am, too. He used to be so thin he looked as if he would break if anyone touched him. As a kid, whenever anyone tried to protect him, he'd say, 'I can do it. I can do it!' All through school everybody called him by his nickname 'Kandoo'.

"When he and I entered Kindergarten I was the only friend he had who was allowed to play at his house. He had a devilish sense of humor, an inquisitive mind and such determination I idolized him. He's four days older than I am and he never lets me forget it. He's still my best friend, and I'd do anything in the world for him and he for me."

Cullen looked at Danita, wondering if he was making this story too long, but he wanted her to understand, to realize that when he committed himself to someone it was for life. "Am I boring you so far?"

"Not at all. Please go on." Danita's smile encouraged him.

"Kandoo's school was next door to mine. His was for orthopedically handicapped children. When we hit second grade, his school started an experimental 'mainstreamed' program with mine. From then on Kandoo and I were in the same classes. We shared the same friends, attended the same parties and hung out together most of the time.

"His prosthesis fascinated me. Showing it to anyone besides me and the kids at his school, his doctors and his therapists embarrassed him. He always wore long socks to hide it peachy-pink lifeless look. Kandoo and I talked about how he could get around better if he had a lighter weight more flexible artificial leg without bulky straps. We were into science fiction movies and TV shows then. Those shows gave us some far-out ideas on how to change his leg."

Danita smiled and refilled their cups with tea. She shifted toward him and trained her gaze on him as if she couldn't wait for the rest of the story.

If she had looked around for their waitress with impatience, Cullen would have cut his story short, but she seemed engrossed in his past.

"Sometimes Kandoo's mother took me to the rehab center with them. I got to know his doctors, and met Phil Mann, the Research Director of The Center for Orthotics-Prosthetics Research(COPR). Mann pioneered some of the changes in prostheses which made his clients more mobile. Kandoo called him 'My Main Mann' because he tested his experimental limbs on Kandoo. Those legs allowed Kandoo to get around without a wheelchair or a walker."

Cullen paused, letting those long-ago memories spring to life in his mind's eye. "In high school Kandoo fell in love."

Danita smiled. "Good for him. He sounds like he deserved a nice girlfriend. How old was he then?"

"About fifteen. He was in the ninth grade. Kandoo couldn't keep his eyes off this girl named Gwendolyn Turner. Gwen was sweet, quiet, studious, and as cute as the proverbial girl next door. He talked to me about her all the time. Although her parents tended to overprotect her, she attached herself to the group of kids who hung out with us. She had two brothers who were as big as bears and twice as mean, but they liked Kandoo and believed he was harmless."

"A harmless fifteen-year-old male? I'd like to meet one," Danita quipped with a knowing smile.

Cullen snorted. "Her brothers must have thought the same, because when Kandoo started calling her, they didn't like it. They let him know they wanted him to stay away from their sister. They said he wasn't man enough to take care of her. When he told me what they'd said to him, I was mad as hell. Kandoo, however, agreed with them and backed away from Gwen."

Danita made an inelegant sound at the back of her throat. "Some kids can be totally stupid. I hope Kandoo kept seeing her."

"I'm afraid he didn't. Not long after his run-in with Gwen's brothers, I spent the night at his house to study for a big test. We had dressed for bed when he started talking about Gwen and her brothers. He damned his handicap, damned his 'white' leg, and damned her brothers."

"He shook me up the most when he damned himself. I felt helpless rage at the unfairness of life. He got so upset he took off his prosthesis, threw it across the room and broke the mirror on his closet door. Before I could get him to calm down, he started crying. He scared the hell out of me. I'd never seen him cry before. It was also the first time I'd ever seen him give up on anything he wanted."

A suspicious bright sheen glistened in Danita's eyes. "I hope you convinced him Gwen's brothers were just plain stupid."

Cullen swallowed a thick lump in his throat. He had started this story, but he was having trouble telling Danita of his pain and anger over the way Gwen's brothers had intimidated his friend.

"I tried, but it didn't do any good. I ended up crying with him. In one breath he swore he'd prove himself as good as anyone else, and in the next he belittled himself—called himself half a person who didn't deserve Gwen. When I said he should let her decide who she liked, he got even wilder. He said he didn't want some girl who could only feel sorry for him."

Cullen tightened his fingers around his tea cup. The memory of his failure to change Kandoo's mind that night still stung after all those years. "By the time his mother came to see what caused the commotion, Kandoo had quieted down. We made up some excuse for the broken mirror and promised to fix it. Years went by before Kandoo said another word about Gwen or girls in general, but I never forgot. I decided then and there to help my friend and other people who found themselves in the same situation, but it took me a while to figure out how."

"What did you do?" Danita asked as if the answer held great importance to her.

"During my senior year in high school I signed up for a work-study program and asked for an assignment at COPR. The moment I walked through the lab door I knew what I wanted to do for the rest of my life. Mr. Mann suggested I get a business degree before I started a training program in orthotics and prosthetics. With his encouragement I enrolled in San Diego State and majored in business administration. Then I went to L.A. and later New York and worked for my certification in O and P. After I completed my studies I got a job at COPR. Armed with a small business loan and every dollar we could scrape together, my partner, Mitch and I bought the business from Mann when he retired.

"The events of that night changed my life, and I'll never forget them."

"Do you ever see Kandoo?"

"Yeah. But he still hasn't gotten over his lack of self-confidence with women. He treats all of them like buddies."

Danita laid her hand on his. "Funny how what happens to us in our pasts can change our whole lives."

The haunted look in her eyes startled him. Before he could ask her what she meant he looked up to see their waitress bearing a huge tray loaded with food.

The evening unfolded for him like a flower blooming in a time-lapse film. Cullen stored each gesture, each word, and each expression Danita shared with him in his heart. Her appreciative exclamations over the meal gratified him. When she discovered she had no fork, she allowed him to feed her the first few bites. His heart jumped into his throat when she touched his fingers with her tongue. Then she got the knack of how to fold her bread around her food, and he had to content himself with merely watching her eat.

His body remained in a state of arousal until they reached the Civic Center and took their seats for the Rock show. Her peals of laughter at Rock's stories made Cullen almost burst with pleasure. He wanted to hold time in his hands and make it stand still.

After the show they stopped for drinks at The Golden Hyacinth. Each time the small combo played a dreamy standard they danced, barely moving in a tight circle on the large floor.

Bound by his arms she snuggled against him. She locked her hands behind his neck, and pillowed her breasts against his chest until he thought he would go up in flames. He had to put some distance between them before the evidence of his desire telegraphed his need to her.

"Let's get you home," he said.

During the ride to her apartment she leaned her head against his shoulder and allowed him to place her hand on his thigh where he covered her left hand with his right. As he parked in front of her building she slowly eased away from him and sat up straight. "Thank you for a wonderful evening," she murmured.

"I enjoyed it, too." He helped her from the car and walked her to her door, wondering how she planned to get rid of him. He refused to make it easy for her.

"Would you like to come in for a cup of coffee?"

"Are you sure?" Did she know she was playing right into his hands?

She paused as she turned her key in the lock and lifted her face to his. The street lamp cast a soft warm glow over her face. Somehow she managed to look shy and seductive at the same time. She tilted her face at a determined angle. "Yes, I'm sure."

In a haze of uncertainty and caution he followed her to her living room. He seated himself on the far end of the couch and listened to the sounds of water running and cabinet doors opening in the kitchen. He had longed for this moment—dreamed of sitting there while a willing Danita signaled she had stopped running and wanted to take a step in his direction.

He would have asked her what had changed, but he wasn't sure if he was only imagining her about face. He loosened his tie and unbuttoned his jacket, prepared for a frustrating end to a perfect evening.

She sat beside him and put her hand on his. "The coffee will be ready in a minute."

He jerked as if she had burned him. If she was putting him on, he was curious to see how far she would go. He turned toward her and took her in his arms. She melted against him and parted her lips expectantly. He said, "Danita, are you playing a game?"

"Not at all." She closed the distance between them and brushed her lips against his. "Does this feel like a game to you?"

He searched her eyes which were soft with desire. Her open expression encouraged him. Her body tilted and strained toward his, tempting him, telling him she didn't expect him to hold on to his control any longer. She had to know where their kisses would lead. She seemed willing, but could he trust her? He captured her lips with his. If she bolted, she bolted.

She returned his kiss with such unexpected ardor she burned him. She lifted her arms and curled them around his neck, clinging to him as if she never wanted to let go.

"Danita, do you know what you're doing to me?" Not waiting for an answer, he swooped down for another taste of her sweet mouth. When he nibbled, she nibbled back. When he ran his hands down her back, she caressed his shoulders and his nape. When his cell phone vibrated he wondered if he were tingling from her touch.

Oh, hell. I can't believe this! I should have left the damn thing at home. His chest heaved as if he had run a four minute mile backwards. He pulled away to check the caller ID on his phone. "I need to answer this. Hope you don't mind."

She slumped against him, her unwillingness to end their lovemaking obvious in the small voice whispering against his chest. "Go ahead. I'll get the coffee."

While she waited for him to answer his call she went into the kitchen. She sat at the breakfast bar which separated the kitchen and living room and watched him, her lips swollen and moist. She folded her hands in front of her as if to steady them.

"Cullen Powers, here," he barked into the phone. The party on the line breathed into the receiver but didn't answer.

Finally a tear-laced voice sliced through the mist of passion clouding his mind like a search light on a foggy night. "Cullen. Can you help me? I don't know what to do?"

Kay! "What's the matter?"

Nine

"WHAT THE HELL'S GOING ON? Where are you?" Cullen held the phone in a tight grip.

Kay's voice shrilled with panic. "Don't say my name, and don't repeat my instructions, or I'll be gone when you get here."

"All right. Calm down. Where are you and what's the problem?"

"I'm at the hotel by Montgomery Airfield. You know, the Four Corners. Room 326. Don't mention to *anyone* where I am. Aaron has lost his mind. He...he...hit me. If he finds me I don't know what he'll do."

Cullen's hand pressed the receiver tighter to his ear. He struggled to keep the anxiety out of his voice. "Be right there."

He hung up and turned to Danita. Her puzzled expression told him she expected an explanation, but he had made Kay a promise he couldn't break.

Danita's voice wavered. She looked at her watch and then at Cullen. "But it's after midnight. What's happened?"

Cullen hesitated a fraction too long before he said, "Nothing I can't handle. I don't have time to talk right now. I have an emergency."

Danita sat erect. She set her jaw at a determined angle. "It's Kay, isn't it? She's in trouble and needs our help."

Our help. Words of denial rose to his lips, but he couldn't lie to Danita. Yet he didn't want her involved until he found out the seriousness of the situation. He strode to the door and turned the dead bolt. "Look, Danita, I don't have time to play twenty questions. I have to go."

"I'll bet she asked you not to tell anyone she called, but you can trust me."

"I know I can trust you when it comes to Kay, so maybe you've guessed wrong."

"Who else would you call 'honey'?"

Cullen made no answer, but yanked the door open. "Lock up tight. I'll call you in the morning."

"You'll come back here as soon as you can tell me what's happened, I don't care what time of day or night. You hear me, Cullen Powers?" she shouted at his back.

Cullen swung around to face her. Hands on hips, eyes flashing, and lips set in a determined line; she looked like a tigress ready to defend her cubs.

He met her stubborn gaze head on. He had to keep her out of this until he found out how seriously Kay was hurt. "An unexpected emergency. It'll take too long to explain right now. I need to take care of this immediately."

"Of course you do. I understand," she whispered.

He turned away, knowing he had to withhold any reassurances for the moment. "I'll get back to you as soon as I can."

He stalked to his car. He fought the impulse to reverse his steps, to wrap his arms around her, and admit Kay had called.

First he had to assure himself Kay was safe. Vowing to make things right between him and Danita as soon as he could, he drove to Kay's hotel.

Cullen parked in the spacious lot in front of the Four Corners Inn. The lot was half empty. An eerie feeling skittered up his spine. He closely studied each car. All of them appeared vacant. The only familiar vehicle he saw was Kay's little bug.

He took his time locking his car, peering through the darkness for any movement. All was quiet. He walked to the hotel's entrance. His heels tapped an ominous cadence. When he reached the doors, he checked its reflections to make sure no one was watching.

He forced himself to adopt a casual pace through the large double-doored entrance. Spotting a house telephone by the restrooms, he dialed Kay's room number.

The phone in her room rang several times before someone picked it up but said nothing. Cullen spoke in a near-whisper close to the mouthpiece. "It's Cullen. I'll be right up."

Soft breathing, half sobs, half sighs let him know someone was on the line. "Kay, are you there?"

Kay's unsteady voice responded, "Knock four times or I won't answer." Then he heard a click and the line went dead.

Damn, this must be serious. Kay was not one to panic. Whatever the problem, he'd take care of her.

He strolled past the hotel bar to a bank of elevators and punched the up-button. He gave the lobby and hallway a furtive but thorough examination. Except for the soft hum of background music and the murmur of conversation from a few people in the bar, all appeared quiet.

Cullen checked the lights above the elevator. Its slow descent strained his patience. Five...four.... "Come on, come on," Cullen mumbled under his breath. Three…two... "At last."...Lobby. The bell dinged. Slowly the door slid open.

Thank God it was late at night and there were no other passengers.

He rode to the fifth floor. He exited the cage and ambled down the hall. He examined the room numbers to determine if he was in the correct wing for room 326. He found 526 midway down the long corridor. He went to the stairs and ran down to the third floor and directly toward room 326. He chuckled in self-derision. His favorite fictional detective Easy Rawlins couldn't have done it better.

Cullen examined his surroundings with the sharpness of an eagle. No sound or movement greeted him. Silently he moved down the blue-carpeted hallway. He looked left and right one last time before he halted in front of Kay's room.

When he knocked four times, nothing happened. He placed his ear against the door. He heard the soft padding of feet on carpet. He stepped back. The footsteps stopped and he felt, rather than saw, an eye peering at him from the peephole. The door opened the width of a safety chain. A bruised eye stared out at him.

"Just a minute." The door closed and then swung abruptly open. With a trembling hand, Kay reached out, seized the sleeve of his jacket, and pulled him into the room. She quickly closed the door and replaced the chain. "Thanks for coming so soon," she mumbled between swollen lips.

At the sight of her puffy face and defeated expression Cullen's blood raged in his veins. Anger choked him. Gathering Kay in his arms, he closed his eyes against the fury scalding him. She trembled against him; her sobs buffeted him. If he lived to be a hundred he knew he would never forget the heartbreaking sounds of her anguished weeping.

"It's all right. I'm here for you now. Cry if you need to. It's all right," Cullen crooned.

Kay's tears undid him. He held her for a long time, awkwardly patting her back and murmuring words he hoped would calm and comfort her.

When her tears subsided he led her to one of the upholstered chairs which flanked an oval table standing in front of tightly drawn drapes.

The monotonous, unrelenting rumble of the air conditioner sounded almost menacing. When he spoke, he kept his voice calm, though he had to struggle to do so. "Have you seen a doctor?"

"N-no, I'm f-f-fine. A little bruised and battered, b-b-but nothing's broken."

"Can you tell me what happened?"

She inhaled several deep shaky breaths. "I told you. Aaron lost control and hit me."

"The bastard. Kay, he's lost his mind."

Her shuddering sighs stopped Cullen's flow of words. He covered her clenched hand with his. Hers was ice cold and trembled under his fingers.

If I were a violent man, I'd track Aaron down and take him apart limb by limb. Instead, I'll have to wait it out and let the law handle Aaron. But while I'm waiting I'll do everything in my power to make sure Aaron spends a good long time reflecting on what he's done. When he gets out of jail, he'd think twice about attacking another woman.

"Do you feel up to telling me about it?"

Kay kept her eyes glued to her wedding band. "When I got home this evening at five, he was already there. He'd been drinking and was in a foul mood."

Cullen was afraid to interrupt, but questions surged to the tip of his tongue. How long had this been going on? Why had she stayed? Why hadn't he known and done something sooner? He bit back his questions, hoping his silence would encourage her to talk. As if recalling a nightmare, Kay poured out her story.

❧

When Kay finished telling him what happened she twisted her wedding band around and around with the fingers of her right hand. "I don't know if he meant his threat, but I can't take the chance, and I can't forgive him for hitting me."

Kay's recitation had set a fire in Cullen's gut. A red haze nearly blinded him to the misery in her eyes. He tamped down the urge to find Aaron and kick his sorry ass. "Do you want me to go with you to the police station?"

"I can't do that!"

'Why not? He committed a crime—assault and battery."

"I just can't. I'd be too ashamed."

Cullen fought to control his voice and keep the anger from coloring his words. "You have nothing to feel ashamed about. Aaron's the one who should feel shame. The way he's treated you is a disgrace to everything it means to be a man."

"You don't understand. If this gets out it will ruin his career—all he's worked for the last fifteen years. He'll be an object of contempt."

"Who gives a damn?"

"What about me and my reputation? I'll never be able to hold up my head again. People will either scorn me for living with such a man or pity me for my weakness. I don't think I could live with either."

Cullen jumped to his feet, too angry to sit any longer. Struggling to understand her reasoning, he ran his hands across his face and over his hair, willing his temper to cool. He knew he would make her feel guilty and cowardly if he badgered her, and she didn't need that.

He calmed himself down. "What do you plan to do?"

She straightened. "First, I want to thank you for giving me the brochure and card on domestic violence when you did. At the time, I was getting ready for my trip and I didn't want to think about Aaron's problem. Though I wanted to deny it, I knew I needed help, so I did prepare for this moment even before I left for D.C."

Cullen looked at her with renewed respect. "What do you mean?"

"I took the advice in the pamphlet you gave me. I gathered my medical records, bank books, and other important papers and packed them in my suitcase. Then I went to the bank and withdrew most of my savings and converted them into cash and travelers checks."

Thank goodness Kay had taken steps to protect herself. As soon as he could he'd tell Danita how much she'd helped Kay already.

He wanted to assure Kay she was in charge. "You're calling the shots. Where do we go from here?" he asked.

"Right now I'm waiting for Cathy from the YWCA's battered women's shelter to return my call. She's working the night shift so someone's available for women...like me." She stumbled over the words "battered women's shelter" as if wanting to deny she needed the shelter's service. "They said they were full, but would search for a placement for me somewhere in the county. Until the call comes I'll have to ask you to help me find another place to stay. I'll need to use your credit card to get me in there. Aaron might find a way to locate me if I leave any kind of paper trail."

"What about clothes and...women's stuff?"

Kay smiled, then flinched as if at the pain in her swollen lips. "Fortunately I never got around to removing my luggage from my car after my trip. I've plenty of clothes and 'women's stuff'."

Cullen advanced to the bathroom and got a hand towel. He strode to the small refrigerator under the bar, yanked out a tray of ice cubes and dumped them onto the towel. He wound the fluffy cloth around the ice and handed it to Kay. "Here, use this while we wait."

She accepted the ice pack and placed it against the swollen left side of her face. "Thanks." She looked up at him, tears brightening her eyes. She blinked them away. "Did I get you away from something important?"

When Cullen recalled the way he had left Danita he bit back a wry chuckle. "You're what's important to me. Never, ever forget that. You can call me anytime, anyplace and I'll come running. Now, no more foolish questions. Would you like me to fix you something cool to drink?"

"Nothing for me, but help yourself."

Cullen was in no mood for a drink. While they waited for Kay's call, he found himself giving voice to a question which had plagued him since Ayana's death. "Has Aaron always had a mean streak?"

Kay didn't hesitate. "No, just the opposite."

Cullen grunted in disbelief.

"He claims I spend too much time with my art and my friends, and neglect our home. When he complained about my housekeeping I hired some help. Lately he's begun to quote his father about respect in his own home and says he's not getting it. He accuses me of only pretending interest in what he's doing, and of constantly nagging him about drinking too much."

"From what you say, you had a reason to."

"Yes, but since Ayana died he's had problems sleeping and claims he drinks at night to relax. He says it's the only way he can block out the memory of the way Ayana looked at the morgue when we went to identify her."

The phone shrilled, cutting off Cullen's next question. Kay looked at Cullen who answered on the third ring. "Yes, Cathy, she's here."

He handed the phone to Kay who took it. At the same time she grabbed a sheet of hotel stationary and a pen. She scribbled some notes while she spoke into the phone. "A week? Yes, I think I can take care of myself that long... No, I won't tell anyone else.... No, I can check out of here in about an hour.... I'll call you back as soon as I have my new number...thanks."

Kay hung up and folded the sheet of paper. She stood, retrieved her bag and carefully put the paper into her wallet. "Let's take a look in the phone book and find another place for me to stay. Somewhere Aaron won't think of looking."

They leafed through the directory and discussed the pros and cons of each possibility. They finally chose a large motel that catered to relatives visiting the men and women assigned to the Marine Air Station at Miramar which was about fifteen miles north.

It was three in the morning before Cullen got Kay settled in her new digs. Before he left he told her of his discussions with Danita and how much she wanted to help.

"Please don't tell her yet. She'll only think less of me for letting Aaron treat me badly all this time, and there's nothing she can do to help right now. Besides, Cathy asked me not to tell anyone else where I am." Kay's voice held a sad note.

"I'm certain Danita won't think less of you. She's not the judgmental type. She understands. She gave me the material I passed on to you. She cares what happens to you. Apparently she's had some experience in this area. We could use her expertise."

"I need a female friend right now. Someone who doesn't know Aaron. But Cathy thinks the fewer people who know where I am or what happened, the safer I'll be. Besides, I can't face anyone else. I need time for my...my bruises heal."

Cullen put an arm around Kay's shoulder and walked toward the door. "Okay. I understand," Cullen said wondering how he'd explain his sudden departure to Danita. "Now, get some sleep. I'll call you around eleven tomorrow. Keep this locked and the chain on. If you need me before eleven, call me on my cell."

Kay opened the door of her small room. "You are one lucky guy. Don't let that woman get away."

Cullen gave her a salute. "Don't worry. I won't."

He headed for his car. As was usual for May, dew misted his windshield. A soft breeze cooled his brow and pulled him wide awake. He had a feeling Danita was waiting for word from him, but he needed time to decide what to tell her. He'd made a promise to Kay, and he'd have to keep it.

He only hoped he could come up with an explanation that would satisfy Danita's curiosity...and soon.

Ten

WHEN CULLEN'S RADIO BLARED a rousing gospel song, he knew it was Sunday morning, but for a moment he had no idea what he had scheduled. Memories of Kay's problems with Aaron surfaced, and a wave of energy propelled him from his bed.

Dressing quickly in black jeans and a blue chambray shirt, he ate a quick breakfast of dried cereal before he roared off to his local supermarket, bought groceries and a bouquet of spring flowers. He called Kay on his cell to let her know he was on his way. As he drove to Kay's hotel he continually checked his rearview mirror to make sure no one followed him.

Kay gushed over the flowers. She arranged them in a cheap-looking glass vase she found in the sparsely stocked cupboards before she stowed the groceries in a small refrigerator. On a table in front of the balcony windows she set the blooms. "Doesn't that look homey?" she asked with a sad smile.

Her obvious pleasure in such a little thing moved him. "They're just a supermarket variety, but I couldn't resist them."

When the phone rang Cullen answered. It was Cathy. Kay took over the phone before he could exchange more than a few words of greeting.

After talking to Cathy, Kay hung up with an optimistic air. "Cathy called to check on me."

Cullen handed Kay Danita's business card. He'd added Danita's cell phone number. "When Cathy gives the okay, give Danita a call. Knowing her, she'll want to help if only to give moral support if that's what you need. She cares about you, and she'd never meddle."

Determined to keep Kay's mood light, Cullen shared some of the pranks his employees played at COPR. She chuckled at the message on the latest post card he had received from his parents whose trip to Africa was nearly at an end.

Finally he told her the grant would be announced on Friday. They talked about the clients who would benefit should he win.

At five o'clock, Kay pushed Cullen out of the door. "I want to watch my TV shows, and you need to see Danita."

"Before I go, promise me you won't contact Aaron for any reason—not to let him know you're okay, not to find out how he is, not to ask about your mail. Promise?"

Kay hesitated.

"I mean it, Kay. We don't know what he's thinking or what he'll do. Don't write, don't call, don't tell any of your friends where you are or how to contact you. Understood?"

Kay sighed. "Yes. I promise. And thanks again for everything. I love the flowers."

"You're welcome, and see you keep your word. If you get lonely and want to talk, call me any time of the day or night. I'm here for you. Oh, by the way, I'm leaving tomorrow around noon for my monthly consult at the VA hospital in L.A., but I'll be back Tuesday night. You have my cell number. Will you be all right?"

"Sure. Now, have a good trip, Sweetie, and don't worry about me."

Cullen hugged her, gave her a lingering worried look, and headed for the door. He hated the thought of leaving her for even an hour, let alone two days.

It was late in the afternoon when he arrived on Danita's stoop. He felt wrung dry and depressed. She opened the door to his ring. She was bare footed and still dressed in an outfit he was certain she'd worn to her family's weekly after-church meal. The sight of her lifted his spirits so much he couldn't seem to stop grinning.

Hips swaying, she led the way into the living room. His gaze lingered on her beautiful graceful legs and the sweet curve of her derriere which fit snugly into a green knee-skimming skirt topped with a black blouse. The sight of her revived his flagging spirits.

She gave him a wary look. "I just got home," she said. "Give me a minute to change. I want to be comfortable while you tell me all about your day. Want a beer?"

"Do I have another option?"

"Sure. Wine, soft drinks or something stronger."

"Since my choices don't include watching you change, I'll take a brew."

She raised an eyebrow and smiled. "In your dreams," she retorted. "Have a seat." She marched to the kitchen and returned with a can of beer and a glass. "I think this should keep you occupied for a few minutes. I'll be right back."

On his way to the sofa he spotted a brown leather-bound photo album lying on the coffee table. While he waited and sipped his beer, he sat and leafed through it.

One group of pictures caught his eye—a teenaged Danita at the beach with a tall slender girl who could only be Virgie. They wore lettered sweatshirts over their shorts. They seemed to struggle to get a box kite off the ground. Danita's carefree look tugged at his heart. He wished he'd known her then.

The last photo showed a long shot of the two teens watching the kite take off. On the grass, a shadow of a male with a camera gave the only clue of who took the pictures.

Unsmiling, Danita returned to the living room. She'd changed into an oversized blouse and a long denim skirt. Cullen noticed how little she had changed from her high school pictures.

He pointed to a close-up of the other girl. "This is Virgie, right?"

Danita moved to his side, leaned over and took one look. She gave a wide smile, the first since he'd arrived. "Yes. We've been friends since elementary school. She's the best."

"She's made quite an impression on Mitch."

"He'd better not hurt her. She's more vulnerable than she appears."

Cullen nodded and set the album on the coffee table. He patted the cushion beside him inviting her to join him. "So is he, but I think they can work out their own affairs. Right now I'm worried about you and me. I wanted to clear the air before I leave tomorrow for my monthly consult in L.A."

Danita stood where she was, pushed her glasses into place and searched his face as if struggling to read his mind. Apparently unsatisfied with what she saw, she said, "Oh?"

"Ever since I got here you've kept me at a distance. Care to tell me what's up?"

"I think I should be asking you that question. Is everything all right? You left in such a hurry last night, and I haven't heard from you until now."

"Danita, honey, I told you it was business. An unexpected problem I needed to take care of."

Danita began to pace. "Anything I can do to help? Or... "

"I want to think about it awhile. It's a question of confidentiality. Trust me. I'll let you know when I can. There are some things I'm not free to discuss."

Danita seemed to close up inside herself. "I see."

Cullen felt torn between his promise and his need to share with Danita his concern for Kay. From the dubious look on Danita's face it was plain to see he'd nearly lost the trust he'd so carefully tried to build between them. He needed a plan, but for the life of him he couldn't think of one.

Maybe if he knew what caused her to be so cautious he could get things back to the way they were before he'd left Saturday night, and still keep his promise.

"This has nothing to do with you and me," he said.

"Does it have anything to do with the grant?"

"The grant? Of course not! What made you think that?"

"Well, you're so secretive. It's not like you. I guess I just wondered what it was that you couldn't tell me."

Cullen rose, went to Danita and gently took her hand and led her to the sofa. When they were seated facing each other, he held onto her hand. "Tell me about Robert."

Danita started to move away, but he kept her hand firmly in his.

Cullen looked into the eyes. "Your distrust of me, and the fact that you brought up the grant makes me wonder if you think I'd go behind your back and do something that would hurt you."

Danita slowly shook her head as if about to refuse to talk about Robert.

Cullen shifted closer to her. "J.V. suggested I need to know about him, but he said it was your story to tell. From what J.V. said, I think your suspicion has something to do with this Robert. Maybe if I understood what happened I'd have a better idea how to prove to you that you can trust me."

૨૨

Danita took a deep breath. She searched Cullen's face for any sign of duplicity. All she could see was puzzlement and sincerity. It was time...maybe past time...to let go of the pain Robert had caused and trust a man again.

"It's an old story. Robert Rattner and I started out as friends. We worked together at a social service agency. He was the CPA there. When my grandmother and I came up with the idea for WAIT FOR ME, I talked to him about it. It was just a dream for me and Momma Dee, but he encouraged me and even offered suggestions which I shared with her."

Danita combed her fingers through her bangs then smoothed them into place again. "Of course I didn't have any extra money to start a business, so it was a fun exercise in dreaming. Then Momma Dee died. She left me money to help me start my own business, some family heirlooms, and a video tape in which she told me to bring our dream to life."

Danita closed her eyes at the memory of that videotape. Behind her lids Mamma Dee's face and voice appeared. If she reached out her hand she could have sworn she could touch her.

Danita shook her head and opened her eyes. "I knew I had no choice. To make a long story short, I quit my job and set up WAIT FOR ME in memory to my grandmother. Robert helped me get a small business loan to supplement my inheritance, and I convinced him to join me as my accountant."

Cullen squeezed her hand. "Sounds like a smart business decision to me."

"I thought so, too, but before I knew what happened Robert changed. He came after me as if I were the last piece of Godiva in the box. Our working relationship soon led to a more...intimate relationship. I thought he was perfect for me. He understood my commitment to the business; he'd come in with me when it was still on the ground floor, and I could rely on his competence so that I didn't have to deal in depth with the fiscal side of the company."

Cullen frowned. "Something tells me I'm not going to like what's coming next. Don't mind me if I swear."

Danita almost laughed. "If I'd used my head instead of my heart, I would have figured something was wrong with that picture, too. Once we started to make a nice profit, his ardor for me seemed to increase. I thought the stress of setting up a new business might have made me start to take him for granted. But I loved Robert and I believed he loved me. I made up my mind to put more effort into our relationship."

Danita dashed a tear from her cheek. "I did everything I could to spend more time with him, to show him how much I cared, to give in to his increasing demands for my time."

Cullen clenched his teeth so hard the muscles in his jaw bunched into hard ridges, but he didn't interrupt.

"When the business had to shut down because of the fire at the mini mall, we decided to work from my apartment. I took care of the job of starting up again and Robert managed the books.

"A week after WAIT FOR ME got set up in its new place,

Robert disappeared. I was frantic with worry until I found his Dear Jane letter. He told me he was sorry and asked me to forgive him. He said he'd pay me back by Christmas. He needed money to pay off some gambling debts. Seems he got hooked on on-line poker. When I tried to pay some business bills I discovered he had cleaned out our business accounts and had gone into hiding. Christmas came and went and no Robert."

Cullen swore in such a creative stream of invectives he nearly shocked her. "Sorry," he said when she winced.

"I understand. I was so humiliated and felt totally betrayed. I pressed charges and he was arrested and is now in prison. He's been in there over a year, but WAIT FOR ME never recovered any of the money. Now we're barely hanging in there. We need that grant to keep the business open, and all because I trusted the wrong person.

"I've had to borrow money from my family and their friends to keep things going. Then I heard about the grant. The rest you know."

Cullen looked stunned. He pulled Danita into his arms and said, "Oh, baby. It's no wonder you're so suspicious of my sudden attraction to you. But believe me I care about you and would never hurt you. If I ever get my hands on Robert I can't say the same for him."

His threat made Danita smile through her tears. He tilted her face and kissed them away. Cullen always seemed to know what to do to chase away her demons.

At his healing touch her bitterness at Robert's treachery faded until the only person she could think about was Cullen, his tenderness, his strength. She hoped she wouldn't be sorry she believed Cullen wouldn't deliberately hurt her. She pulled back and said, "But, Cullen, what if I do win the grant? Will you..."

Cullen hauled Danita into her arms and silenced her with a gentle kiss.

ε⋒

Cullen wanted to comfort her, to let her know she was safe with him. He poured all the love and tenderness he felt for her into that kiss. He cherished her with his mouth, giving her the sweet passion he had held inside just for her.

With a soft sound of surrender, she melted against him and returned his kisses. When he eased his mouth away from hers, she said, "You haven't..."

"Hush, Danita." Cullen sank his fingers into her lush, tousled hair and kissed her again.

"All right," she whispered. Eyes closed, she sought his lips. "Please touch me."

At her mumbled plea, his heart felt as if it would trip out of his chest. He cupped her breasts through her blouse and found delight in their perfection. He stroked his fingers across her peaked nipples. His gratification in her response stunned him. The desire to give her pleasure intermingled with his intention to comfort her.

The need to touch her flesh claimed him. His fingers brushed the buttons on her blouse, and one by one he slipped them out of their holes until her blouse hung open. Her lacy beige bra peeked out at him and teased his senses.

She undid his shirt, and blood rushed through his body. Danita's tantalizing scent swirled around him. He tasted the sweet flesh between her breasts.

His heartbeat tripled. He craved more than a taste. He needed sustenance.

In spite of the haze of his desire he hesitated in order to give her time to consider where this passionate exchange was heading. Once he made love to her, he'd never let her go. Her surrender would bind him to her; make him hers for as long as she would have him.

When she moaned into his mouth and settled into his arms he gave in to his need for her.

An ache like fire coursed through him. Rigid with desire, he leaned against the throw pillows on the arm of the couch and shifted her until she lay atop him. When she moved against him, he thought he would explode. The passionate sounds she made told him she needed him as much as he needed her.

He gathered her to him and cushioned her breasts against his heart. When he unhooked the front fastening of her bra, her beasts spilled into his hands. He drew first one perky tip then the other into his mouth, and tugged with his lips and teeth until she whimpered and sought his nipples with her fingers.

"Be still, Dani. I'm not sure I can hold on if you keep moving around like that."

She froze and buried her face in the crook of his shoulder. He rested his fingers on the racing pulse at her throat. Her lashes fluttered against his skin, sending sparks of sensation to the heart of his manhood.

He rebuttoned the top buttons of her blouse to conceal her tempting flesh. He forced himself to ask, "Do you understand

where this could lead?"
Her voice held a shy but determined note. "Yes."
"With a word, we can stop right here. I'll be a wreck, but I'll survive to tempt you another time."
She slid her arms around his waist.
"You must know by now, I want you, Danita. You've taken over my dreams. I think of you at the craziest times—when I'm talking on the phone, in meetings, while I'm playing cards with the guys. You're driving me nuts. I need you, honey."
She lifted her lashes and revealed passion-glazed eyes, her full lips swollen and moist. Her stormy gaze searched his face. "I need you, too."
At her response his restraint almost deserted him. He returned her gaze unwilling to hide the love he knew must shine in his eyes. He had to assure himself he understood her meaning. "What do you want?"
Her hand skimmed his body. She smoothed the cloth of his shirt across his chest. "I want you. Now."
The heat of her touch through his clothing nearly undid him. He captured her restless hand in his. "You have to be sure. Once I love you, there'll be no turning back for either of us."
"I'm sure. I want you to make love to me."
He didn't ask why. He would love her, make her his, then find a way to convince her the past was just that—the past.
Cullen carried Danita to her bed, lowered her to the comforter, and settled himself beside her. He removed her blouse and bra and planted hot kisses on every inch of skin he unveiled. "Your skin is like silk."
He tugged her skirt and skimpy panties down her legs and tossed them over the foot of her bed. Raining kisses on her stomach, he trailed his fingers to the juncture of her thighs. "Open to me, Dani."
Danita caressed his shoulders. Distress laced her moans.
"What is it?" he asked.
She pouted. "I want to touch you, but you're wearing too many clothes."
He gave a husky laugh and sat up beside her. From his hip pocket, he removed his wallet. He reached into it and found three foil-wrapped packets. Placing his wallet on the night stand, he unwrapped one condom, turned to her and guided her hand to his waistband. "Undress me."
Her hesitant touch branded him as she fumbled to strip him of his clothes. Aching to touch her he held himself still. "That's it,

sweetheart. Show me how much you want me."

When he was naked she stared at his erect manhood. She reached out to touch him.

His indrawn breath hissed between his teeth. "Easy, girl, or it will end before we begin."

He eased down beside her and enclosed her in his embrace, scattering kisses on her lips. He found the nest of curls between her legs and stroked her until she was hot, wet and trembling. She twisted against him; she wanted him to explore all of her secret places.

Danita watched him with desire-drugged eyes while Cullen rolled the condom into place.

He lay on his back and pulled her over him until she straddled him. Placing his hands on her waist, he lifted her and guided her until she sheathed him. Her welcoming heat bathed him with pleasure. He would remember this moment as long as he lived.

He held a tight rein on himself until her body seemed to adjust to his. Encased in the tight embrace, he rocked his hips in a gentle motion until she matched his rhythm. With soft urgent cries she held nothing back while she sought her pleasure.

He took her hips in his hands, encouraging her, loving her until she tightened and rippled around him, gasping out her completion.

Her sounds of satisfaction washed over him. He clenched his jaws at the rush of sensations. Heart pounding, slick with sweat, he rode a wave of sheer sensation until he followed her over the edge.

Still joined with him, she collapsed against him. "I didn't know...I never guessed..."

A weak chuckle escaped Cullen. "I didn't know either. You pack quite a wallop, little Dani."

Moments later she moved against him as if testing her feminine power. When he slipped from her body, she uttered a surprised "Oh"

He grinned. "Greedy lady. If you want any more of me tonight, you'll have to give me time to recover." He rose and went into the bathroom.

When he returned, he tucked her under the covers and joined her there. She turned on her side to face him, laid her head on his chest and wrapped her arms around his waist. He held her close to his heart, replete in body and spirit for the first time in a long, long while.

When her breathing slowed and she lay limp in his arm, he

whispered in her ear, "Rest sweetheart. We've had quite a day. I'll have to leave soon, but I'll call you tomorrow before I leave for L.A."

Though she drifted off, he remained wide awake, watching over her. The memory of her response to his lovemaking overwhelmed him. Watching her at the peak of her pleasure had blown his mind.

He questioned his good fortune. This woman, full of life and fire, had healed his lonely heart. He had hoped that in the throes of passion she would have expressed her love for him, but she had revealed only her fierce desire. They'd reached for each other again and again until late into the night. Tenderly he kissed her lips as she fell into an exhausted sleep.

The way she'd responded to him made him believe she had to feel more than physical desire for him. After the intimacy they'd shared, he knew he loved her and would remain unsatisfied until she admitted she loved him, too.

If I can get through the next few days without mishap, I'll make her acknowledge it—to herself and to me.

꙳

At her desk at WAIT FOR ME, Danita shifted to a more comfortable position. She found it difficult to concentrate on her mail. She missed Cullen already. Even though she knew his day would be busy she wished she could see him one more time before he left.

Her thoughts kept drifting to the night she had spent in Cullen's arms. Every tiny ache brought pleasant memories of the unrestrained attention they had lavished upon each other. She had discovered a deep well of passion within herself she hadn't known existed. He had taken her there again and again to fill her cup. If he had intended to prove to her that she was a sensuous, desirable woman, he had succeeded.

Thoughts of their lovemaking made her pulse quicken. She gloried in his virility. The memory of the way his muscles had bunched beneath her hands, and the power of his taking sent a melting sensation inside her womb.

Only a strong man like Cullen gave up control to let a woman discover her own strength. All through the night his words of appreciation and encouragement had released her inhibitions and increased her confidence in her femininity.

She was glad now that she had chosen Cullen to...what? She opened the door on her reflections, and the word "love" slipped through. She couldn't reveal her feelings to him but she relished them. She hoped he felt the same way about her, but she was old-fashioned enough to want him to declare his feelings first. Until he did, she'd wait and love him with her heart.

She returned to her mail. When her secretary buzzed her, she was happy for the interruption hoping it was Cullen. Then he said her advisor, Frederickson, wanted a word with her.

Eleven

"MS. JOHNSON, THE COMMITTEE has made its decision. Though you and Mr. Powers should receive your official notifications in Friday's mail, the chairman directed me to communicate their selection today," Frederickson said.

Danita was glad she was sitting. His words made her heart thud and her hands moisten so much she had to grip the receiver or drop it. "Why...why did he want you to do that?"

"He knows this is the end of the month. Past experience tells us that a small business like yours can deal with its creditors more effectively if it knows whether or not it will be granted a substantial sum of money."

Danita pressed her free hand against the fear churning in her stomach. "I see."

"Since you are especially in need of funds, Mr. Rawley suspected you might want the information today."

"Thank him for me, please." She crossed her fingers.

"Let me be the first to congratulate you for being selected this year's recipient of the Penn-Atkinson Foundation for Change Award. We hope your business continues to enrich the lives of the senior citizens of our community."

Danita was speechless. They'd done it. They'd saved WAIT FOR ME and she could get her family's inheritance back without anyone knowing how close she had come to losing it.

"Ms. Johnson, are you there?" This time the voice was that of Mr. Frederickson.

"Yes. Thank you, thank you, thank you for the good news! All of us are grateful to The Foundation for having faith in us. Please tell the committee how much we appreciate this opportunity to help our staff and the working people who depend upon them."

Mr. Frederickson's voice rang with self-importance. "Your concept of cross-generational interaction swayed the committee in your favor. Of course your greater financial need was also a factor. Keep up the good work. We want to see you at nine o'clock Wednesday morning at The Foundation's office where we will hold a small ceremony and explain how you may access your funds."

"I'll be there. And thanks again for letting me know."

"You're welcome. Now don't forget our agreement. Keep out of trouble from here on out."

Danita assured him she would, and, in a daze, replaced the receiver in its cradle.

With a raised fist punching the air and a victorious "Yesss!" Danita sprang from her chair and ran straight to Virgie's door. Balancing on tip toes, she surveyed Virgie's office through the window in the door. Except for Virgie peering at her beloved computer, the office was unoccupied.

Danita knocked once and burst inside. "We did it! We got the grant! Print a congratulations banner. We'll hang it first thing tomorrow morning. We'll have a party. I'll spring for the treats and drinks."

Virgie swiveled in her chair until she faced Danita. "Hold on. Back up. Today's Monday. What makes you think we won?" Danita recounted her conversation with Frederickson. "Do you know what this means? I can pay you what I owe you, return the loans my relatives made to us, and get our creditors off our backs."

"Fan-tastic. And with the changes we've made within the last month, we'll be back in the black from now on if we stick to our new business plan."

Danita dropped onto a chair facing Virgie. "If WAIT FOR ME had closed, our workers would have been out in the cold."

The thought of all she had risked in the name of love made a queasy wave of regret roil in her stomach. *Never again will I take such a gamble. I could have lost my family's heirlooms, too. I'll always remember what I learned from this experience. Never spend more than I have, and never wager more than I can afford to lose.*

"I've truly learned my lesson. A good manager always keeps on top of every aspect of her business. I'll work harder to master our bookkeeping program, and stop trying to weasel out of those weekly budget meetings you insist on. I promise. Cross my heart."

Virgie gave Danita a hearty laugh and a thumbs-up sign. "Have you talked to Cullen yet?"

Danita's joy waned. How could she talk about celebrating? She had won the grant and probably lost Cullen. "No. I'm not sure I should. I'll let Frederickson break the news to him."

Virgie said, "I know he'll be disappointed he didn't win. I hope this doesn't change things between the two of you. You both seemed so close in the last few days."

Danita attempted a brave smile. "I'm surprised you noticed. You and Mitch have been inseparable. Has he given you any clues how COPR will manage without the grant?"

Virgie actually blushed. A broad grin lit her face. "We don't talk much about COPR or WAIT FOR ME. We keep our personal lives separated from our business lives."

Danita nodded. She wondered if she and Cullen could do the same. If she had lost, she would have had to struggle night and day to save her business. She would not have had time for Cullen. Her fears and regrets might have put an end to their relationship.

Virgie's buzzer sounded. She snatched up the phone and listened. "It's for you. Cullen Powers on line two. Want to take it here or in your office?"

"In my office."

Sitting on the edge of her desk, Danita picked up her phone with trepidation, twisting the cord around her index finger. "Hi, Cullen. I guess you heard the news."

"Yes. Congratulations. I'm proud of you."

Danita wished she could see his face. From the tone of his voice he sounded disappointed...or frustrated...or worried. "Thank you. I'm sorry my good news means bad news for you," she said.

Cullen remained quiet for a long moment. "No need to worry about me. I talked to Rawley. He said he would help me explore some other options for COPR, but he may have been trying to make losing easier for me to take."

"Oh, Cullen. Maybe not. After all, Rawley could have let Frederickson make the call. I'll bet Rawley will find some way to help you."

Cullen paused a few beats. "Never mind COPR. We'll survive. I know this is your night, but I'm frustrated because I have to go to Los Angeles today and we can't celebrate tonight. When I get back we will, okay? I'll call you."

Danita's spirits plummeted. *Yeah, right. Cullen's dumping me already. I should never have expected so much.*

Before Danita left for the day she called Kevin. While she waited for him to come on the line she caressed one of the dozen red roses Cullen had sent her, then reread the note he had enclosed promising a special evening when he got home. She wondered if they were his kiss-off gift or whether he really meant to see her again.

Kevin came on the line. "Hi, Danita. News travels fast in your family. I'll bet you called to congratulate me." He sounded as cheerful as a man who'd won the lottery.

Always formal, Kevin never said "Hi". Danita thought fast. "Sure did. Tell me all about it."

Kevin's laughter rang with pure pleasure. "I can't tell you all about it. Suffice it to say Lu and I are getting married."

Danita was so surprised she nearly fell off the edge of her chair. "Have...have you guys set a date? Did you tell the family? I'll bet Mom will want to plan the wedding for Aunt Lu. Wow, Kevin. Congratulations. I'm happy for both of you?"

His chuckle held a rueful note. "All right, Danita, it's obvious you didn't call about Lu and me. What's up? Another problem at WAIT FOR ME?"

"No, in fact just the opposite. I received word that I won the Penn-Atkinson grant. I'd like to come by your place as soon as it's convenient to arrange to return your loan, and I want to give you time to plan a replacement for your display."

"Glad to hear your good news. Thanks for the lead time."

"My pleasure."

"No hurry to repay me. In fact I think we should keep the arrangement we made just between the two of us. You know Lu. If she finds out the details she'll get mad. Might even call off the wedding. I don't want that to happen."

The anxiety in his voice carried clearly over the line.

"I won't say a word. Thanks for your help," she said.

"Feel free to call on me any time you need it. Our families go back a long way. I'm concerned about your welfare."

Though Kevin had hoped to own her bronzes, Danita knew he meant every word. He had helped her when she'd needed him, and she would always be grateful.

Suddenly Danita remembered how Kevin, a Texan, used his gallery to keep alive Juneteenth, the June nineteenth celebration of the emancipation of slaves in his home state. On impulse she said, "You're welcome to keep them until after your Juneteenth exhibit is over. It's the least I can do after all your help."

Kevin's voice regained its usual smoothness. "I'll look forward to doing just that. And to show my appreciation, until you're back on your feet, I'll let you keep the money you owe me. I know Penn-Atkinson will deliver, and I'm sure you have more pressing business than to rush over here to pay me."

"Thanks, I am a little overwhelmed right now. Talk to you soon."

Danita hung up, grinning from ear to ear. Lu married to Kevin. That she had to see. As Momma Dee would say, "Would wonders never cease."

When Danita arrived home it was still daylight. Nevertheless she rushed to take a warm relaxing shower. Her day had drained her, and when she'd told her family the good news, they'd insisted on throwing an impromptu party over the week-end. Better get some rest while she could. Skin still damp, she put on her bathrobe. She went into the kitchen to make herself a cup of hot chocolate, hoping it would help her relax.

She set a cup of milk into the microwave and pulled out the step she kept handy for getting boxes down from high kitchen cupboard shelves.

She climbed it, and then reached back into the corner of the cupboard for a box of cocoa one of her seniors had brought to her from a trip to Senegal.

She stepped down and glanced out of her kitchen window. And froze. A shadow moved. Something that resembled a man's head seemed to duck down out of sight.

She wondered for a moment if her imagination were playing tricks on her. She'd lived in that apartment for two years and there was never a problem with prowlers. The security around the complex had always provided her with a sense of complete safety.

She inched slowly to the window and peered out. Nothing moved. Then a cat howled and skittered from the bushes bordering the walk. It dashed across the walk and raced down the street.

When the microwave dinged she started. "All right, Danita. Mix your drink and go to bed. You'll need something warm and soothing after a day like today. And stop talking to yourself."

Still slightly shaken, she mixed an extra big spoonful of cocoa and sugar into her milk.

Before she took the hot chocolate into her bedroom, she checked all of her doors and windows, fastened the security chain on her front door, and placed the cutoff broomstick her mother had given her along the groove of the sliding glass patio door. She closed all of her drapes and dusted her hands. "That should do it. Now take a nap."

Just a few more days. What could happen in a couple of weeks?

When her cell phone chimed she picked it up and fumbled for the talk button, hoping foolishly for it to be Cullen.

It was Kay Burdell. "Danita, I hope I didn't get you at a bad time. I need a favor. Cullen's out of town, and I hate to call him to come back now."

Danita didn't hesitate. "What do you need?"

"It's a long story. Do you think you could come over here? I think it would be better if I told you in person."

"Sure. Where are you?"

When Kay told her where she was, Danita was puzzled, and when she added, "Don't tell anyone where you're going," Danita was totally mystified.

She wanted to ask questions, but had heard a frantic note in Kay's voice. Danita said instead, "I'll be there in thirty minutes."

"I'm in B 114, but call me from the lobby. I'll meet you there. It's a little tricky to find my bungalow."

"Okay. See you soon."

As Danita hurried to her room to get dressed she wondered what she would find when she saw Kay. Whatever had happened, Kay had turned to Danita for help and she was determined to help her new friend.

❧

Thirty minutes later Danita phoned Kay from the motel lobby. She took a seat facing the entrance. When Kay appeared Danita just stared in disbelief. Kay's face was puffy, she had a black eye, and her lip was swollen.

Danita rushed to her side and gave her a careful hug. "Were you in an accident?"

Kay pulled away and looked around the lobby. With a nervous flutter of her hand, she said, "You could say that. Let's go to my rooms. I'll explain there."

Kay led the way down a path that skirted around several cottages. Each cottage had a small yard with beds of flowers surrounded by stone borders.

The evening sky was crimson and painted an eerie glow along the walks and reflected in windows with a fiery light that seemed to warn of lurking danger. Except for their footsteps and the rustle of a breeze through the palms, all was ominously quiet. Danita shivered and quickened her steps as she followed Kay.

Kay stopped at door number 114. She peered into the shadows, took a key card from her pocket, slid it quickly into the slot and rushed inside, motioning for Danita to hurry.

She shut the door behind them, slid the security chain in place and turned on the lights. Kay asked in a subdued voice, "Can I get you something to drink? Cullen brought me regular and diet drinks, or I can brew us some coffee?"

Danita looked around the cheerful motel rooms. The drapes were drawn so tightly together she couldn't even see a sliver of light from the fixture above the stoop outside. A suitcase full of neatly folded clothes sat on the bed. Danita wondered if Kay was packing or unpacking.

"I'll have a regular cola. Why don't you join me?"

"I believe I will." Kay bustled around the neat little kitchen as she collected glasses and ice cubes.

Danita frowned. *So. Cullen knew about this...this...this whatever it was. It was obvious Kay was in trouble. Why hadn't he trusted me enough to tell me? Kay needed a friend. How could he leave Kay here alone and go to Los Angeles?*

Danita wanted answers, but from the sad expression on Kay's face, Danita knew she'd have to let Kay tell her story in her own time and her own way.

Kay set ice-filled glasses on the table and poured their drinks. Her hands shook so much she spilled some of the soda. "I'm sure you're wondering what's going on," she said as she grabbed a paper towel and wiped up the moisture.

Kay took a seat at the table and stared for a moment at the wedding band on her finger. Haltingly she told Danita about Aaron's abuse. As she talked, she closed her eyes and twisted the ring around and around. Tears slid down her face.

Kay said, "I wanted to let you know what had happened, but Cathy my social worker at the women's shelter said I couldn't tell anyone. She made me swear Cullen to secrecy. He wanted you to know, but he respected my request."

She sighed and opened her eyes slowly. They had the unfocused look of a woman awakening from a nightmare. She brushed the tears from her cheek, and with a shake of her head she seemed to come back to reality, a reality filled with pain and uncertainty.

Danita was silent for a long moment, uncertain what to say.

She knelt at Kay's feet, took Kay's hands and gently squeezed them. "I'm so, so sorry, Kay. What can I do to help?"

"Just being here is a help, but I do have a favor to ask."

"Ask away. I'll do anything you want me to."

Kay smiled for the first time since Danita had arrived. "I know, Honey, I know."

"Cathy called me a little while ago and said she has an unexpected opening if I'd be willing to take it tonight. She asked me to meet her at her office before nine o'clock. I told her I'd be there. I'm getting cabin fever here all by myself. I'd love to have other people around, especially people who would understand my circumstances. Since the shelter doesn't allow men there, I need someone to drive me. I'm in no condition to drive myself."

Danita stood, glad for a chance to do something practical. "Let's do it. What about your car?"

Kay placed the last of her belongings in the suitcase and zipped it closed. "Cullen and Mitch can pick it up in the morning. He'll keep it in his garage until I'm ready to make further arrangements."

She took a shopping bag out of a cupboard drawer and loaded soft drinks and snacks in it.

After Kay packed the last of her belongings in the suitcase, she checked the drawers, closets and cupboards. When she looked under the bed she found a pair of house slippers. She placed them in the shopping bag. A shuddering sigh escaped her.

Danita went to Kay and put her arm around her shoulder. "Would you like to rest a few minutes?"

"I'm fine, just a little tired. I'll be glad to get settled in tonight."

Danita stood and moved toward the phone. "I'll call the front desk, if you want me to. We can do a courtesy check out."

At Kay's nod, she dialed the front desk. "Could you send someone to bungalow 114? We're checking out and need help with our luggage."

A pleasant male voice answered, "I'll send someone right away."

When Danita hung up, Kay said, "Too bad I won't be here when you and Cullen tie the knot. As soon as I get things arranged, I'm moving to Washington, D.C."

"You'll love Cullen's parents. They remind me of yours. They're good people. They'll adore you. I do."

"How can you be so sure they'll accept me?"

"When they see the joy you've brought into his life, how can they feel otherwise?"

Before Danita could reply, a knock sounded on the door. She looked out of the peephole. A college-aged man with a cart peered back at her.

"It's the porter for your bags."

She swung the door open and pointed to the suitcases standing ready beside the door. "Would you mind loading these in my car? It's over there beside that blue van."

The tall blond grinned at Danita as he wheeled his handcart into the room. "Hi. I'm Mac." He pointed to his tag. "You folks using the courtesy check-out?"

Kay called from across the room, "Yes. We'll drop the keys off on the way."

Thanking him, Danita collected the key card and the envelope with the evaluation sheet and the room keys inside and handed them to Mac.

He pocketed the envelope and left whistling out of tune.

Danita grabbed her shoulder bag and hurried to catch up with Kay's luggage. She needed to unlock her car trunk for the bags. She hurried back to the room and strode into the bungalow. "Ready, Kay?" she called.

When she entered the bedroom, Aaron Burdell's tall, bulky figure rose from the foot of one of the double beds. Danita gasped in horror.

Fists balled at his side, Aaron said in a malice-laced voice, "I had a hell of a time finding you, Kay."

୧ଈ

Kay cowered in a corner behind the bed. She held her purse in front of her face as if to ward off his blows.

To Danita the scene was surreal. She wanted to run to Kay and shield her with her body, but she didn't move for fear of setting off Aaron. Maybe she could ease back out of the door and get help.

At that moment Aaron turned toward the door. "Come on in Ms. Danita Johnson. Stand over by the dresser where I can see you."

His comment surprised Danita. She had no idea how he knew who she was. She moved into the room and leaned against the dresser, so shaken she needed its support.

Red-eyed, clothes rumpled, Aaron raked the room with a contempt-filled gaze until it settled on Kay. "You left our home to stay in this dump?"

Kay's voice carried a note of fear. "At least I felt safe here."

Aaron's face relaxed into an apologetic smile. He eased his stance. "You've made your point. Time to quit playing games and come home."

Kay backed against the wall. "How...how...how did you find me?" she cried.

Aaron's mild expression almost convinced Danita he meant no harm. He raised his hands, plainly showing he was unarmed. "Please, honey, I don't want to hurt you. We need to talk. I want to apologize...ask you to come back." He glowered at Danita. "Can't we talk without this busybody in here?"

Kay stood her ground. "I asked how you found me." Her voice sounded stronger.

"I've been tailing Cullen for a couple of days. I even went to WAIT FOR ME where I saw your little *friend* here."

"Friend" rolled off his tongue like a curse. Behind his repentant facade, Danita detected a still-arrogant tyrant.

"You spied on me through my kitchen window, didn't you?" Danita asked in dismay.

"Just checking to see if you had Kay tucked away with you. You women always stick together."

"I didn't even know about you and Kay until today."

"But I knew about you and Cullen. He spent the night with you, and I've been tailing him ever since." He smirked as though he had done something clever. "I knew it was only a matter of time until you butted into my business."

It made her skin crawl to realize Aaron had been spying on her and Cullen. "That's it? That's how you knew how to find us?" asked Danita.

"Not entirely. When I was tailing Cullen up Route 5, I noticed how easy it was to follow him...too easy. When I got to the Orange County line, I slowed. He did, too, so I speeded up and he did the same. He never let me lose him. As soon as he pulled in at a motel, I realized what he was up to. He wanted me to follow him. I hightailed it back to your place in time to watch you leave."

His words revealed his unbalanced mind and how crafty he was—and how dangerous. Danita would have to handle him with caution, or he might blow. "You must have sat in front of my place a long time."

"You had me fooled there for a while when I saw you in your night clothes in the kitchen, but after you came out of your place in such a hurry I knew I had hit the jackpot," he said. "All I had to do was keep out of sight, and you'd lead me straight to my dear wife."

With a dismissive wave toward Danita, he turned his gaze on Kay. "Let's go someplace where we can talk." His clenched fists belied his quiet reasonable tone.

"I have nothing to say to you, and I've listened to you, ad nauseam. Your accusations, your drinking and reckless driving scares me witless. I wouldn't get into a car with you if my life depended on it."

Danita shivered at Kay's words. She wished Kay would tone down her refusal—make him believe she would at least consider his request. Danita was afraid Kay would push him into a desperate move if she provoked him further.

"Then come with me to the coffee shop here at the motel. What can happen there? I'm sorry for what I did. I swear I love you. I didn't come here to hurt you. I'll never do that again."

Kay looked about her as if seeking an escape. The only way out lay beyond Aaron. She backed up still gripping her handbag. "No. Please leave me alone." Panic edged her voice.

"Baby, I know how you must feel, but all I've ever wanted to do was to keep you safe." He spoke in a tone filled with regret and sincerity.

He sank down on the side of the bed and rubbed his hand across his eyes. "When Ayana left us to marry Cullen I should have done more to keep her where I could watch over her. I should have driven her the day she had her accident.

"I've been trying to watch over you, Kay, but you won't let me. You had to go to D.C. For your art career, you said. You knew I couldn't be there with you. The whole time you were gone I was worried sick. Anything could have happened to you there. Now you want to go away for good and all because of a little…

With no sign of her intentions, Kay flung her purse at Aaron. He ducked. Kay dashed past him and out the door like an antelope fleeing for its life.

Kay cleared the threshold. Danita took off after her. Aaron jumped up and followed, shoving Danita aside. Danita stumbled but recovered in time to catch up to Aaron who closed in on Kay. Grabbing Kay's arm he swung her around. With one hand he pinned both of her wrists together.

She screamed and struggled against his grip. "No! No! Get away from me! Let me go!"

"Calm down. I just want to talk. To explain. Everybody in this whole damn place can hear you." he said with a note of desperation.

"I don't care," she wailed. "You want to get me where you can finish the job you started."

Aaron set his lips into a hard line. An ominous note crept into his voice. "You will stop this foolishness and listen to me—now!" Freeing his right hand he slapped her.

Kay slumped against Aaron as if trying to shield her face from further blows. Her muffled sobs tore at Danita's heart.

Danita ran up behind Aaron. She kicked his legs and hammered on his back. "Are you crazy? Let her go. You're hurting her," she yelled.

"Stop shouting," he said to Danita between gritted teeth. "I had to do something. She was getting hysterical. You'll have everyone out here trying to see what's going on."

As if swatting an annoying fly, he swiped at Danita. His blow sent her reeling.

She clamped her hand over her mouth to keep herself from screaming.

When Kay started to cry louder, Aaron shook her. "Shut up. There's no reason to go off your rocker. You act as if I want to kill you. All I want to do is talk."

"You said you would kill me. You said..."

"I didn't mean it."

"Yes you did. You want to get me alone so you can..."

The door in the next bungalow opened. Danita jerked her head around. A husky baldheaded man stood silhouetted in the doorway. He held a digital camera in his meaty hands. When Aaron renewed his struggle to shove Kay toward the parking lot, the man aimed the camera toward them.

Danita turned back to the struggling couple. She knew she had to stop Aaron, but she had no idea how. "If you don't let her go this minute I'll...I'll call the police!

At the word "police", Aaron seemed to lose his tenuous hold on his temper. Still jerking Kay by one wrist. "You bitch. You'd like to see me publicly humiliated, wouldn't you?"

He loomed over Kay. Danita was certain he would hit Kay again. Instead he dragged her toward the door of her motel room. She lost her footing and reached out with her free hand. She crashed into a Bird of Paradise plant.

"Kay, Kay." Still shaken from Aaron's blow, Danita's feet seemed mired in quicksand. She needed all her strength to overcome her nightmarish inertia.

Kay jerked her wrist from Aaron's grasp. Her body pitched forward. With a sharp crack, her head struck one of the rocks that lined the sidewalk leading to her room. Blood gushed from her temple.

Danita flew to her side. Kay lay still as death. "My God, what have you done?"

Then she heard Kay's soft moan. "Thank heavens," Danita whispered. When she looked up, Aaron's face held an expression of such horror she thought he had received a death blow.

He gaped foolishly at Kay who lay on the glistening sidewalk, still damp from the motel's lawn sprinkler. He groaned. "She's dead. She's dead."

Danita called to the man taking pictures, "Don't just stand there. Call the police."

Aaron bellowed, "No! No police!"

He glared at the lens trained on him. "Damn all of you," he yelled over his shoulder at the gaping people standing outside their rooms. Swinging around, he sprinted toward the parking lot.

A car door slammed, followed by the squeal of tires. A horn blared. Someone yelled, "What the hell's going on?"

She returned her attention to Kay. "Don't move," Danita whispered. "I'll get help."

Danita ran into the room, snatched a spread from the bed, carried it out and covered Kay. Danita ran back inside and dialed 911. While she listened for her call to go through, she grabbed a handful of tissues and pressed them to her lips.

The operator's questions seemed to go on and on. "What's your name? Where are you? What happened? How did your friend get hurt? What signs do you see that indicate your friend is seriously injured? What did you do? Where is the victim at this moment? Is she able to speak? Is she alert?"

Danita wanted to scream, "Just get someone over here and fast." Instead she answered the operator's questions as calmly as she could.

When at last the 911 operator released Danita, she returned to Kay's side. Ignoring the people who stood in front of their doors watching she waited impatiently for help to arrive.

The man with the digital camera approached Danita. He aimed it at her. "Wasn't that Aaron Burdell fighting with his wife? She's a famous artist hereabout, isn't she? I'm sure I recognized them."

Danita kept her gaze trained on Kay. "Can't you see we have a serious problem here? Please give her room. She needs air."

"Yeah, I can see," he said.

A woman asked, "What happened, Irving? Why's that woman lying on the ground?"

"Her and her man had a whale of a battle. I got it all on tape. It wasn't just anybody fighting. It was that guy who used to be a councilman. His wife's going to have one hell of a headache."

Their voices receded. "I gotta make a phone call," he said.

A buzz of comments swirled around Danita. Kay's problems had become a subject of public speculation.

Humiliation stung Danita–humiliation for Kay, for Aaron, and for Cullen. God only knew what that Irving person intended to do with the film. No doubt they would be plastered all over TV.

The minutes dragged like hours. Danita prayed Kay's injuries were not as serious as they looked. Kneeling next to Kay's still body, tiny bits of wet stones and twigs dug into Danita's knees and palms. She welcomed the pain. She deserved it and worse. She had underestimated Aaron's persistence. Instead of protecting Kay, Danita had let her own puny efforts lead to Kay's getting seriously injured.

Kay had been right to fear Aaron's threats. Danita knew she had been stupid, and Kay, not Danita, would pay the price.

Tears streamed down Danita's face. She looked up and saw Irving had returned and was aiming his digital camera at them again. "Please...turn off that thing, for God's sake. Have you no decency? Have some consideration for this woman's privacy."

The tone of her voice or the anguish she felt must have hit a responsive cord because when he lowered his camera its beep indicated he had turned it off. He backed away.

Danita heard approaching sirens. She prayed help had come in time. Kind heaven would not let her lose her friend to that abusive man.

Twelve

KAY REMAINED IN THE emergency room for what seemed to Danita like forever before the doctor assigned Kay to a semiprivate room.

Eight in the morning arrived before Danita could speak to him.

"We did a CAT Scan," Dr. Gittleson said. "Mrs. Burdell has a mild concussion. We want to keep her quiet and have her stay overnight for observation. Go home. Get some rest. Have something to eat. You can see her again during visiting hours."

In spite of the doctor's advice, Danita went to the visitors lounge, too upset to drive home.

She left a message on Cullen's answering machine telling him where Kay was and her room number. She didn't want to call him on his cell phone until she had something concrete to tell him.

In the meantime she contacted her parents and told her mother the whole story. Her mother provided her usual no-nonsense support. "You have enough to worry about with Kay," Nita Johnson said. "I'll call Virgie and explain the situation. Get back to her when things settle down. I'll tell her not to expect you at work until the hospital releases Kay."

After a few more words from her mom, Danita made a final call to Cathy, the shelter's contact person. To Danita's surprise, Cathy offered comfort instead of blame.

"I know you did all you could," Cathy said. "Don't blame yourself. I'll come by in the morning. Kay's release will go more smoothly if I help her check out of the hospital. The staff there knows me."

Bolstered by Cathy's caring words, Danita dragged herself

home, checked her e-mail and answering machine, cleaned up and hurried back to the hospital.

Magazine in hand she stood abruptly and paced back and forth in front of the windows overlooking the parking lot. With apprehension she scanned the lot for Cullen's car though she'd have been surprised to see it. She had no idea how to tell him that she was the one who'd led Aaron to Kay. She was the one Kay had trusted. She was the one who'd left the bungalow door open. She was the one who didn't protect Kay from Aaron. She was the one who'd let Kay down.

No matter what she told Cullen, nothing would change what she'd done. Well, she'd just have to face him. Whether or not she'd lost him when she'd won the grant, she knew she'd lose him when he found out what she'd done to Kay.

But first things first. She'd make sure Kay was okay, and then she'd get some advice from Cathy on what to do about Aaron.

A nurse's aide walked into the room. "Mrs. Burdell is awake. She's had her medication and is waiting for her breakfast."

"May I see her now?"

"Yes. I'm sure she's looking forward to your visit."

With unsteady hands, Danita replaced the magazine on the lamp table, dropped her water bottle into her voluminous shoulder bag and headed toward Kay's room.

Kay sat up in bed and listlessly took small bites of the light meal before her. Danita glanced around the room and noticed the other bed was stripped and empty. She sat on the side of it facing Kay.

"Danita. How nice to see you. I hope you haven't been worried about me," Kay said in a weak voice.

"You've had quite a time. How do you feel?"

"Fine except for the pain in my head. I'd love to get out of here, but Dr. Gittleson says I have to stay overnight. He says I have a mild concussion from the spill I took. I don't know why I'm so clumsy lately, but I'm glad you were with me. I hope you haven't told Cullen about any of this."

"Not yet, but you know he'll have to be told."

Kay gave a dismissive wave of her hand. "Let's not worry him. It was silly of me to fall that way. I think I was on my way to see someone, but right now I can't remember who. Well it will come to me, and when it does, I'll give whoever it was a call and explain."

Kay looked toward the door. "Has...has Aaron been looking for me?"

Danita gave Kay what she hoped was a reassuring smile. "Not that I've heard, but don't worry. He'll get in touch as soon as he can."

Kay looked down at her breakfast, resignation written all over her face. "I'm sure you're right, dear," she said and pushed the food around on her plate as if searching for an especially tasty morsel.

To delay any further discussion of Aaron, Danita attempted to entertain Kay with some of the more unusual assignments her seniors had taken. Kay chuckled in all the right places, and demonstrated that she was properly distracted by finishing a good portion of her meal. She leaned against her pillow and smiled as if she'd won a ribbon for the best eater in the hospital.

Kay and Danita continued to talk until Kay's eyelids started to drift shut.

Danita stood. "You look a little drowsy. Why don't you get some sleep? I'll be back later."

Before Danita could move the tray table under the window and tuck the covers under Kay's chin, Kay had dozed off.

Danita returned to the visitor's lounge where she checked to make sure she had left nothing.

She looked up at the television set hanging from a wall and gasped in dismay. A picture of Aaron Burdell flashed on the screen, while a voice-over reported, "Aaron Burdell, prominent political figure, dies in a freeway accident."

Danita froze in shock, unsure she had understood the newscaster's words. She moved closer to the set, one hand covering her mouth as she listened to the reporter describe the event.

Oh, God. Aaron's dead? Who will tell Kay?

A picture of a crumpled car appeared on the screen. The unseen newsman continued. "The police, acting on complaints of a domestic dispute at the Canyon View Motel in the Mira Mesa area, arrived in time to follow Burdell, sixty-three, speeding toward the freeway.

"Authorities said they pursued Burdell who attempted to enter the Interstate 15 onramp and lost control of his vehicle. He was killed instantly when he slammed into a guardrail. His chest was crushed against the steering wheel of his car. An open bottle of whiskey was found in the wreckage. He was not wearing a seat belt. He was pronounced dead at the scene."

A picture of a reporter interviewing Irving, the man with the digital camera at the motel, appeared on the screen. "I was at the

Canyon View Motel to take some out-of-state friends to the zoo," Irving said. "I had my digital camera with me for the trip. When I saw Burdell beating his wife I took my camera and started shooting. I recognized him and his wife. She's famous, you know." He puffed out his chest as if proud of his familiarity with an artist.

A picture of the altercation flashed on TV. Irving's camera had captured the screams and struggles with almost professional clarity. Mercifully the reporter's voice finally drowned out the sounds of the fight.

"Injured in the fracas, Burdell's sixty-year-old wife Kay, a well-known local artist, was rushed to a hospital. As of this report, her location and her condition are unknown. Friends of the Burdell's expressed surprise to learn the forty-year marriage was a troubled one."

A close-up of Danita's tear-stained face filled the screen. Though she clutched a bloodstained wad of tissue to her mouth, anyone who knew her would have recognized her at once.

The reporter intoned, "This unidentified witness to the incident between Burdell and his wife is being sought for questioning. If you have any information as to the identity of the witness, please contact the police." A phone number was displayed across the screen.

I have to tell Kay, but she doesn't remember what he tried to do to her. And Cullen. If the media discovers his connection to Kay, they'll splash his face all over TV, too. I've got to keep him out of this. If the committee finds out he's involved they won't give him the grant when they take it away from me, as I'm sure they will. And the police. I'll have to call them, too.

❧

A shadow fell across her shoulder. She spun around and met Cullen's furious eyes.

He took her hand. "What happened?"

At the sight of him, tears sprang to her eyes. She struggled to speak, but had to swallow several times.

Cullen's piercing gaze examined her face. "Did Aaron do this to you?" he asked.

Danita uttered only two words, "Its Kay," before she collapsed against him and released the terror of the day in a flood of tears.

He put his arms around her. "Sh-sh-sh. I'm here now. Everything will work itself out. We can handle whatever happened."

His murmured words comforted her. Her sobs turned to hiccoughs and gradually subsided.

"The doctor says she has a concussion, but he's pretty sure she can go home tomorrow. I need to call Cathy. She's supposed to meet us here to drive Kay to the shelter. She won't need to go to the shelter now."

Danita stepped away from him and struggled to stiffen her spine and stop babbling. With the back of her hand she dashed away her tears and steeled herself for his questions.

"Ready to tell me what happened?" he asked.

Danita described everything–from the time Aaron had forced his way into the motel room until Kay's admission to the hospital.

How serious is Kay's concussion?"

"She has five stitches on her temple, but the doctor said it's a mild injury. Within a half hour after they admitted her, she gained consciousness. She complained of nausea, dizziness and a headache. Kay doesn't remember that Aaron pushed her and caused her fall."

Cullen patted Danita's shoulder. "Loss of memory after a concussion is pretty normal."

"The doctor wants her to rest, but he says she answered most of his questions and appeared alert."

"How soon can I see her?"

Danita removed a tissue from her bag and dried her eyes. "She's sleeping now, but I'm sure you'd like to look in on her. Visiting hours started about an hour ago."

They walked the short distance to Kay's room.

Cullen leaned over Kay and kissed her cheek. "I'm sorry I wasn't here for you." Then he left.

Standing just outside Kay's door, Danita wished she could deny her part in the tragedy but she couldn't. It had jumped out at them from the television screen.

He took her elbow and guided her away from the doorway. Her heart lurched and her throat burned while she fought back the cry of remorse rising to her lips. *I never should have left that door open. It's all my fault.* "I've got to contact the police."

"But first we need to tell the nurse in charge what's happened to Aaron," Cullen said.

They walked back to the desk. With a quiet chill in his voice Cullen told the nurse Kay's husband has been reported killed in an auto accident. "I'd like to break the news to Kay myself. Can we hold until she's awake and I tell her? If there's a TV in Kay's room it needs to be turned off before she sees the news reports."

The nurse scribbled on a pad. "I'm certain it can be arranged. I'll talk to her doctor."

"While you're at it, can you keep the press away from her until she's informed?" Cullen asked.

"I'll get Dr. Gittleson up here right away." She made a call, and they waited for the doctor. Danita fought to rid herself of the feeling of unreality that settled over her, but to no avail. She felt like a bystander watching someone else's drama.

When Gittleson arrived he asked, "What's the problem?"

In a fog Danita listened to Cullen explain their dilemma.

"We need time to talk to the authorities and arrange for Mrs. Burdell's care when she's released," Cullen said. "Her husband's death will come as a shock to her, and I know she won't want to face the media."

The doctor ordered Kay reassigned to a private room where no visitors other than family would be allowed. While Cullen and the doctor talked, Danita's numbness thawed. In its place settled a resolve to shelter Kay and Cullen from the storm to come. She could do it. All she had to do was figure out how.

 ༄

After the doctor left, Cullen leaned over and whispered in her ear, "Let's go to my place. It's only a matter of time before the press or the police track us down here or at your apartment."

"Not a good idea. I'll meet you at WAIT FOR ME," she said. "There are several telephone lines out of there. We can both make our calls at the same time, and decide how to handle this situation." Danita didn't wait for his response, but set out straight for an elevator.

They rode down in silence in the crowded car. Danita was pressed so close to his side she could feel the heat from his body. She almost leaned into him but caught herself just in time.

They took a roundabout way out of the hospital, peering over their shoulders to make sure their departure went unnoticed. Though she was glad they had escaped without detection, Danita felt like a wanted criminal on the run and didn't like the feeling. She wondered how much more skulking they'd have to do before the nightmare ended.

All the way to WAIT FOR ME questions assailed her. What could she have done differently? Not fall in love with Cullen? Never. He was the best thing to happen to her. Could she have refused to help Kay? No, she had come to Kay's rescue solely because she was a friend in need. She would have assisted Kay no matter what.

Danita brushed back her bangs. It was too late for second guessing. She barely had time to plan what to say to Cullen once they finished their calls. She knew he would stand with her through the coming ordeal, and she could not permit him to do it.

The committee had warned her—no scandal or no grant. Danita knew her face would soon grace every newsstand between San Diego and San Francisco.

What good would it do for both of us to lose the grant? At least it was still possible for Cullen to help his clients. If he ended up in the public eye, he wouldn't have a chance for the grant which she knew she had lost. If she played it right, he would still get it. She had to come up with a way to support Kay while keeping Cullen from any further involvement with her and Kay.

By the time Danita arrived at the entrance to WAIT FOR ME, Cullen already stood there. A plan formed in her mind as she coolly slipped her key into the lock and opened the door.

She ushered him into the employees' lounge and kept the right distance between them to discourage any acts of consolation on his part. She had to stand on her own. After creating this mess, she would get herself out of it without taking Cullen down, too.

She plastered a smile on her face. "Have a seat while I fix us some coffee. You're welcome to make your calls from here."

Quivering inside, she strode to the lounge and started the coffee. While she waited for it to brew, she removed her cell phone from her bag and retrieved Frederickson's office phone number. A woman answered.

"This is Danita Johnson. May I speak to Mr. Frederickson, please?"

While she waited for him to come on the line, she prayed for the right words to say to him. The last thing she wanted to do was give away Cullen's part in all this. If only Frederickson didn't ask too many questions.

"Ms. Johnson. You just caught me. What can I do for you?" Frederickson's voice held such friendliness, she dreaded telling him the reason for her call.

Danita tightened her grip on the receiver. "Mr. Frederickson. This will take a few minutes."

"No problem. For the winner of this year's grant, I have all the time you need."

In a halting voice Danita gave Frederickson the gist of the events of the last twenty-four hours. "I wanted you to know what happened before you or anyone on the committee saw the story on TV. I plan to contact the authorities right away."

"Let me get this straight. Not only did you witness a fracas between two prominent San Diego citizens, but one of them is dead, you were involved, your picture was on TV and the police are looking for you?"

"Well...yes."

"You know what this means, don't you?"

"That's why I called as soon as I saw the story on the news."

"You understand the agreement you signed?"

"Yes, Mr. Frederickson, but I can explain."

"There's nothing to explain. You're involved in a scandal, and you'll have to forfeit the grant."

Danita groaned and clutched the phone even tighter. "Surely the foundation gives its recipients an opportunity to defend themselves in cases like this. I have an appointment with the committee tomorrow."

"I don't expect you to keep it. I'll explain the situation to the committee."

"I'll be there. I'll use my time to explain what happened and why. If, at the end of my presentation, they still want to withhold the grant, I'll give it up without a challenge."

Frederickson's voice hardened. "A challenge, Ms. Johnson? As in legal?"

She let an evasive tone creep into her voice. "I'm sorry. I guess that was a poor choice of words. I meant we would all feel better if the foundation had all the facts in case anyone asks why it withheld the grant promised to WAIT FOR ME. After all, I'm sure there's not a person on the committee who wouldn't have come to the aid of a woman in danger."

Frederickson remained silent. Now it was her turn to sweat. Danita feared her ploy had failed. After all, what could she say to change the committee members' minds? They had warned her, and by her blunders, she had lost the right to a second chance.

"All right, Ms. Johnson. We'll see you tomorrow."

Danita hung up. She was relieved she still had time to take the responsibility for the fiasco on her own shoulders and ensure that if the committee took the grant from her, Cullen would still get it.

She closed her eyes and massaged them. It was time to make the call to the police. Too many people knew her. She hadn't a hope in hell of remaining anonymous.

She placed her call, identified herself, and answered a number of questions before her call was switched to Sergeant Larson the officer in charge of the case. When the sergeant told her where to report, she said, "I'm on my way."

Cullen came up behind her and squeezed her shoulders, "I wondered what was taking you so long to make a pot of coffee."

He poured coffee for both of them, set the steaming mugs on the card table in front of Danita, and turned off the pot. "I heard most of your calls."

"Eavesdropping again?"

"I thought you saw me come in."

She longed to turn into his arms; lay her head on his chest, breathe in his special scent, and feel safe again. Instead, she held herself aloof. Knowing Cullen, he would rush to her defense if she gave him the slightest encouragement.

"While you made your calls, I phoned Cathy at the YWCA and explained," he said. "She offered her regrets and said to call her if you needed her."

Danita's heart softened. "Thanks." She loved this caring thoughtful man with all her heart. She hated what she had to do.

She forced an unwavering gaze on him. The pain she saw in his eyes reflected her own misery. Though Aaron had hurt Kay, none of them had wished him dead. She and Cullen would have to find a way to give Kay comfort and support through this crisis.

"After Kay's settled in her home, I'll stay with her," Danita said.

"Good idea. She'll appreciate having you near at a time like this."

Cullen covered her hand with his. "When you're ready I'll go with you to the police station. We're in this together, sweetheart. Tomorrow we'll talk to the committee. I'm sure they'll understand when I explain how I got you into this."

Danita drew away from his touch and looked him in the eye. *Might as well get this over with.* "No way. I can't let you do that. You're not going anywhere with me. My own carelessness got me into this. I have to take care of the fallout...alone."

Cullen stared at her as if she had spoken in an unknown tongue. "Wait a minute. I share some responsibility in this situation. I'm the one who introduced you to Kay. What's going on here?"

Danita realized Cullen wouldn't listen to reason. She had to say something to stop him. "Nothing's going on. I've had all the help I want from you. You know what your trouble is? You fix people. You love it, don't you? Mr. Fix-It. I don't want or need your assistance. You've done enough."

Cullen clenched his teeth as if struggling to hide his

frustration. "You're talking nonsense. I know you're upset. Who wouldn't be? But we need to be a team."

"Not anymore, we don't. Well, except when it comes to Kay. We can still work together on Kay's behalf."

Afraid her trembling fingers would betray her; Danita turned her back to him, picked up the phone and punched in some numbers. She needed a few minutes to harden her resolve. "We'll finish this after I talk to Laureen."

Cullen pushed down the disconnect bar, interrupting her call. "We'll finish now."

She rose to her feet and injected an angry tone in her voice to disguise her desperation. "All right then, here it is. Ever since I met you, you've done nothing but hound me. You used every trick in the book to divert me in order to make me lose the grant. When you didn't succeed, you took me to bed."

"What? You have to know that's not true. I care about you. I have since the moment I met you. How can you..."

Danita interrupted with a raised hand. "Really? Funny, this is the first time you've mentioned it. If you care about me, prove it. Stay the hell away from me. Keep out of my affairs. Let me handle this situation on my own. Or do you think I'm too stupid to take care of myself?"

"Of course not. I didn't mean it that way, and you know it. I care for you, care what happens to you. You don't have to do this by yourself. Together we're strong—we can work this thing out."

"You don't get it do you? Let me put it into words of one syllable. I don't need you. I don't want you. Leave me alone."

Cullen clenched his jaw. "Okay, Danita. Have it your way. I wondered why you made your about-face and decided to let me get close to you. I should have known your sudden change of feelings for me was phony. But tell me—why did you encourage me?"

Danita stalled for a minute. What convincing enough reason could she give to drive him away until her got the award?

"I figured two could play the same game," she said. "If I could get your mind off of the grant and onto me, you'd lose and I'd win. My plan almost worked. But then this thing came up. Well, I haven't lost yet, and I don't intend to without a fight. Stay out of it. You'll only sabotage my chance for the grant, again."

"I don't believe you mean what you're saying." Cullen turned her so she faced him. "I want you to listen to me. You did all you could. Aaron set himself on the road to destruction long ago. When he found nobody would join him there, he tried to force

Kay to become his companion in hell."

"I know that."

"I wonder if you do. I think you want to take responsibility for Aaron's insanity."

Her unease increased under his scrutiny. She clung to her fragile control, praying she would not betray her true feelings. "I intend to deal with the committee alone. I don't blame myself for what Aaron did, but…"

"No 'buts'! Aaron's life ended the way it did because he couldn't accept Ayana's death. We all loved Ayana. I miss her—probably always will. I grieved over losing her and our baby. I was angry, too. My wife left me without warning and no good-byes. Eventually I learned to accept what happened and stopped fighting against it."

Miserably, Danita watched Cullen's apparent struggle to make her understand. He placed his hands on her shoulder. When she moved under his hold, he tightened his grip and held her in place.

Cullen closed his eyes for a moment as if to gain control. "Then I met you and suddenly my life had meaning again. I knew it was hard for you to trust my motives. When I learned why, I understood you might need more time to believe in me. After we made love, I truly thought you felt for me what I felt for you. Now you tell me you never cared for me. It was all a game with you."

"What you say changes nothing. I'm the one who led Aaron to Kay. I left that damned door open so he could get in. Kay could have been killed."

"But she wasn't, Danita. I'll go with you, Monday. I'll explain everything."

Danita shook her head vehemently. "I can't let you do that. Even though I made a mess of things, I can salvage something out of all this, and I intend to try…without your help." She moved away from him, her steps agitated. "Please, you'll only make things worse."

Cullen smoothed his hand over his hair. "When I met you I was lonely. Your fire and enthusiasm for life healed my soul. Even though I need you, I'd rather spend the rest of my life without you than live in the past with ghosts—any ghosts—mine or yours."

Cullen's words hit her like a wrecking ball. Danita studied his face. He had put up a wall she feared would be unbreachable when the whole miserable mess ended.

He wasn't simply talking about Kay, Aaron and the grant. He meant her part in nearly losing WAIT FOR ME because she had trusted the wrong man.

She paced the room. She had to protect Cullen.

Cullen blocked her path and lightly gripped her upper arms, halting her steps. "Though we can each do without the other, we'd be stronger as a team," he said. "We can't change the past, but together we could change the future. I love you too much to watch you destroy your life."

Danita bit back a protest and a declaration of her love for him. She shook off his touch and moved away. She knew any words of love would destroy the distance she had tried so desperately to put between them.

She studied Cullen's expression. He looked like a man who had come to some sort of life-altering decision. An uneasiness skittered up Danita's spine.

She lifted a hand in a plea for understanding and whispered, "Please leave now. I need time to think."

"You do that. I need you in my life, but I need you whole, free of the past, ready for a future without regrets. The choice is yours."

He turned to leave. "I'll see you at the hospital when Kay checks out."

She followed him to the exit and opened the door. "Good-bye, Cullen."

"Then there's no future for us. You don't trust me, you never have and you never will." He turned, kissed her until she was reeling, then pulled away and searched her face as if to read her soul. Whatever he saw appeared to satisfy him. He shook his head and murmured, "Good-bye, Danita? We'll see."

જે

Though the door closed on Cullen, his parting words hung in the air. Still shaken from his kiss and her uninhibited response to it, she wished she could call him back—tell him her awful words were lies. *Forget it. He'd never believe me now.* She shook her head. *I can't think about how I've hurt Cullen. I know I did the right thing.*

If the foundation withdrew the grant, she would have no way to save WAIT FOR ME. What little money she could salvage she would use to retrieve the family heirlooms. She had learned one important lesson: never give up without a fight.

She didn't want to face her family's disappointment when she told them she couldn't repay their investment in her, but she had no choice. More than anything else, she didn't want to face the future without Cullen. She wanted to share her love and her life with him. But she'd gone too far to turn back.

She prayed for strength to survive her meeting with the police and face the next day when she and Cullen would have to tell Kay what had happened to Aaron.

She went to the employees' lounge to make sure everything was in order. Hands trembling, she gathered up her bag and jacket, as fatigue threatened to overwhelm her.

One thing at a time. First the police. She hoped the sergeant would be brief. When she got home she would prepare her presentation for the committee.

⁂

Danita marched toward the front door, flipping off lights as she went. When she jerked the door open, a strobe light blinded her.

Someone pointed a microphone at her. She blinked against the light and held her hand in front of her eyes to shield herself from the glare. When her eyes adjusted to the lights, she recognized the anchor woman from a local TV station. The woman asked, "Danita Johnson?"

Feeling she had lost the last bit of control, the blood froze in her veins. "You're Joan Chevette the TV reporter. What are you doing here?"

"I came to interview you. As soon as I saw our piece on Kay and Aaron Burdell on the noon news I recognized you as the missing witness."

Danita swallowed against the knot in her throat. Her voice wavered. "But I've never met you."

"I read an article about WAIT FOR ME in the *Union-Tribune* a while back. In fact I clipped out the piece. I thought I might need to call on you in an emergency."

Danita winced. Tonight her every word, every gesture, every emotion would be featured on the evening news. Too late to run and hide, she garnered her wits and controlled the desire to deny she was indeed the witness the police sought.

"I see," Danita said. "I'm on my way to the police station this very moment. If you'll excuse me…"

Joan smiled. "I'd appreciate a few minutes of your time. I'm sure the public would be disappointed if you left us without making a statement."

Given the persistence of the media, Danita knew she couldn't avoid talking to the reporter. Might as well make the most of it. She'd show Joan Chevette who was in charge. After all, they were in her territory. She would decide when and how this interview would be conducted.

"All right," she said to Joan. "Come into my office."

Danita led the way and deposited the two cameramen and Joan into her office. "Give me a minute to freshen my make-up."

Without giving Joan a chance to reply, Danita slipped into the powder room and closed the door. *Some of the committee members are bound to see me tonight or tomorrow morning on the news. I'll make this an interview to remember. Even if I lose the grant, I can give important information to women who are watching.*

The more Danita thought about the coming interview the better she liked it. She brightened. Joan Chevette had a great reputation. She had won an Emmy for her series of stories on spousal abuse.

Danita combed her hair, put on fresh lipstick and powdered her nose. "Lights, camera and aces-high," she muttered under her breath. She intended to come out of this interview holding all high cards.

With a few words of directions, Joan put Danita at ease.

Joan asked, "From the tapes an interested bystander gave us, it appeared obvious Kay Burdell had fled from an abusive situation, am I right?"

"Kay and her husband had some serious issues to resolve, and she needed time to calm down and determine how to proceed," Danita said.

"I'd like to focus on your involvement."

Here it comes. I can't fail now. "I'm her friend. Friends are often the best and only people a battered woman can turn to for understanding and support. I had to show Kay I cared. Kay needed to know she could count on at least one person to follow through on her behalf."

Joan nodded. "Then you helped in her escape from violence?"

"Kay needed a safe place to stay until she could assess her problems—contact with people who would care for and counsel her."

"But you were with Mrs. Burdell at a motel."

"We were on our way to one of the YWCA's counselors for the Battered Women's Shelter. An unexpected opening had come up and Kay was next on the list. Because of the number of women who need to go there has increased, Kay had to go on a waiting list. It's a shame we don't have more shelters, but without increased public support, things will get worse, and women like Kay will be put in jeopardy."

"Did you encourage her to leave her husband?"

"No, I didn't. Kay had already left when she called me for help."

"What made you fear for her safety?"

"I didn't know what her husband might do. I wanted to minimize the danger for her. I couldn't encourage her to return to her husband. Her circumstances might have worsened. I had to take precautions on her behalf and I did. We made the mistake of trying to keep their difficulties quiet. If I had it to do over again, I would have alerted the police. She could have gotten a restraining order so they could have taken measures to protect her."

One of the cameramen moved closer. "Why didn't you?" Joan asked.

"Kay wanted to guard Aaron's reputation. Some folks think only less affluent people have this sort of problem. Not true. And when socially or politically prominent people are involved, the victims and their friends often, unfortunately, engage in a conspiracy of silence."

"One last question," Joan said. "In light of the tragedy that developed, are you sorry you got involved?"

Danita paused. Her words could make the difference in how the viewers she wanted to reach might react in similar circumstances. "Never! My grandmother a very wise woman once said, 'Friends stand by you when others stand aside.' If friends and neighbors don't respond when asked for help, everybody suffers. As a nation we've kept quiet and accepted spousal abuse for too long. Now is the time to speak out for these victims."

At a signal from Joan, the cameramen doused the strobes and packed up their equipment. Joan turned to Danita. "Thanks for the interview. I'll run it as a feature story and add a hotline number for abused women to call."

Danita nodded. "I hope the interview encourages the friends of abused women to give support if they're asked. Shelters and police protection will never take the place of those who love you."

Joan shook Danita's hand. "I won't keep you. Give my best to Mrs. Burdell. I'm an admirer of her work."

The moment Joan Chevette left, Danita locked up, hurried to her car and headed for the police station. Thank God that was over. She hoped when Cullen saw the story he would understand why she had to try to salvage the grant on her own.

She had hurt him when she had tried to get rid of him. She didn't deserve him, but she loved him. Missing him already, she hadn't the heart to deal with the coming days alone, but she had

no choice.
    One day he would thank her. One day he would forgive her. He had to, because a future without him would be bleak indeed.

Thirteen

GRITTY-EYED FROM LACK of sleep, Danita stood beside Kay who sat in a wheelchair on the sidewalk in front of the hospital's exit. An attendant waited beside them.

Danita fought her weariness and concentrated on Kay. The sight of her bruised and bandaged face made Danita want to weep. She whispered in Kay's ear, "You'll be home soon."

Cullen drove up and parked at the curb. Danita held open the car door while Cullen and the attendant helped a stricken Kay into Cullen's car.

During the ride to Kay's house, Danita recalled the gentle patience Cullen had exhibited when he gave Kay the news of Aaron's death. Dr. Gittleson had stood by while Cullen explained to her what had happened. Except for giving her a prescription for a sedative in case she needed it, the doctor's silence indicated Cullen had handled the situation well.

Danita sat in the back seat beside Kay and searched for a way to console her, but nothing came to mind. She held Kay's hand in hers and hoped, by her touch, to transmit her sympathy.

"I have my suitcase in the trunk. I'll move in with you for a while if you don't mind," Danita told her.

"Thanks, I'd like that," Kay whispered. She turned her head and stared out of the window.

Danita's cut lip burned and made it uncomfortable to speak. Except for the desultory comments between Cullen and Kay, little conversation was exchanged on the drive to Kay's home.

Cullen carried Kay's suitcases upstairs to the master bedroom, then returned to his car for Danita's luggage. "I'll wait downstairs while you get her settled," Cullen said to Danita. "Then we'll talk."

Unwilling to create a scene in front of Kay, Danita resisted the urge to tell Cullen to go home. Instead she murmured, "Okay," and set about finding a nightgown for Kay.

When his footsteps receded down the stairs, Danita turned from the dresser, a gown in hand. One look at Kay, and Danita dropped the garment on the foot of the bed and went to her.

Kay stood beside the bed, the fingers of one hand pressed against her mouth. Tear-brightened eyes stared at a pair of men's pajamas and a robe which hung on a hook on the open bathroom door. Shaving paraphernalia lay scattered on the beige marble sink. The faint scent of sandalwood aftershave lingered in the room.

Feeling helpless, Danita put an arm around Kay's shoulder. "I'm so sorry, Kay. So sorry."

Kay blinked back her tears. She patted Danita's hand. "I know," Kay whispered. "I think I'll use one of the guest rooms." She picked up her nightgown and hurried out of the door.

Watching her go, Danita wondered for the hundredth time how she could have changed what had happened. When she had gathered some of Kay's clothes and personal items, she joined Kay who had slipped into her nightgown and climbed into bed.

Kay looked up with an air of resignation. She raised her hand to the bandage on her head and winced. "I know the doctor ordered me to take it easy for the rest of the day, but I should attend to a few things. Insurance, funeral arrangements, police reports. Something. I hardly know where to begin."

"We'll do it together. Let's wait until later. I have a meeting in the afternoon. My mom will drop by here to answer phone calls for you. As soon as I get back, we'll sort out what needs to be done first. Rest for now."

Danita went into the adjoining bathroom and got a glass of water. From her bag she took a small container of medicine she'd had filled at the hospital's pharmacy.

Back at Kay's side, Danita handed her two tablets. "Take these. They'll help your headache."

Kay wrinkled her nose but complied. "Thanks. Between this pain in my head and the nurses waking me up every two hours, I didn't get much sleep last night. I could use a little nap." She searched Danita's face. "So much has happened. It's hard to adjust. Don't worry, though. I'll be fine."

Danita tried for a reassuring smile, but her face felt as rigid as wood. "You're doing great."

Kay's gaze settled on a picture sitting on a tall oak chest of drawers. "Who would ever have thought I'd lose them all?" She turned away and settled under the covers as if to shut out the misery waiting for her in the coming days.

Danita followed her gaze. A family photo from happier times caught and held her attention. A smiling Aaron posed between Kay and a young woman whose resemblance to him was unmistakable. Tall and slender, she had a soft open look about her eyes. Cullen stood next to Ayana, his hand gripping hers. His look of devotion was so profound her throat clogged with tears.

"No one would ever choose this to happen." She gave Kay a hug. "Cullen and I are here for you, and we love you."

Though she knew Kay was not ready to respond to her words of sympathy, Danita had to say them. She turned on the radio next to Kay's bed. With one last look at Kay, she left, closing the door softly behind her.

Danita found Cullen sitting in a recliner in the family room. With his long legs stretched out before him, he nursed a cup of coffee.

He came to his feet. "You must be exhausted. I made a pot of coffee. I'll get you some."

Grateful for a few minutes to garner her strength for the discussion she knew would follow, she sank into an armchair.

She heard him open a cupboard. A cup rattled against a saucer. She had only a few seconds to shore up her resolve. She had to keep Cullen away from the committee.

Cullen set a steaming cup of coffee on the low table in front of her. "Smells delicious," she said.

He returned to his seat and said without preamble, "We need to get something settled." He set his jaw at a stubborn angle and narrowed his eyes just enough for her to know he was not prepared to give an inch.

"Is this another one of those talks where you lay down the law and I meekly obey?" She stared him down—or tried to—but he didn't bat an eye.

"In this case, yes."

"I made myself perfectly clear last night. I can take care of myself. I don't need a Sir Galahad."

"You're one hardheaded woman."

"Look who's talking."

Cullen glared at her. "We need to get something straight." He leaned forward. "I won't hide behind a woman's skirts. Make up your mind. Kay's my responsibility, not yours. This isn't about you. This is about how I got you involved with Kay and her problems with Aaron."

"And just why do you think I can't deal with the committee on my own?"

"That's not the issue. A man doesn't stand by and allow another man to mistreat a woman. Neither does he allow a woman to pay his debts. It's my responsibility to explain how I got you involved in this situation with Kay."

Danita stared at him. Her heart dropped into her stomach, and for a moment she could barely catch her breath. He had made up his mind. How could she protect him when he was bent on protecting her? *I can't let him. He has too much to lose.*

His argument had cut the ground from under her. Surging to her feet, she raised her voice. "No. I told you, I don't want your help. I know it's about Kay, but it's about WAIT FOR ME, too. Play macho man some other time. Stay out of it."

"What's going on down there?" Kay demanded. Leaning over the upstairs banister, she looked unsteady on her feet. "What about WAIT FOR ME? What's happened?"

Danita's face burned with guilt and shame. How could she have lost her temper and disturbed Kay? She opened her mouth to speak.

Not waiting for an answer, Kay turned to Cullen. "Why are you and Danita arguing? Haven't we had enough turmoil to last us a lifetime? Cullen, I think you'd better leave before this gets out of hand."

Cullen moved to stand below Kay. He looked up at her. "I'm sorry we disturbed you. To answer your questions, you're not involved with WAIT FOR ME. Danita and I had a difference of opinion. We got a little excited. I'm leaving now, but I'll be back tomorrow morning around nine and we'll get started on the arrangements. Get some rest."

Kay looked relieved. "I will, but first I want both of you to kiss and make up, otherwise I'll think I'm the cause of your disagreement."

Danita backed up a step. *Oh, Lord, if he touches me I'll break.*

When he shrugged and turned, he gave Danita a look that dared her to resist his embrace.

She almost laughed when he reached out and cupped her shoulders. He reminded her of a kid who have been forced to shake hand with his rival after a playground fight. He pulled her close. The soft touch of his lips against hers held the hint of a challenge. A shaft of sorrow mixed with desire pierced her heart. She wondered if he would ever again touch her in passion.

His soft breath feathered her ear. "I won't force myself into *your* meeting with the committee. You've won this round, but it's not over yet."

She trembled from the power of his touch and from relief when he agreed to give up his plan to go with her. She stood motionless while he went up the stairs and kissed Kay on the cheek.

"I'll let myself out," he said to Kay as he retraced his steps. "Promise you'll take a nap." At her nod, he left without a backward glance.

Danita could not believe she had finally convinced him to stay away from the committee. "Cullen Powers is one stubborn man. Sometimes he makes me so mad I say things I don't mean."

"But you love him anyway."

"Yes. I love him anyway." *And I can't let him get hurt again, though I can't tell him that. At least he won't turn up tomorrow morning, thanks to Kay.*

As she led Kay back to bed an uneasy feeling stole over her. The warning he had whispered in her ear left her wondering. What did he mean "it's not over yet"?

ૐ

Danita glanced at the entrance to Penn-Atkinson Foundation's suite of offices again, expecting Cullen to turn up at any minute. His parting words had worried her more than she wanted to admit. She wanted to get this meeting over and leave.

She shifted on the waiting room couch and glanced at her watch—five minutes after two. Only one minute had passed since she had looked at it. What was taking them so long?

The previous night her mother had talked for an hour, devising ways to help Kay. The press continued to bombard Kay with phone messages she was in no condition to return. Though Danita had fielded all of their calls, the effort had exhausted her. Thank goodness, her mom would take care of the press and any other curiosity seekers, Cullen would help Kay make plans, and Danita could meet with the committee without worrying about Cullen.

When Mr. Frederickson's secretary contacted Danita to say he had rescheduled her ten o'clock meeting for two, her anxiety increased. She didn't ask why he had changed the time, but it added to her worries.

Mr. Frederickson opened the door to the committee room.

"Sorry to keep you waiting, Ms. Johnson." He ushered her inside, indicated her chair, and sat down across from her at the long mahogany conference table.

He looked anything but sorry. Trembling, she scanned the group. Except for Mr. Rawley, she faced the same men she had first met with months before. Her heart sank. She had counted on Mr. Rawley's friendly presence.

Mr. Frederickson must have noticed her disappointment because he said, "Mr. Rawley's been held up. He asked us to start without him. You may go ahead and make your case now."

Danita leaned forward and scanned the group. Not a single encouraging smile met her gaze. Garnering all of her courage she straightened her spine.

"Gentlemen," she said, "on behalf of my employees and my clients, I've asked you for this opportunity to plead for a chance to continue my work at WAIT FOR ME. Your original benevolence tells me you recognize the value of our service to the community."

Moisture gathered under her armpits. She willed herself to relax. "I won't discuss WAIT FOR ME. Instead I'll address my remarks to the so-called scandal you seem to believe makes me ineligible to receive your grant. I'm asking you to use that same benevolent spirit to consider what would have happened if I, or someone like me, had ignored the pleas of a woman whose life had been threatened."

A murmur went around the table, but not one member of the committee addressed a remark to her.

Danita paused and met each man's gaze with steady regard. "Some of you have met Kay Burdell. She's a strong, talented woman, but no woman is strong enough to withstand physical and emotional abuse from the man she loves and trusts."

Each man's gaze dropped and focused on the note pad in front of him while Danita waited for her words to sink in. "From the days when British Common Law's rule of thumb permitted a man to beat his wife as long as he used a rod no thicker than his thumb some men believed it their duty to do so. Since then, women have been systematically disenfranchised, leaving them at the mercy of their husbands."

At the thought of such treatment, her indignation rose. "Even some Western religious teachers gave men the right to scold, bully, terrify and beat their wives for their own good to make them obey.

"Well into the twenty-first century our laws still don't protect women from spousal abuse. Even now women have little recourse and few places to go for shelter. In this city alone, there are more shelters for animals than for women. That's why Kay and women like her find themselves on waiting lists for beds in safe houses."

The men shifted in apparent embarrassment at her last statement. *Good. I see I have your attention now.*

"I believe not one of you would stand idly by and permit your daughter, granddaughter or family friend to be victimized. Violent men use their physical advantages and their wives dependence to brutalize and control them. I had to help. I had no choice."

The silence in the room held such intensity Danita felt crushed by it.

"Good morning, Ms. Johnson. Sorry I'm late, but I believe I heard most of your presentation."

From the back of the room, Rawley's familiar voice made her swing her head in his direction.

He walked to his place at the head of the table and took a seat. "Any questions, gentlemen?"

The men muttered they had none.

"I have one, Ms. Johnson," Mr. Rawley said. "In view of the agreement you signed regarding scandal, why didn't you call the authorities or let someone else handle the problem?"

Danita knew her answer stood between her and the grant. She shook off her fears and met his questioning gaze.

She said, "In spite of Mr. Burdell's mistreatment, Mrs. Burdell wanted to protect her husband from public humiliation. She asked me for help. I knew what was at stake, but she is my friend. I could not turn my back on her. The authorities would have given her one choice—file charges. Ultimately it may have come to that, but Mrs. Burdell was not ready to take that step."

Mr. Rawley nodded. "I see. Thank you for coming. We'll notify you this evening around six o'clock of our decision."

He rose and escorted Danita to the door. She searched his face. Except for a frown creasing his brow, she found no clue to his thoughts.

"Thank you for listening," she said. She turned toward the waiting room feeling as if she had taken a gamble and lost WAIT FOR ME.

As she walked Danita's heart pounded all the way to the underground parking lot. Her blouse clung to the perspiration on her back. Her mouth felt dry and her stomach ached. When she arrived at her Ford Taurus she slipped into the driver's seat and leaned back against the headrest. She needed a minute to mend her frayed nerves before she tackled the freeway traffic.

The committee members had hated the presentation. She may have made them uncomfortable, but she had seen little sympathy or understanding in their detached gazes. They must have agreed to hear her out to avoid legal problems, but their behavior indicated they had already made a decision. Even Mr. Rawley had let her down.

Instead of condemning her, Cullen should thank her for meeting with the committee without him. His presence would have served no purpose other than to earn the committee's disfavor.

She had to talk to him—make him see the uselessness of the sacrifice he had planned.

How and when she could explain her actions to him presented a problem. With both her mother and Kay about, she would have little opportunity to talk to Cullen in private. She knew when she saw Cullen again he would be too angry to listen. Besides, the phone rang continually. If she and Kay had some uninterrupted time, they would use it to deal with the details of Aaron's cremation services. She couldn't risk the possibility Kay might overhear her discussing the meeting with Cullen for fear Kay might blame herself for Danita's problems with the grant.

Danita would just have to go to Kay's and wait for an opportunity to get Cullen alone. Perhaps she could lure him onto the patio with a promise of sharing the details of her meeting. If he would listen, she knew she could convince him to forgive her.

Eyes brimming, she started her car. One thought kept her from bursting into tears. She may have to forfeit the grant, but she had saved it for Cullen.

She pulled out of the dimly lit underground lot. At the exit, she blinked against the dazzling sunlight and the moisture in her eyes. As she sat there she noticed a tall muscular male figure with a confident stride disappear through the revolving doors of the Penn-Atkinson building. The man's gait and build reminded her so much of Cullen, she strained to see if she had imagined him.

The sharp honk of a horn behind her made her ease into traffic and head for the freeway. She shook her head in denial. *I've got Cullen on the brain. He wouldn't come here. He promised.*

ટે&

Cullen rang Kay's doorbell at exactly four o'clock. Danita

schooled her face to hide her joy at the sight of him. He looked tired and distracted, as if he had a lot on his mind.

"How's Kay?" he asked.

"Fine." Danita murmured. She controlled her desire to throw herself in his arms and kiss away his tightlipped wary look.

"Who is it?" Danita's mother called.

"It's Cullen," Danita replied.

Nita Johnson hurried to greet Cullen. "I'm glad you're here, son. You look exhausted. Come on into the family room. Looks like you could use some lunch."

Danita followed the pair into the back of the house. *Son?* Her mother had adopted Cullen. The whole family had. Every time Danita talked to Laureen, Adam and J.V., they raved about what a great guy Cullen was and tried to find out what progress she had made in her relationship with him. Danita had sidestepped their questions so far, but she would soon have to tell them there was no relationship unless she could get Cullen to listen to her and forgive her for accusing him of using her. With her mother hovering, she would have a hard time getting him alone.

Nita brought two steaming mugs and set them on the table. "This ought to perk you up. Lunch will be ready soon. Why don't you both take a breather on the patio until I call you." She said to Cullen, "You look as if you need to relax."

Bless your heart, Mom. Danita picked up her cup and moved toward the patio. She slid the glass door open and turned to Cullen. "Coming?"

When he hesitated she knew he would rather be anywhere than alone with her. She held her breath. Maybe he would insist on keeping her mother company.

"Sure." He walked past her and took a seat at the round glass-top umbrella table. Danita closed the door behind her. This might be her only chance to talk to him before Mr. Frederickson's call.

She joined Cullen at the table. A tall brick wall enclosed a large backyard.

The tension seeped out of her body at the sight of the peaceful scene. "I wish we had more than a few minutes. We need to discuss my meeting with the committee."

"How *did* your meeting go?" Cullen asked. He took a sip of his coffee but didn't meet her gaze.

All right. So what did you expect from him? Instant forgiveness? Open-minded interest? A fair chance? Danita rubbed away the frown between her eyes. *Yes. All of the above. He said he loves me. Surely he should care what happened.*

She covered the top of her mug with the palm of her hand. The steam soothed her tangled nerves. "The committee listened politely to everything I had to say, but I think they had already decided."

She gave him an imploring look. "Try to understand. There was no reason under heaven for you to subject yourself to their rejection. I gave them every argument in the book for involving myself with Kay. They never batted an eye. Except for Rawley, they didn't ask me one question—they just sat there. Robots show more animation than they did."

"Yeah, I know."

His words jolted Danita. "What do you mean, you know?"

Cullen gave her a dead-on look, his expression both resigned and unapologetic.

"Of course," she said. "Mr. Frederickson must have called to let you know where you stand now that WAIT FOR ME no longer gets the grant."

"Not exactly."

"No, I guess he wouldn't. Mr. Rawley did say he'd let me know their decision this evening around six. He wouldn't let me off the hook 'til then. What did Mr. Frederickson say?"

"Not much. None of them did."

Danita stared at Cullen. There was something wrong with this picture. She checked the rush of words behind clamped lips. In slow precise words she asked, "What do you mean 'none of them did'?"

"You must have figured it out by now. After I left you last night I called Mr. Rawley and told him my role in Aaron's tragedy. I asked for a hearing before the committee. He and Mr. Frederickson arranged for me to address them this afternoon at three o'clock."

"Oh, no! Cullen, I asked you not to get involved. You promised."

"I promised to let you meet with the Penn-Atkinson group on your own. I never promised to cover up my part in the affair. After all Kay is part of my family. But for me, you'd never have met her, let alone involved yourself in her problem."

The unyielding look he gave her told her better than any words that he had no regrets. His admission jolted Danita. She had fought hard to make sure that his clients would benefit from her defeat. Too late she realized the extent of Cullen's ethical make-up. She should have listened to him. He had wanted to present a united front. Instead he'd had to fight both her and the committee. By trying to save him, she had diminished him. From the cool look he gave her, she knew he would never forgive her.

She bowed her head to hide her shame. Without looking at him she asked, "What did they say?"

"Absolutely nothing. Except for their obvious surprise when I told them Kay was my mother-in-law and I had asked you to help her, they didn't react to anything I said. I gave them my best shots, but I was shooting cotton bullets at a steel wall.

"They listened politely, even when I cited statistics about the thousands of women whose husbands or ex-lovers kill them every year. I tried to make them see that we believed Kay was in real danger. We had to stand by her. Unfortunately, my pleas fell on unresponsive ears."

"Mr. Rawley promised to call me this evening. I had my calls forwarded here," Danita said.

"I did, too." He gave her a wry look. "We're in this together whether you like it or not."

She didn't try to hide her chagrin. She deserved his censor. She took comfort in his use of the word "we". Maybe... "Let's meet upstairs in Aaron's office around six," she said. "Might as well have the bad news confirmed before we say anything to our partners or our families."

"Fine."

He looked so defeated Danita's heart went out to him. Though she had no right, she wanted to comfort him. When she reached to touch his hand, he pulled it away and cupped his mug with both hands. His gesture confirmed her fears. The knowledge that she had lost him settled like a huge painful knot in her chest.

Danita's mother slid open the patio door. "Dani, would you go get Kay, please? Lunch is ready. I'm putting it on the table right now."

Danita stood, and with one last look at Cullen's discouraged expression, left without another word.

❧

Danita's steps slowed as she approached Kay's door. While Danita had fielded phone calls, Kay had spent part of the morning talking to Aaron's partner. Aaron's firm had been in the middle of planning a campaign for an important client, and Kay had given his partner access to all the materials Aaron had brought home to work on prior to his death.

Danita wondered how Kay had survived the meeting. She tapped on Kay's door.

"Come in," Kay replied in a husky voice.

Danita entered and found Kay sitting with folded hands in an easy chair, her bruised face filled with sorrow. Danita could hardly bear to meet her listless gaze. "Cullen's here. And Mom says lunch is ready. Feel like eating?"

Kay nodded. "Instead of sitting here going over what went wrong, I should have come down and helped your mom."

"Don't worry about it. She loves to cook. Are you all right?"

"I don't know yet. I'm trying not to blame myself, but I can't seem to stop. Maybe I could have been a better wife. I should have put him first. I should have set aside my painting after Ayana died. Aaron needed pampering, and I wasn't there for him. He must have felt everyone had deserted him. No wonder he lost control."

With her back to the door, Danita sat on the bed facing Kay. "No. I won't have you thinking like this. Aaron bullied you. I was at the motel, remember. I saw him. He was calm and deliberate in everything he did to you. You're not to blame."

"You sound so sure."

"I *am* sure. My family went through this with my aunt. I know. A very wise man taught me long ago that I had to let go of undeserved guilt or it would cripple me. I didn't listen to him until it was too late. I beg you to listen to me now."

The ring of certainty in Danita's voice must have caught Kay's attention because she stopped twisting her hands and seemed to focus her attention on Danita's words.

Danita placed her hands over Kay's. "Aaron wasn't a child. He was a man—a man capable of making choices. He chose the hell he was in, and he wanted to take you with him. Nothing you did would have satisfied him. You did what you had to do. You left—and just in time. Please, please don't spend even one more minute beating yourself up. You don't deserve it."

"But maybe I could have…"

"No! You were a good and caring wife. You did all you could do. You shouldn't have made yourself an emotional and physical punching bag. You knew it. Cullen knew it, and I did, too. We can't change the past. We have to go on."

A light of acceptance beamed in Kay's eyes. "You're right. I realize that. I promise to work on…"

"Excuse me, ladies," Cullen said from the doorway. "Nita asked me to hurry you two along. The food is getting cold."

Danita watched Kay move toward Cullen. Kay's steps held more confidence than Danita had seen since Aaron's death.

Cullen draped his arm around Kay's shoulder. When he looked at her a smile lifted the corners of his mouth—a small one, but a smile nevertheless.

Wishing he had another such smile for her, Danita trailed Kay and Cullen down the stairs.

Danita straightened her spine. She'd find a way to save WAIT FOR ME with or without the grant. Her biggest challenge would be to save her relationship with Cullen no matter what.

A plan slowly formed in her mind. She'd do it. Just as soon as she could get him alone.

Fourteen

DANITA WAS SITTING ON THE brown leather couch in Aaron's study, leafing through a copy of San Diego Magazine when Cullen opened the door. Her heart danced at the sight of him. She prayed her plan would work and that she wouldn't come across as too bold.

"Hi, Danita," he said with a tentative smile that made her hunger for those fiery kisses which went with his hello's just a few days ago.

She examined him closely. His eyes held the courageous fire she treasured. He seemed subdued but not defeated. She wanted to assure him everything would work out even if both of them lost the grant, but would he believe her?

"Kay's resting in her room. Your mom just left," he said. "She and you dad will be by for Kay in the morning. Your mom asked that we tell her as soon we hear from Frederickson."

"Of course. I'm not looking forward to facing Virgie and my seniors, but as soon as I know something for sure we can start planning for the future."

Danita watched Cullen with a wary eye as he moved to sit in the office chair in front of the computer. He swiveled around in the chair to face her.

She looked at her watch and cleared her throat. She had no time to waste. "Cullen, we have to talk. I can't stand this anymore."

Cullen looked at her with a surprised expression on his face. "You can't stand what?"

She jumped to her feet and paced the room. If she blew it now she might never get another chance. She chose her words with care. "This wall we've piled up between us."

He shook his head slowly as if with regret. "The 'wall', yes. We do have a wall between us, but it's a wall built of immovable shadows. I can't fight them alone. If you're going to tell me you can take care of yourself, don't. I've heard that speech before. I didn't buy it then, and I'm not buying it now."

"You've already helped me. More than you'll ever know."

Cullen looked at her. The light of hope seemed to quicken and grow in his eyes. "How have I helped you?"

"After our talk the other day, I began to realize something. Ever since Robert's betrayal I've beat myself over the head with if-onlys, I-should-haves and maybe-I-coulds until I've nearly destroyed my life."

Cullen sat motionless, gripping the arms of his chair. "And..."

"And suddenly everything seemed so clear. You were right. I can't go through life blaming myself for someone else's sins. What kind of friend would I make—what kind of parent—what kind of ...wife?"

"But what about Kay and Aaron? What about the grant? Are you saying you've forgiven yourself for all that's happened?"

Danita moved to sit on the coffee table in front of Cullen. She lifted her face, praying he could read the truth in her eyes as well as in her words. "No. I'm not saying I forgive myself. I'm saying..."

With a sigh that held a note of disillusionment and frustration he said, "Danita. This conversation is pointless. You'll never change and neither will I. Let's agree to get Kay through the next few days. I'll do whatever you will allow me to do to help salvage WAIT FOR ME. Then you can tell me good-bye."

Danita placed her hand over his. The muscles bunched beneath her touch. A thrill of hope shot through her. Maybe he still wanted her.

"No. Hear me out," she said. "I have no need to forgive myself. I did what I had to do. The result of our actions is never guaranteed. We do the best we can, take the consequences and move on. We learn from our mistakes, mourn our tragedies, but we can't let ourselves drown in self-pity and remorse when things don't go our way. We're each given one life. We have to live it to the fullest."

Cullen leaned forward and cupped her face. "You mean that, don't you?" he asked.

"With all my heart. And there's more. Even though you're one hardheaded, stubborn, obstinate, determined, unyielding…"

Cullen chuckled. "I get the idea, but where are you going with it?"

"I love you. If you can forgive me for shutting you out of my meeting with the committee, I want you to say you still love me. Say you're willing to take a chance on me."

There, she had said it. She held her breath. Her pulse throbbed wildly in her throat. What if it were too late?

Cullen stared at her like a man wearing a Wal-Mart Superman cape who had been told to chance a leap from the top of a twenty story building.

"What exactly do you mean, 'take a chance'?"

Danita leaned closer to Cullen. "Before Mr. Frederickson calls, I want you to say you'll marry me and let me spend the rest of my life showing you it's the future that counts, not the past. No matter how things turn out, we'll deal with it together."

"What if he tells us we've both lost the grant? Will you feel responsible?"

"No."

"What if I can't help you save WAIT FOR ME? Will you blame yourself for turning your seniors away from your door?"

"No."

"How can you be so sure?"

What was the use? Her attempt at reconciliation had failed. The man was impossible.

Danita leapt to her feet. She towered over him—well at least she looked down on him while he sat in the chair. "Cullen Hughes Powers. Have you heard a word I've said?" she almost shouted. "I love you and you love me. If you can't trust my word, there's no hope for us."

She stalked to the window. Turning to him, she fisted her hands on her hips. "Do you want to marry me or don't you?"

She glanced at her watch. "It's two minutes to six. Make up your mind."

In less than two strides Cullen stood at her side. He hauled her against his chest. "I wondered how long it would take you to admit you loved me. And by the way, I figured out why you spouted off all that crap about not caring for me. You were trying to save me from myself. It only took me a few minutes to realize that you couldn't have responded to me as you did if you hadn't cared."

He threw his head back and laughed, pulling her tighter against him. "You know, you have one sassy mouth, but maybe you're sweeter than you sounded."

His eyes darkened. Taking his time, he lowered his mouth to hers. His breath brushed her lips, sending tiny shivers of anticipation up her spine. She leaned into him, afraid he might draw back.

His tongue tasted her lower lip. "Sweet so far," he murmured.

When she opened to his searching, he gently glided inside and sipped the honey there. "Mmm-mm, yes," he said.

She swallowed his words and answered his kiss with a surge of passion. She wound her arms around his neck and nestled against his groin, rotating in a desperate attempt to get closer.

He moaned and kissed her so sweetly her head reeled. He explored every part of her mouth, tasting, seeking, adoring until she heard bells ring.

The phone. Cullen placed his hand over the receiver. A loving smile tilted the corners of his mouth. "Yes, Dani, I'll marry you. I can hardly wait."

೭❀

Cullen motioned for Danita to join him. She sat on his lap while he tilted the phone so that she could listen in on what Mr. Frederickson had to say.

"Hello, this is Cullen Powers."

"Hello, Powers, is Ms. Johnson there with you?"

"Yes, she's here."

"Good. The Penn-Atkinson Foundation has reached a decision on conferring this year's grant."

When Frederickson hesitated just a moment too long, Cullen held Danita tighter.

At last Mr. Frederickson continued, "By unanimous vote of the committee the foundation wishes to confer this year's award upon Ms. Johnson. The committee further asked me to convey both their congratulations and commendations to you and Ms. Johnson for your bravery in the Burdell matter."

Momentarily speechless, Cullen could not believe his ears, but the look on Danita's face told him he had heard correctly. Tears streamed down her face, but from her wide grin he knew they were tears of joy.

"Thank you for the good news, Mr. Frederickson."

Mr. Frederickson gave a chuckle. "You can thank Mr. Rawley. He championed your causes until he wore us down. In fact he even waxed poetic. He said, and I quote, 'In a forest, tree leans on tree. In a community man leans on man.' Of course, he was right.

President Clinton realized the seriousness of domestic violence. If he saw fit to establish a national spousal abuse hot line, the least we can do is to publicly back your efforts on behalf of a woman in danger of losing her life."

Danita snatched the phone from Cullen. "Thank you again, Mr. Frederickson, and please give our special appreciation to Mr. Rawley."

"You can do that in person, Ms. Johnson. He and the committee invite you to our offices tomorrow afternoon at two if you can make it, to finalize the plans for you to access your funds immediately. In addition, Mr. Rawley is in the process of arranging with a fellow philanthropist to take on Cullen's project."

"Thank you, thank you, thank you. We'll be there tomorrow at two."

When Cullen hung up, he gave a whoop of elation and rose to his feet with Danita in his arms. She slid down the length of his body and into the circle of his arms. Lifting her face, she rounded her lips as if to speak. He tasted her words with the kiss he had feared they would never share again.

They broke apart to come up for air. "We did it. Cullen, we did it!" Danita exclaimed.

Cullen looked at her dear, sweet face. The taste of her joyous tears lingered on his tongue like seasoning for his soul. Mascara smudged his shirt. She pushed her bangs away from her eyes. Her smile was radiant. She was the most beautiful woman he had ever seen.

"Let's tell Kay the good news. Then we'll call your mom, Virgie and Mitch," he said.

"Which good news?"

"That you got the grant, and I talked you into marrying me."

"Let's get this straight. Who did the asking?"

Cullen laughed. "Whatever."

Epilogue

DANITA LAY SPRAWLED ATOP Cullen in their bed. She throbbed from head-to-toe with the pleasure of their lovemaking, her body slick with perspiration.

After a year of marriage, the flame of their desire for one another had grown sweeter, blazing into urgent need at a touch or a glance.

The look of proprietary satisfaction Cullen leveled at Danita filled her with wonder. He fitted her into the protective curve of his body and covered them with the sheet. "God, what you do to me. I think all that practice has paid off."

She wriggled against him. "More than you know."

He raised himself on his elbow, propped his head on his fist and looked down at her. "You sound awful smug and satisfied, and with good reason. If the big earthquake everyone's waiting for hits right now I wouldn't have the energy to duck and cover."

She laughed. "I have news for you, honey. 'The Big One' has already hit."

"What do you mean?"

"Hold onto your pillow. In about seven months you're going to be a papa."

Cullen froze, then a look of pure joy spread over his face. "You're sure?"

"I'm sure."

He sat up in bed and gave a shout of such elation he rattled the windows.

She patted her tummy. "Ssshhh. You'll wake the baby."

He sobered. "Are you all right? Maybe we shouldn't have.

When did you find out?"

Danita chuckled. "I'm fine. We definitely should and will—lots of times before the big day. And I found out today."

"Hot damn. I'm going to be a father." He gathered Danita into his arms and kissed her with such reverence he brought tears to her eyes.

Soon his reverence turned to passion, and his passion sent them on another sensuous journey.

Later that night as Cullen closed his eyes and drifted off to sleep he murmured, "What a year."

Danita smiled and placed her hand protectively over her stomach. She whispered, "Hi, Junior. You missed all the excitement. This year has turned out to be one of the busiest in my whole life."

Danita smiled with satisfaction and the joy of impending motherhood. With Cullen at her side, their baby would have a stable future. "Loving your father and being loved by him have changed both our lives. By supporting each other and the people we care about we discovered the secret to a lifetime of love and happiness."

Danita snuggled against Cullen. "Your dad's some kind of man. I'm so glad I learned to trust in love," she whispered.

About The Author

When she's not playing bridge, traveling or attending meetings, Vashti Ann Reed is doing what she loves best: reading and telling stories, the more humorous the better.

Though born and reared in the Cleveland, Ohio area, she moved to San Diego with three suitcases, a four year old and her trusty VW bug. After many years of teaching hearing impaired children, rearing a child and taking care of her mother, who was an amputee, she decided to turn her love of fiction into writing.

Email Vashti at Vashann59@att.net